THE
Runaway
YEAR

SHANI STRUTHERS

OMNIFIC PUBLISHING
DALLAS

Omnific Publishing
10000 North Central Expressway, Dallas, TX 75231
www.omnificpublishing.com

First Omnific eBook edition, July 2013
First Omnific trade paperback edition, July 2013

The characters and events in this book are fictitious.
Any similarity to real persons, living or dead,
is coincidental and not intended by the author.

Library of Congress Cataloguing-in-Publication Data

Struthers, Shani.
 The Runaway Year / Shani Struthers – 1st ed.
 ISBN: 978-1-623420-24-6
 1. England — Romance. 2. Relationships — Fiction.
 3. Marriage — Romance. 4. Friendship — Fiction. I. Title

10 9 8 7 6 5 4 3 2 1

Cover Design by Micha Stone and Amy Brokaw
Interior Book Design by Coreen Montagna

Printed in the United States of America

How do I even begin to say thank you? So many of my family and friends (you know who you are) have supported me on this journey, avidly encouraging me, admonishing me on occasion, and believing in me always. Writing can be a lonely profession, but you made it fun—a thrill ride, in fact! Let's do it all again sometime.

chapter one

"You've done what?" Penny asked, choking on her pinot grigio.

"I've left, walked out, told her to stick it," repeated Layla, biting down hard on her lip.

"Told *who* to stick it?"

"Hazel, of course. I told her to stick her job where the sun don't shine." Layla leaned forward in an almost conspiratorial manner. "Honestly, you should have seen her face — what a picture!"

"Oh, God!" said Penny, her jaw dropping. "I don't believe it."

And, in truth, Layla could hardly believe it either.

At precisely 6:05 p.m., she had marched up to Hazel Smith, marketing manager of Easy Travel Holiday Company and all-round dragon of the department, and told her in no uncertain terms what she had decided only five minutes earlier: she was relinquishing her role as marketing executive. Why? She couldn't bear the thought of Alex, her boss and former lover, returning in the morning from his so-called "work" trip to Florida with office assistant Sarah-Jane Johnson. Layla had rent due at the end of the month, numerous bills outstanding, and now, due to her self-imposed unemployment, barely any money to pay them.

"Look, Layla, I know you've been through a lot lately, but a job's a job. There aren't many of them around at the moment. Go back.

Hazel might still be there. Tell her you didn't mean what you said; you were having an off day. Blame it on hormones. No one ever questions hormones."

"But I *do* mean it," said Layla, the cozy confines of their favorite after-work pub beginning to feel really quite stifling. "I can't be there when he gets back. I just can't. Anyway, you know what Hazel's like; I've told you often enough. She'd never let me waltz back in as though nothing's happened. Not after what I said to her."

Penny was stumped. Layla could almost see her brain whirring away, searching frantically but failing to find the words that would inspire her to stay and stand her ground, to face up to Mr. Big Boss Man and demand his explanation for dumping her so callously.

Watching her friend struggle and feeling increasingly guilty at being the cause, Layla placed a hand on Penny's arm. "Don't worry, Pen, I'll be fine. Whatever happens, I'll be okay."

"Really?" asked Penny, clearly not taken in at all.

"Really," said Layla, avoiding Penny's eyes entirely.

She had last seen Alex in late December, a little over two weeks ago. They'd spent Christmas together at his swanky bachelor pad in Sussex Square, just off Brighton's seafront. It had been pure heaven—him, her, and one of those realistic gas-flamed log fires, in front of which they had drunk champagne, made love, and talked about their plans for the future. Okay, his plans had been mostly work-related and not once had the subject of love been mentioned, but deep down she knew this was it: *the real thing.* That he felt the same way was confirmed when he presented her with a diamond-studded bracelet on Christmas morning. Everyone knew diamonds were forever; it was obvious he was hinting at something.

Drowning in romance, she had been certain an engagement ring would follow and then, of course, the wedding itself. A lavish affair held in some ultra-posh country hotel. She would lower her eyes demurely as she whispered, "I do," transforming in that magical moment from Miss Layla Lewis, twenty-eight-year-old girl-about-town, to Mrs. Alex Kline, wife of the managing director of Easy Travel.

The dreams hadn't stopped there. As a bona fide member of the upper echelons, she imagined swanning down the aisles of Waitrose instead of hunting for BOGOF bargains in Asda, swapping her Topshop clothes for Stella McCartney, and riding her newly acquired horse (a magnificent chestnut with a white flash on its nose) across the sunny Sussex Downs, freed from the need to work for a living.

Intending to laugh at how carried away she'd become with dazzling dreams of a brilliant future, her vision blurred instead, and try as she might to stem their flow, rebellious tears dampened her lashes anyway.

"Hey," said Penny, "don't cry. Not over a rat like him."

"A diamond bracelet!" Layla burst out, startling herself as well as a group of four sitting at a nearby table. "Who gives a diamond bracelet to someone they're going to chuck in a few days?"

Alex, that's who. He was so rich, an expensive trinket was hardly going to make a dent in his fortune. In fact, he probably thought it would serve as some sort of consolation prize. Something to buck her spirits through the long, lonely nights she would spend without him. Maybe even a thank-you for services rendered?

"Where is it, the bracelet?" asked Penny, tucking a few strands of hair behind Layla's ear in an almost motherly fashion.

"I chucked it in the bin this morning before I left for work." Layla sniffled and dabbed at her nose with a tissue one of the four had kindly handed over.

"The bin?" shrieked Penny, withdrawing her hand in horror.

"It was mocking me, I swear," said Layla, rushing to her own defense. "Glittering away like some shiny little demon, laughing at my downfall."

"It's a bloody bracelet," Penny replied in exasperation, "and an expensive one at that! You could sell it on eBay, make a bit of money. You're going to need every penny you can get now you're jobless, you know."

"I don't want the money from that bracelet," said Layla emphatically. "It's his money. It would make me feel…I don't know, used somehow, unclean. I don't want anything from him anymore."

At a temporary deadlock, both girls went back to their drinks, as did the crowd around them. Despite not wanting to go over and over it again, Layla couldn't stop herself. It was all she could think of. *He* was all she could think of.

They'd parted the day after Boxing Day. He had dropped her back at her flat, explaining he had business to attend to over the next few days and promising to call her on New Year's Eve to make arrangements to spend the evening together. That had been okay, situation normal. Alex was a busy man; he often had to disappear at short notice. And usually he was as good as his word. But not this time. This time it was radio silence. Unable to bear it any longer, she had left messages on his landline and iPhone. Still nothing. Hurrying round to his flat, she found the door stubbornly shut.

Concerned but not yet panicked, she had instead spent New Year's Eve with Penny and her husband, Richard, trying in vain to ignore the cutthroat atmosphere between the pair of them. When she heard nothing from Alex on New Year's Day either, she was unusually eager to get back to work, positive he would be there with a perfectly reasonable explanation as to why he'd vanished into the ether. He wasn't. Hazel, however, was.

As soon as Layla had stepped over the office threshold, Hazel had rushed up to her as if facing a particularly aggravating opponent on the rugby field. In that screechy voice of hers, she had yelled, "Have you heard? Alex is away on business. There's a note for you on your desk."

Of course she hadn't heard, something she suspected Hazel well knew. Desperate to escape her manic gloating, Layla had tottered over to her desk in killer black heels — Alex's favorite — and scoured the mess she'd left pre-Christmas for his note. There it was. Not a proper note, written on decent company headed paper and tucked away discreetly in an envelope with her name on it, but a bloody Post-It note stuck on a pile of random papers.

> *Called away on business. Will be gone two weeks.*
> *Keep you-know-who at FarScapes sweet until*
> *I return. Alex*

And that was it, nothing more, nothing less, not even a kiss for old times' sake.

The note barely had time to register before Hazel was at her side again, itching to fill her in on the gory details.

"Oh, yes," she said. "I popped in just after Christmas to help Alex with a few last-minute details, and there he was with Sarah-Jane in his office. Both of them in rather a state of, well, how can I put it? Undress, I suppose. They were so embarrassed, they didn't know where to look!"

Cackling with laughter, Hazel had wandered blithely off, leaving Layla feeling as though someone had reached inside her chest, located her beating heart, and squashed it into one big, red, pulpy mess.

The next few days had passed in a blur. Quickly she had found out (Hazel again) that Alex had taken Sarah-Jane to Florida with him. Quite a coup, considering she'd only been with the company for two months. Layla had chatted to her by the photocopier a few times, and she'd seemed sweet enough, around twenty-four, with poker-straight blond hair, gray eyes, and slender limbs. Layla had noticed, however, that during their conversations, Sarah-Jane's eyes would flicker toward Alex whenever he happened to pass by, slight color flushing her pale features. At the time, she'd dismissed this as nothing out of turn—most of the girls at Easy Travel had a crush on Alex. And no wonder. He was good-looking with an easy charm. But as far as she'd been aware, Alex hadn't even known Sarah-Jane existed. Certainly, he had never mentioned her.

Since the news had broken she'd been dumped for the new girl on the block, Layla had had to endure sympathetic stares and sighs of condolence from most of her colleagues. Even Rob in Accounts had emailed her with, "Heard the romance with God is over. How about giving me a chance?"

For others, though, she had become a laughingstock. Hazel and several of her sycophantic sidekicks clearly thought she had overstepped the mark and was back where she belonged: on the shop floor.

Still, if the last two weeks had been hell, it would be worse than hell once Alex and Sarah-Jane got back and continued their romance right under her nose. She'd rather be broke and on the streets than suffer that—which, of course, she would be if she didn't find another job, and soon.

"Have the bin men been?" asked Penny at last.

"No," said Layla sulkily, "not till Friday."

"Have you still got your keys to the office?"

"I think so. Why?"

"Check," Penny insisted.

Although perplexed at this line of questioning, Layla did as she was told. Rummaging in her handbag for a few moments, she pulled out her purse, her makeup bag, a dog-eared paperback, a chewed pencil, and a couple of as yet unopened but official looking letters before she found them.

"Right," Penny said, setting her glass down on the table, "this is the plan. We're going to pop back to your flat, retrieve the bracelet, and go back to the office. You can leave it on his desk with a note of your own."

"What's the point?" Layla began.

"There's every point. Come on, drink up. We're going."

Sighing, Layla grabbed her bag and coat and rose from the table. As they left, she saw disappointment cross not just all four of her neighbor's faces but several others too and wondered why. But then again, in between Penny's shouts of disbelief and her own heartfelt sobs, she supposed they had put on quite a floorshow.

It took five minutes to reach her flat, one half of a tiny terraced house optimistically billed as two-bedroomed. She'd been renting it for a couple of years now, and it was okay. Partly furnished when she moved in, a few trips to Ikea in Croydon had taken care of everything else she'd needed. It was in a nice, handy location too. The neighbors were friendly, and the town center was only a short walk away. But it did feel crowded, and trying to park her car, an old but much loved Mazda MX-5 MK I (red, of course), was a nightmare. The streets were crammed.

Opening the front door, they stepped into a long and narrow dimly-lit hallway. There was a door immediately in front and another to the right, the one that led to her ground floor flat. Taking the key from Layla, Penny let herself in and headed straight for the kitchen. Swiftly removing the bin lid, she poked around for a bit, grimacing as she did so, before emerging triumphantly with the brutally discarded object.

Turning it over and over in her hands, she asked, "Are you sure you want to part with this? It's actually very tasteful considering who bought it."

"I'm sure," Layla replied. "It either goes back in the bin or we return it to Alex. I don't care which."

"Okay, okay, fair enough. Let's go."

The headquarters of Easy Travel Holiday Company was only a few streets away, in Brighton's Old Steine area. As they neared the large, double-fronted white building, Layla hung back.

"What if Hazel's still there?" she said, looking nervously ahead.

"We'll just tell her you've come to return your keys or something. That's perfectly believable. Anyway, she won't be. It's after eight. Surely even Hazel has a home to go to."

"Shall we ring the doorbell though, just in case?" Layla asked, still uncertain.

"There's no need. Look, there aren't any lights on. Everyone's gone home. Come on, don't be such a wuss. Open up."

It was indeed empty inside: computer monitors eerily blank and desks left in various states of abandon. As usual, everyone had downed tools as soon as decently possible and sprinted for the exit, glad Monday was done and dusted at least.

"Where's Alex's office?" asked Penny.

"Over here," Layla replied. "Follow me."

When he wasn't casually sauntering between floors, Alex sat tucked away in an office divided from the marketing crew by glass and white vertical blinds. The door was locked, but she had the key to that too. Steeling herself, she walked in. Sarah-Jane hadn't been the only one in a "state of undress" within such hallowed confines. Memories of their own love-ins came flooding back—as soon as the last person had gone, he would call her in, clear his desk with one fell swoop, lay her down on it, and "do the business" as he laughingly called it. She'd never found that quite as funny as he had, but had laughed along nonetheless.

"Didn't you say something about Easy Travel merging with FarScapes?" asked Penny, one eyebrow raised in thought.

"Yeah. I've been in charge of overseeing that whilst Alex has been away." Then a horrifying thought hit her. "Oh, God, I forgot to email them with possible dates for the next meeting. I was supposed to do that today."

"Were you, indeed?" said Penny. "Can you log on to his computer?"

"Yeah, of course I can. His password is 'SexBeast.'" Then sensing Penny's distaste, she countered, "It's just a joke."

"Hilarious," said Penny, rolling her eyes. "Come on then, do it."

"Good idea. I should let FarScapes know about those dates, at least."

"Whatever. Just get me in, get a blank email to the managing director of FarScapes up, and I'll take care of the rest."

"Penny," said Layla, really worried now, "what are you up to?"

"Revenge, that's what I'm up to. Alex gets off with another woman, disappears to sunny climes with her, and leaves you nothing but a Post-It note by way of explanation. All that and still you're worried about him and his company! I don't think so. He needs to be taught a lesson."

Three glasses of wine had made Layla's head buzz. She was tired. All she wanted to do was write a Post-It note of her own, leave the bracelet, and scram. Still, if it were just a tiny lesson, maybe it would be okay. It might make him think twice about cheating on his girl-friends in future.

"Okay, then," she conceded, "but go easy, Pen, please. I've been dealing with Jack Thomas. He's nice, actually. We get on well. The first meeting's supposed to be this Friday. Wangle it so that they turn up at different locations or something, something that will embarrass Alex."

"Yeah, yeah." Penny nodded dutifully. "Something like that."

Leaving Penny to it, Layla turned away to search for the Post-It pad in the top right drawer of Alex's desk. In the past fortnight, she'd come to hate their neon handiness. They were an all-too-pertinent reminder of how little Alex respected her—how dare he leave noth-ing but a sticky square of paper to say goodbye!

Pressing down hard with his favorite Mont Blanc fountain pen, she wrote her reply.

Thanks for the bracelet, but no thanks. Give it to your next victim. Good luck with FarScapes. You'll need it Layla

She looked up just as Penny pressed the send button.

"What did you say?" she asked, her eyes widening at Penny's daring.

"You don't want to know." Penny smiled enigmatically. "But one thing's for certain: Alex will have a bit of groveling to do when he gets back."

"Serves him right," said Layla, surprised at how hollow that senti-ment sounded.

Digging out the diamond bracelet from her coat pocket, she looked at it one last time, turning it over and over in her hands as Penny had done, before placing it beside the Post-It note.

"Another drink before we call it a night?" Penny's voice was sud-denly gentle, understanding.

"May as well," replied Layla, shrugging her shoulders dejectedly. "After all, it is the end of an era."

Taking one last look around at the place she'd spent the last eight years of her life—practically all of them fawning over Alex Kline until he had finally deigned to notice her—Layla switched off the lights, locked the door behind her, and headed into an uncertain future.

chapter two

Later that night, as Penny lay in bed beside Richard, who was absorbed in the latest John Grisham novel, she began to wonder if the email she'd written to the director of FarScapes had actually been a bit over-the-top.

"Jack, how are you?" she had typed. *"Just got back from a trip to Florida. Really loved it and can see plenty of ways to expand our business over there. That's the good news. The bad news is we don't want to take it any further with FarScapes. Although you're a solid company, I think Easy Travel is strong enough to grow bigger and better on its own. I hate to say it, Jack, but my gut feeling is that FarScapes could become a burden that drags us down instead of taking us to the top. It's the survival of the fittest in business, Jack, as I'm sure you understand. It's nothing personal. Good luck with your proposals elsewhere. Alex."*

She knew from Layla that Easy Travel was, in fact, relying on the merger with FarScapes for continued success. Joining together would make Alex's company one of the most formidable in the South East, boosting his already over-inflated ego to unbearable proportions.

What *did* Layla see in him anyway? He was nothing more than a glorified hustler, and he lied about his age too, she was sure of it. Forty-three? And the rest. Okay, she couldn't deny he looked after himself. He was gym-trim with a thick head of dark hair and nice, even teeth, but she wouldn't put it past him to shave a few years off for the sake of the ladies. He lied about everything else, why not that too?

And Layla was so pretty, although she'd deny it every time, annoyingly pointing out all the things that were wrong with her. Things you'd need a magnifying glass to see if you could see them at all. She had long, dark hair that was naturally shot through with gold, huge green eyes, and a figure that stayed slim despite an almost phobic aversion to exercise. She could have any man she wanted, but she always seemed to go for the older ones. Penny supposed Layla had a bit of a thing for father figures, having lost her dad when she was young. She'd be better off with somebody her own age, though, somebody she could have a laugh with. Somebody she wasn't so bloody in awe of.

Alex had never been right for her from the start. Always eyeing up other women — and never discreetly. And Layla still didn't know that he'd made a pass at Penny one night when they'd all been out in town. While Layla was at the bar getting a round in, he'd leaned over and suggested they meet, just the two of them, later on that week, to "get to know each other properly." After nearly biting his head off, Penny had resolved to tell Layla as soon as possible, but every time she tried, she failed. Layla was so over the moon that finally — after years and years of working for him — Alex had noticed her. Penny didn't have the heart to burst her bubble. She had decided to sit tight instead, knowing he would show his true colors sooner or later, and he had, big time.

"Good book?" she said to Richard at last.

"Hmm."

Typical, thought Penny. *More interested in his book than me.*

They had been married for three years now. When they had first tied the knot, after a whirlwind romance, they'd been smitten with each other. It had been perfect, like a fairy tale. At times she had thought she'd burst with love for him. And he felt the same way, she knew it; he couldn't get enough of her. But now, they were more like strangers than lovers. He spent virtually every waking hour working, and Penny felt bereaved somehow, often having to remind herself she was married at all. No wonder she hadn't been able to resist Dylan when he came along. She wanted to feel desired again, and he had certainly done that. He fancied her to distraction, telling her over and over again how much she looked like Scarlett Johansson, his favorite actress apparently.

Extremely flattered, as anyone would be she supposed (especially someone feeling severely neglected by their other half), she had at last succumbed to his persistent charms—not fully, of course, just a few kisses and cuddles in the corner of a darkly lit club one night. But enough to feel horrendously guilty about it afterward. Enough to feel she'd have to come clean. Big mistake. Richard had been like a block of ice since. Nearly two months had passed, and there was still no sign of a thaw.

"Layla left work today, just walked out. All because of Alex," she said in an attempt to kick-start a conversation.

"Really?" he said, one-word replies his specialty of late.

"Yes," answered Penny, working hard to keep the irritation out of her voice. "I don't know what she's going to do for money. Jobs aren't exactly easy to come by at the moment."

"She'll manage."

That was an improvement, two words at least.

"How exactly will she manage?" Penny persevered. "I'm worried about her."

Closing his book shut, a little too pointedly she thought, he said, "It's late. I'm tired. I've got a meeting early in the morning. Good night."

And with that he placed his book on the bedside table, switched off his light, and turned his back on her.

For the second time that day, Penny was lost for words. She knew he cared about Layla, but such was his determination not to engage in any sort of meaningful conversation since "Dylangate," he was able to resist asking any more about it.

Looking at the mound beside her, she wanted to scream. Tell him for the hundredth time that her fling with Dylan, if you could call it that, had been a mistake. To drum it into his stubborn head that what had happened, had happened for a reason—because he worked too hard and because she missed him. She worked hard, too—as funds manager for Charity Now!—but not to the exclusion of everything and *everyone* else. He just worked and worked and worked. She wanted to grab him by the throat, stare manically into his eyes, and yell, *Why do you do it? Because you don't love me anymore? Because you can't stand being with me?* But she didn't say a word. She knew it would end in tears. Hers.

All she said was "Night," before turning her own light off and falling into a troubled sleep.

When Richard left for work the next morning, Penny was only vaguely aware. He had slipped from the covers early, like a ghost, silent and fleeting. An hour later, the alarm clock rang, shaking her rudely out of the comfort of sleep. A few seconds passed whilst she collected her thoughts, groaning at the prospect of spending another day at Charity Now! She used to love her job, her enthusiasm for fund-raising unrivaled. Event after event she had tirelessly organized, exceeding target after target, passionate about making life easier for Brighton's deprived families. Layla had often helped out during her spare time, the pair of them really enjoying themselves and meeting some inspiring people along the way, Dylan being one of them. A bit of a bad boy, he had been in trouble with the law in his youth, but he'd managed to turn his life around since then. He worked for a local charity too. "Atoning for my sins," he had laughingly told her one night over a couple of drinks as he flicked his shaggy brown hair out of his eyes. At twenty-four, he was younger than her by five years, with one hell of a naughty smile. Since their "liaison" and her consequent bust-up with Richard, however, she seemed to have little enthusiasm for anything.

Stop thinking about Dylan, she admonished herself as she flung her legs over the side of the bed and made her way to the bathroom.

Dying to phone Layla, she thought she'd leave it until she was walking to work. If the girl had any sense, which was debatable considering she'd just made herself jobless in the middle of a double-dip recession, she'd be enjoying a lie-in.

Grabbing her coat, Penny walked out the door. It was freezing. An icy cold wind blasted her awake as she headed from her modest Victorian terrace in the trendy Fiveways area to New Britain House, an eyesore of a building close to Brighton Station. It was popular with companies like the one she worked for because the rent was fair. And not without reason, the inside was just as grim as the exterior. Richard worked in plush offices on Queens Road; he had his own magnolia-painted office and a secretary who catered to his every whim. Well, not every whim — Dawn preferred the ladies and very obviously so.

"Hi, you awake?" asked Penny, barely having reached the bottom of her road.

"Yeah, have been most of the night actually," replied Layla, her voice distinctly groggy.

"Poor you, you must be feeling rotten. I've got to get to work, but I can meet for lunch if you feel up to it."

"I don't think I do, actually, Pen, but thanks anyway. I'm just going to stay at home, work out my next move, that sort of thing. Probably ring round a few agencies, see if there's any temp work going."

"Good idea. Give yourself the morning off and then get back into the swing of things. Show that idiot you don't need him or his job."

"Yeah, yeah, that's what I thought. Thanks, though. Speak later, yeah?"

"You bet. I'll call you on my way home."

Penny rang off, feelings of concern for her friend growing. Layla was definitely out-of-sorts and not just because of lack of sleep. If heartbreak had a sound, she supposed she'd just heard it. God, she was angry. If Alex were standing in front of her, right here, right now, she would slap him. Honestly, she would. If he didn't want to continue his relationship with Layla, fine. People break up all the time. But why spend Christmas with her, buy her an expensive gift, and then run off to Florida with another woman? What was that all about? Men were crap sometimes when it came to matters of the heart. They just didn't understand women at all. Richard certainly didn't understand her.

Thinking of Richard sent her thoughts spiraling in another direction. Surely he must love her still? He wouldn't have reacted so badly when she told him about Dylan if he didn't. And he was hurt, that's why he could barely bring himself to talk to her. He probably thought she didn't love him if she needed to kiss and cuddle someone else. Oh, the irony of it! If he kissed and cuddled her more, she wouldn't need to look elsewhere. She'd be content.

It was Tuesday. He'd be working late again, no doubt. Well, she'd get through the day, then go and surprise him. Grab a large pepperoni pizza with extra chilies from that place on the London Road and a bottle of merlot, take dinner to him. She'd never done that before. It would be fun. He would see she was trying to make an effort, trying to put the whole Dylan episode behind them, and hopefully melt a bit.

Once things were back on a better footing, she would enforce a few ground rules to ensure their relationship never crashed and burned again. No more working after seven p.m., that sort of thing—and certainly not at weekends. The weekends would be their time to spend together, sacred time, spent lingering over breakfast in one of Brighton's many bustling cafés or leisurely looking around antique shops in nearby Lewes. Just being together, rediscovering each other. He would see sense; she would make him. She had her ways.

Just after six p.m., Penny left her desk, hurried down several flights of stairs, and made her way to Get Your Pizzeria. She then popped into the Eight Till Late a few doors along for the wine before heading up Trafalgar Street to his office.

Dylan might be sexy, but he couldn't hold a candle to Richard. Richard was tall, just a smidge under six foot, and always impeccably turned out. His black hair, which had been longer when she first met him, was close cropped, and there was never a sign of stubble on his finely chiseled jaw. His favorite shop was Gresham Blake in the North Laines, a fine purveyor of hand-tailored suits, all with a bit of an edge to them. He had about three suits from them, maybe four now, and looked like a male model in all of them. She, on the other hand, liked to slob around in jeans; there was no need to look particularly smart in her job. In fact, her muesli-crunching colleagues would think she was mad if she turned up in a designer number. Still, she knew she scrubbed up well when she had too, channeling that Johansson look with her blond hair piled high, bright red lipstick, a figure-hugging dress, and heels. Richard had always appreciated her efforts at least. Well, Richard and Dylan.

She knew Richard had his reasons for working the hours he did; perhaps she should be more understanding. He didn't talk a lot about his childhood, and they rarely saw his surviving parent, Bill, who lived in Portsmouth—she'd gleaned early on that he hadn't come from too comfortable a background. He and his two brothers had often gone without. But he was as bright as a button. He had made it to Sussex University, scored top marks in Law, and was taken on straightaway at solicitors Torrence and Higgins. It would be Torrence, Higgins, and Hughes one day, he had told her, and even the partners had hinted at such. Despite being held in high regard by both bosses, however, he still felt he had a lot to prove, she knew. And she understood, really she did, but he needed to understand something too: that working all possible hours wasn't exactly doing wonders for their relationship.

Deep in thought, she was taken aback to find herself coming to a standstill outside his office. Excited about seeing him, a smile spread over her face as she pushed open the double glass doors in front of her. Marianne, the receptionist, was just leaving, but stopped long enough to tell her Richard was still in the building and to go on up. Having run up and down the steps of New Britain House all day long, she treated herself to a ride in the lift. He worked on the fourth floor. As the doors slid open, she noticed straightaway that Dawn's desk was empty. *Good,* she thought. *It looks like everyone's gone home. We've got the place to ourselves.*

She could see the door to his office was slightly ajar and made her way to it, treading lightly so as to keep the element of surprise. She stopped short when she heard voices. *Damn, we're not alone, after all.* Oh well, the pizza was getting cold; she'd go in anyway. Praying she wasn't disturbing him in the middle of something important, she was about to knock politely on the door when laughter from within stopped her. Not exactly laughter. No, if she had to describe it, she would say it was giggling. Giggling with a highly flirtatious edge to it.

Her curiosity aroused, she lowered her hand and decided to peer though the crack of the door instead, feeling the need to get a handle on the situation before barging in. And there they were, the pair of them. Richard and some woman she had never seen before. Standing so close, their foreheads were practically touching, her well-manicured hand resting lightly on his arm, both of them *giggling.*

Richard was the jealous type; Penny was well aware of that. He often told her off for flirting, even when she wasn't. But she had never considered herself a slave to the green-eyed monster. Not until now. Now it seemed to wake from some slumber deep within her and come crashing to the fore.

"Richard!" she yelled, kicking open the door in fury. "What's going on? Who is *she?*"

"Penny," spluttered Richard, his face coloring straightaway, "I wasn't expecting you."

"You weren't expecting anyone by the looks of it. You and this—" she struggled for words to describe the startled woman before her

"—this…floozy," she said at last, slightly dismayed she couldn't come up with a more lurid description.

"I'd better be going," said the woman, who actually looked quite annoyed she'd been called a floozy. "Let you deal with this mad woman."

"Mad woman? Me? Damn right I am!" Penny was sure her own face was as red as Richard's by now, but not with embarrassment, with anger. "And keep your hands off my husband in future. He's out of bounds."

As the woman sidled nervously past her, Penny had to resist the urge to hit her over the head with the pizza box. She could just imagine it: tomato, pepperoni, and extra chilies flying everywhere.

The split second the woman had left, Penny slammed the door and turned to do battle. Instead of squaring up to her, ready to put forward his case as was his line of expertise, she was surprised to find Richard slumped in his chair, head in hands.

"Oh, God!" he was saying. "I don't believe it."

It was the same sentiment she had uttered yesterday, when Layla broke the news to her that she had quit her job. That Richard was now saying it, and this time to her, served only to inflame her more.

"I don't bloody believe it either," she screamed at him. "You're a hypocrite, you are. Putting me through hell because of Dylan whilst you're busy having an affair with some old bag at work."

"I am not having an affair," Richard countered, anger at last pushing him to his feet. "And that 'old bag' happens to be Diane Tyrrell, a very important client of ours. Your behavior just now probably cost me any hope of a partnership."

"My behavior just now was perfectly justified," Penny continued, undaunted. "Whoever the hell that woman is, you were flirting with her. Not only were you standing so close you were practically morphing into each other, she had her hand on your arm."

"Oh, right, and her hand on my arm means I'm having an affair, does it?" he replied, every word dripping with sarcasm. "Think about it, Penny. It's hardly on a par with kissing and groping someone in a nightclub, is it?"

"There was no groping involved," Penny slammed back, indignant.

"Maybe not, but a fair bit of tonsil tennis. I think that's bad enough."

"At least I told you about it. I didn't keep it secret."

"Yeah, thanks for that, Pen. Did me the world of good, hearing every last detail," replied Richard, his voice still scathing. "Here I am, working like a dog, trying to raise our standard of living, and all you can do is whine that you're lonely and then snog someone else."

"I do *not* whine!" Penny was furious at the insinuation. "And believe me, Richard Hughes, I'm capable of a whole lot more than snogging."

As soon as it was out, she knew she'd said the wrong thing, had pushed him too far. His face was filled with rage.

She tried to claw back a bit of ground. "Richard, I didn't mean that. I'm angry, that's all. I'd never be unfaithful. I mean, not *properly* unfaithful." But it was no use. He walked menacingly toward her and then straight past her without uttering another word.

"Richard!" she yelled after him, but he was gone, the ting of the lift confirming his departure.

Sinking down in his plush office chair, she mirrored his head-in-hands pose, the pizza box and the merlot pushed aside, forgotten. What on earth had possessed her to say such a thing? To goad him like that? Considering the circumstances, it was not a clever move.

So much for her notions of a romantic impromptu dinner, a dinner which would miraculously smooth out the boulder-sized lumps in their relationship. All she'd done was make a dire situation ten times worse. It seemed her marriage was going down the pan faster than Layla could tell Hazel to stick her job where the sun don't shine. And right now, it didn't seem there was a damn thing she could do to stop it.

chapter three

Hannah's eyes widened as she read Layla's text. Quickly she texted back:

> I'm so sorry to hear that. What u going to do? ~H

Layla was equally as swift.

> Don't know. Go into hiding when the rents due, I suppose.
> Do a moonlight flit. I doubt work will pay me the money they
> owe me. Not after I walked out without notice. ~L

> U know where I am if u want me.
> If I can do anything to help I will. ~H

> I know, Hannah, thanks. I'll be fine though, I'm sure.
> Hope all is well with you in sunny Cornwall. ~L

Sunny Cornwall? If only. This part of the world hadn't been sunny for what seemed like an age. Rather, the rain and wind reigned supreme and, with them, rapidly dipping temperatures. The mere thought of the weather they'd been suffering lately made Hannah shiver, despite being warm and toasty indoors. She would have to venture out in a while, though, to work her shift at the pub she ran in the village high street. She didn't want to, not least because she'd be surprised if any of the locals bothered to put in an appearance (it was so filthy out there) but mainly because she wanted to stay at home and paint.

"Hey, babe, what's happening?" Jim came up behind her as she sat at her easel, putting his arms round her waist and snuggling into the nape of her neck.

"I'm just about to attack this picture again," she replied happily as he nuzzled away. "It's missing something. I can't quite figure out what, though."

"It looks great to me. And so do you. Sure you don't want to attack me instead?"

"No," she laughed, batting away his hand. "You've had your quota for today."

"Spoilsport," he murmured, but good-naturedly so. Flinging himself on the sofa next to her, he picked up his guitar and began to strum.

Hannah continued to stare at her picture, full of swirling grays and blues, her trademark colors. After a few moments, she spoke again.

"I've just heard from Layla. That boyfriend of hers has dumped her, you know the one I was telling you about, her boss or something, or ex-boss, I should say. She's walked out of her job, too. I feel so sorry for her."

"Layla from Brighton? Ah, that's a shame. What's she gonna do?"

"No idea. She doesn't know yet. It's only just happened."

"Invite her down; a change of scene might do her good. Be nice to see her again," replied Jim, plucking at the strings and starting to sing softly to himself.

What a lovely idea, thought Hannah. It *would* be nice to see her again. It had been so long. What was it now? Well over a year since they'd last hooked up, more like eighteen months. Just after she'd started going out with Jim, in fact. They had crashed at Layla's flat whilst Jim and his band, 96 Tears, had played in the Brighton Fringe Festival. May, it had been. Prior to that, they hadn't seen each other in years, not since their early twenties. Thanks to Facebook, she had managed to trace Layla again. The need for a place to stay during the festival had been the spur she'd needed to get back in touch.

Despite not having seen each other for so long, not even talking on the phone, there had been no awkwardness when they'd come face-to-face once more. For the first few moments, they had simply stood and stared at each other, drinking each other in. She remembered thinking how little time had changed Layla: same old warmth in those green eyes of hers, same big grin. Then they had hugged—hugged, laughed, and cried, all at the same time.

Instead of a few days, Hannah and Jim had stayed a week. Layla had taken obvious delight in showing them all her favorite haunts: pubs, clubs, cafés, and restaurants—Brighton was chockablock with them. Now they were in touch several times a week by phone, text, or via Facebook.

Layla kept saying she wanted to come back to Trecastle, to revisit old haunts, but she hadn't made it yet. Maybe, as Jim suggested, now would be a good time, especially after the boyfriend bust-up. Escape for a while.

"I'll call her later and ask," resolved Hannah, "when I'm at the pub. At least talking to Layla will stop me jabbering away to myself; it's going to be dead in there tonight."

"Hey, I'll come and see you," said Jim, a twinkle in his eye.

"I know you will," Hannah replied, grinning back at him.

Such a small show of support, but it meant a lot. He was so loyal, showing how much he loved her in so many ways. And she loved him too, of course. She was lucky to have him. Quite why he put up with her, though, she didn't know, all things considered. But he did.

"Better get ready, I suppose," said Hannah with a sigh.

As much as she enjoyed working at the pub, she'd rather just paint for a living. The walls of their flat were a showcase for her artwork: modern interpretations of seascapes mainly and usually a riot of color. Jim was always telling her she was a genius. She scoffed at him, but actually her work was beginning to sell well, all up and down the Cornish coast. Not selling for thousands, of course, not even hundreds, but bringing in a bit extra. They rented the flat they were living in, just off the high street, but wanted to buy eventually. Perhaps in Trecastle, perhaps elsewhere. Maybe "elsewhere" would be kinder in the long run, and not just to herself. Jim had regular gigs and picked up local work in between, mainly from Joseph, his best friend, so they were doing okay. At this rate, fingers crossed, they'd have enough for a deposit by the end of the year.

Grabbing her coat, Hannah checked herself in the mirror. Her shoulder-length hair was pulled back in a scruffy ponytail, and she had not a scrap of makeup on to brighten her features. Who cared? Like she'd said to Jim earlier, it would be dead in the pub tonight; no one to look at her. Jim preferred the natural look anyway. He told her all the time she was beautiful. It had taken a while to believe it again, though.

"See you later," she said, leaning over him and planting a kiss on his cheek.

"You will," he replied, and as ever, the love in those gorgeous eyes of his, green like the ocean on a stormy day, took her breath away.

"Hey, Lenny, you're brave, aren't you, coming out in this?" called Hannah as local botanist, Lenny Dryden, came through the door.

"Ah, this is fine Cornish weather, this is. I'll miss it when I'm gone."

Frowning at his words, Hannah watched as Lenny approached the bar, weaving his way round empty chairs and tables.

"Miss it, Lenny? Why? You going somewhere?"

"To Scotland, as soon as I can. I've been commissioned to study and paint the flora and fauna of the Hebrides. I've been to the islands before, in the dead of winter, and I can assure you, a couple of weeks up there and you'd never complain about the rain down here again. It's brutal."

Pulling a pint of Tribute for him, Hannah said, "Wow, I'm sure it is! What are you going to do about your place, then? Sell up?"

"No," replied Lenny as though the thought appalled him. "I'm only going for a year. I need a home to come back to. Ideally, I'd like a house sitter. Someone to look after the place until I return. They'd pay the bills but no rent. It's a pretty good deal. Trouble is, no one's biting."

"Really? I'm surprised. Your cottage is lovely."

And indeed it was, right next door to Joe. *I should move in there myself,* she thought and then stopped. Amazed and disappointed in equal measures that she could think such a thing. Still…

Taking the five-pound note he handed her, she was counting out his change when the idea hit her. *Layla. Why not?*

Swinging back round, Hannah said, "When do you need to get going?"

"As soon as possible, really. Everything's ready and waiting. I'll be staying in an old crofter's cottage on the Isle of Harris first, but

I'll be moving around. There's a lot of work to do. I really need to get cracking."

"I might be able to help you," Hannah replied tentatively. "A very good friend of mine—my best friend, in fact—might be looking for somewhere to stay. Layla Lewis, she's called. She's lovely. I could ask her."

"Thanks, Hannah. Any friend of yours would be more than welcome."

"No worries. I'll do it right away, whilst we're quiet. Let you know."

And with that, Hannah took herself into the confines of the pub kitchen and dialed Layla's mobile.

"Come to Trecastle? To live? Are you serious?"

"Deadly serious," said Hannah, disregarding the sound of sheer horror in Layla's voice. "It sounds to me as if you've got yourself into a sticky situation, and as far as I can see, this is as good a way as any out of it."

"But I live here, in Brighton. I always have done."

"You're no stranger to Trecastle, though. You know it well. For a long time it was almost like your second home. You used to say it was."

"Yeah, when I was a kid," Layla scoffed.

"It hasn't changed much, believe me. A place like this never does. But think about it. You can work as many shifts as you want at the pub, and you've got a decent place to live for next to nothing."

"But I've never worked in a pub."

"Oh, Layla." Hannah couldn't help laughing. "There's nothing to it. It's easy. I know it isn't what you're used to, but is that such a bad thing? Look, you haven't got a job, you're worried about paying the rent, and you don't want to see Alex ever again. Move down here, and it's all fixed. And remember," she reiterated, "it's only for a year. An extended holiday, really."

"An extended holiday? Hmm," said the voice on the other end of the phone, but Hannah knew she had swung it, that Layla was giving it serious consideration. Finally, after a bit more nudging, Layla agreed she would give it a go, that Hannah was right, she had nothing to lose. By the end of the phone call, both girls were squealing with delight.

Lenny had been delighted too, especially when Hannah told him that Layla could be down by the weekend if he wanted her to. He had finished his pint and hurried off, insisting he needed to "spruce up the place a bit for the young lady" and start packing. Hannah had been in Lenny's cottage once or twice. He wasn't an overly neat man, but he didn't exactly qualify for a stint on *How Clean is Your House?* Either. After a quick whip round with a duster, Layla would love it, she was sure.

Polishing the top of the bar for the umpteenth time, Hannah started to reminisce about how she and Layla had met as children. Layla had come down on holiday with her mother, Angelica, and stayed in a cottage just outside the village. They had spent a lot of time on the beach, as did everyone for miles around when the sun decided to shine. Theirs was no ordinary beach; it was a gorgeous swathe of golden sand, framed by granite cliffs upon which stood the crumbling walls of an ancient castle. There were caves to explore too, hidden in the cliffs. Children and adults alike would venture deep into them, discovering a dark world that belonged predominantly to birds and sea creatures.

It was at the beach that they had met, both of them taking part in a sandcastle competition, their earnest attempts failing to bag either of them a prize. Hannah remembered feeling quite disappointed. She'd put a lot of hard work into sculpting those turrets, scouring the beach for colorful shells to use as windows. Sensing her disappointment, Layla had leaned over, pointed to the winning castle and said, "I thought yours was much better than his. It's prettier." The kind words and a warm smile had made her feel instantly better. Hannah had asked the little girl her name, kick-starting what was to become an enduring friendship.

Hannah had introduced Layla and her mother to her own mum, and the two women had also clicked. Hannah's mum, Connie, had invited them to supper at her house in the village that very same evening. Whilst they sat downstairs, discussing life over a glass of wine, the two girls had raced upstairs to Hannah's bedroom and chatted some more. Hannah couldn't believe it; she had never met anyone she got on so well with, not like this, not straightaway, not even Molly Cardew, her best friend at school.

At the end of their holiday, Angelica and Layla had promised to come down for a fortnight again the following year, which they did, as well as every year after that until Layla was seventeen. The two families spent nearly every day of those two weeks together. Hannah didn't have a father either — he had left the family when she was a toddler — so it was just the four of them, laughing and letting their hair down. If there had been a boyfriend in either of their mothers' lives at the time (and there would certainly have been in Angelica's case), no invite was ever issued. This was *their* time, the four of them — an unwritten but strictly-adhered-to rule. Hannah knew Layla didn't feel that close to her mum, certainly not as close as she had been to her dad once upon a time, but the pair of them always seemed to get on okay during their time in Trecastle.

Between holidays, the girls would write to each other regularly until their early twenties when, for one reason or another, they'd drifted apart. It had been brilliant to be in touch again, and now Layla was coming to live here. Hannah could hardly believe it. This was something they'd dreamed of so often as children, living on each other's doorstep, and finally that dream was coming true. It felt a little surreal.

It was also just a teeny bit ironic she would be living next door to Joseph. Hannah wondered how the pair of them would get on. Both of them were single. What was to stop them from *really* getting on? But no, surely not. Layla had just split from her man. Getting involved with another one was probably the last thing on her mind.

Uncomfortable at where her thoughts were leading, she was relieved when the pub door burst open for only the second time that night. In walked Jim, just at the right moment. A knack he had.

As he walked toward her, she admired the fluid way he moved, his tall, broad-shouldered frame toned from surfing. Holding his body always felt good, his arms a cocoon of warmth and safety. She loved his hair too, almost as long as hers and slightly darker than her honeyed tones, although it lightened to an exact match in summer. He looked as though he didn't have a care in the world. And lived like it too.

"Pint?" she asked as he reached the bar, her eyes lowered in a purposefully coy manner.

"And a kiss from the barmaid," he replied with a wink.

chapter four

"I think you're mad. You know that, don't you?" Penny snipped.

"I should do," replied Layla irritably. "You've told me about a thousand times already this morning."

"All I'm saying is that this isn't the answer. Running away never is. If it was, don't you think I'd have done a bunk by now?"

Ignoring the jibe, Layla looked up from packing. "How's it going… with Richard, I mean? Still in separate bedrooms?"

"We most certainly are," replied Penny, becoming as irritable as Layla at the mention of his name. "I won't have him anywhere near me since that Diane Tyrrell episode. It'll be separate houses next, I'm telling you."

Layla sighed and went back to packing. That was the trouble with Richard and Penny: hot heads the pair of them, stubborn as mules. Once upon a time, Layla had admired the passion between them. It was so intense you could practically feel the air sizzle. She'd even felt a bit jealous, if she was honest. That instant chemistry had never happened to her, although she'd read about it often enough in the romantic books she devoured. Sadly, the sizzle had fizzled, and the divide between them was so enormous now, tumbleweed could blow through it.

Poor Penny, poor Richard. If only they could find their way back to how it used to be. Come to some sort of compromise: Richard working just a few hours less every week and Penny reining in that flirtatious nature of hers. Layla knew that more often than not Penny wasn't even aware she was flirting; she simply considered herself friendly. Her "friendliness," however, often landed them in hot water, with Layla having to smuggle a bewildered Penny out of a nightclub or pub because someone she'd been "chatting" to had gotten the wrong impression. With Dylan though, she *had* crossed the line. But why go and tell Richard about it? Why hadn't she just filed it away under "Things never to do again" and saved herself a whole lot of trouble? Coming clean had only added to their problems.

"That's it. I'm done," she said, looking at the pitiful pile in front of her.

"Is that it? Is that all you're taking?" asked Penny in amazement.

"There's only so much I can fit into that old heap of mine. It's a sports car, remember, not a mini bus. The cottage has everything I need anyway, Hannah's assured me."

"But what about all the stuff you've bought? You've practically furnished this flat."

"Which is why my lovely landlord is letting me off paying the rest of the rent. We've traded—my furniture for the money I owe him."

Eyeing the bits and pieces she'd picked up over the last couple of years, none of it shabby but none of it too impressive either, she continued, "It's a good deal as far as I'm concerned. He gets to charge the next punter more for a fully furnished flat, and I get my deposit back in full. At least I won't be landing in Trecastle completely destitute."

"Don't go!" Penny burst out suddenly. "*Please*. It's a stupid idea. There's nothing for you in Trecastle. It's the middle of nowhere."

"It's the edge of nowhere, actually," Layla countered. "Go a few steps further, and you'll fall into the sea."

"Oh, don't be so pedantic. You know what I mean."

"I do," Layla conceded. "But there's not a lot for me here either, is there?"

"Of course there is. You were born here; you belong here. And what about your friends?"

"My ex-work colleagues, you mean?" Layla shook her head derisively. "They're not friends, not really. They're people I haven't got anything in common with unless we've chucked at least three, preferably four, glasses of wine down our throats beforehand. I won't miss any of them."

"What about your family, then?"

"Penny…" Layla was getting exasperated now. "I'm an only child, remember? Mum's in Milan with Giorgio and shows no sign of ever coming home. As for my aunt, I hardly know her. She and Mum never got on."

"You still ought to stay, though," replied Penny. "Have your say with Alex."

"Alex?" Layla couldn't help shouting. "Do you realize he hasn't even texted me since he got back on Tuesday? He doesn't give a damn. He's made that crystal clear. No," she continued, shaking her head determinedly, "there's nothing more to say to Alex. Nothing at all."

"All right, then," Penny replied, her voice small this time. "What about me? How can you leave me?"

"Oh, Penny," said Layla, softening. "I'm not that far away. You'll come down and see me. I'll be back after a year. It's not a big deal."

"It's a big deal to me." Penny threw her arms in the air. "It feels like my whole world is falling apart!"

No stranger herself to that feeling, Layla attempted to give her a hug but was rudely brushed aside. Clearly Penny was not done.

"Richard and I are on the brink of divorce, and now my best friend is deserting me, leaving me alone to face life and all its battles."

Surprised at how dramatic she was being, Layla tried again to console her.

"I'm not deserting you. We can talk every day on the phone, text like it's going out of fashion. I'm here for you whatever happens."

"But you won't be here though, not *physically* here. It's not the same; nothing's the same anymore."

She was right about that at least; nothing *was* the same anymore, for either of them. Seeing her friend in such distress was upsetting, though. Was it a stupid idea to leave Brighton? Should she stay and confront Alex? The temp agency had said they would probably have work for her over the next week or so. All she had to do was ring them again, and she could be earning in no time. Then a voice surged up inside her, the same one she'd heard whilst on the phone to Hannah. A voice that had worried her at first, making her wonder if she had schizophrenic tendencies. A voice that said, *Go. Leave here. Have an adventure. It'll do you good.*

All she'd ever known was office life. All she'd ever known was Brighton. If she stayed, it would be the same old same old with a constant fear of bumping into Alex and Sarah-Jane mixed in for good measure. The idea of an adventure appealed to her. And she loved Trecastle, she really did. It was a magical place. The place she had met her other best friend; the place in which she had felt close to an otherwise absent mother; the place where she had found temporary relief from the grief of losing her father, as if somehow it were possible to have a holiday from heartache. She had been seventeen the last time she'd been there. She was dying to see it again, to see for herself if what Hannah had said was true: that time had hardly touched it at all.

No, as much as she was going to miss Penny, her staunchest ally since they'd met at City College over a decade ago, she was not going to stay in Brighton. Not with that voice nagging away inside her twenty-four seven.

Grabbing onto Penny's shoulders, her steely grip ensuring she wouldn't be brushed off this time, she said, "Listen to me, I am *not* abandoning you. And I'm not running away either, not really. I'm not sure if I can explain it, but what I'm doing feels right. When Hannah said to come down, it was as though I could see a way forward again, whereas before, all I could see was a brick wall I'd be constantly banging my head against. I'm going to miss you, you know I will. But I have to go." Then, as an unexpected wave of emotion rose from deep within and threatened to engulf her, she heard herself beg, "*Please,* Penny, please, you've got to let me go."

Penny looked shocked, really shocked.

"Okay," she said at last. "Go. Go and get over this shit with Alex. Go and come back stronger."

"Thanks," whispered Layla, relief replacing despair now she'd finally obtained her best friend's blessing.

Quickly the shoulder clutch developed into a bear hug, both girls holding onto one another as though their very lives depended on it.

Penny was the first to break away, a slight tremor in her voice as she said, "Anyway, I'll be down soon, to see what sort of a shack you're living in."

"I can't wait to see myself," Layla replied, smiling through her tears.

Soon after, they gathered up all that Layla had left in the world — two big black bags stuffed with clothes and toiletries, a duvet and pillow, a clutch of books she'd recently bought (none of them remotely romantic for once) a bag of CDs, and her beloved laptop — and they headed outside to load the Mazda. As Layla pulled away from the curb, the sight of Penny waving, a sad, solitary figure standing alone and lonely, nearly set her crying again. She would miss Penny. And she would miss Brighton, the city she had grown up in.

But she carried on regardless, leaving the crowded streets further and further behind until all that lay ahead was the open road.

The weather was not conducive to a long road journey. The heavens soon opened, and the farther west she drove, the harder it rained. Past Arundel, past Chichester, Portsmouth, and Southampton, she finally stopped in historic Dorchester for a bite to eat in a quaint café. Her phone buzzed on the table.

> The cottage is unlocked. Go straight in when you arrive
> and make yourself at home. Hannah xxx

What a difference! thought Layla. You could never leave your door unlocked in Brighton. If you did, you'd come back and find everything gone—fixtures, fittings, and the family cat. What a trusting lot they were down there. It was nice, comforting.

Quickly, Layla called Hannah.

"I've got to work at the pub tonight," Hannah told her, "so drop off your bags and come down for a drink as soon as you can." She sounded excited, and it was catching.

Layla looked at her watch. It was a few minutes past noon. She should be in Trecastle around three p.m. That would give her plenty of time to check out her new home, unpack, and spruce herself up a bit—perfect. Hannah promised they'd spend the next day together too, revisiting old haunts. As she thought fondly of Trecastle's impressive beach, the ruined castle, and the hustle and bustle of the high street, Layla could hardly wait to see them again.

After chomping away on her smoked salmon, cream cheese, and cucumber baguette, she drained the last dregs of Coke before heading back to her car, which she'd parked down a quiet side road. It was a short walk, but it still left her cold and wet. Her hair, normally smooth and shiny, was starting to frizz at an alarming rate. She turned the car's heater to full blast, grimacing at the slightly burned smell that came from the grill as she did so, and chose a CD. Adele had accompanied her on most of the first leg of the journey, Layla practically screaming herself hoarse to the lyrics of "Set Fire to the Rain." Although it had been quite cathartic, she had wanted something more low-key next and had turned to Lana Del Rey. But all that talk of kissing the object of your desire hard in the pouring rain, of being in love forever, had begun to grate after a while, and she'd turned the music off. She'd had enough heartfelt outpourings concerning boyfriends, errant or otherwise; now she wanted something comforting and instrumental, no lyrics at all. DJ Shadow it was, then, as she departed Dorchester and made her way to Exeter via Honiton.

By the time she reached Exeter, the rain had become fierce, forcing her to go slow. She would be at the cottage in more like two hours at this rate. But that was okay; she was enjoying the journey, just taking it easy. This was a stretch of road she'd always loved, sitting beside her mother as she drove them down in their old Peugeot, anticipating seeing Hannah again. She adored the scenery too, even in this weather, and how it changed from the soft, rolling hills of Devon to the more barren, rock-strewn Cornish landscape.

Turning left at Kennards House, she swapped the main road for the narrow country lanes of North Cornwall. A few miles before Trecastle, she started passing familiar landmarks. There, on the right, was the slate mine, a living monument to a bygone age. The famous Trecastle Piskie House was also still standing, but instead of the lively tourist attraction it had once been, it looked strangely desolate. An odd assortment of gnomes, piskies, and elfin-like statues stood guard, but they had clearly seen better days and the little house itself had fallen into serious disrepair.

I hope that's not indicative of Trecastle itself, she thought with a worried frown. But no, it couldn't be. Hannah was always going on about what a great place it was to live in. Certainly the pub she worked in, the oh-so-imaginatively named Trecastle Inn, attracted a lively crowd.

As she drew nearer to her destination, she caught a flash of silver on the horizon, and once again excitement gripped her. The sea she remembered well. It was different from the often murky waters of the Sussex coast, much bluer in color (when the sun shone), practically azure, and much wilder.

It was nearly four p.m. when she pulled into the village. The rain hadn't quite given up yet, and the wind was starting to thrash the already cowering trees around her. Her TomTom had guided her nicely for the main part of her journey but was faltering at the last hurdle. Hannah had told her exactly how to reach the cottage, however, and Layla had written the instructions down word-for-word, but still she missed the turn-off to her lane an impressive four times.

Finding herself on the way to the village center again, she pulled over, intending to negotiate a three-point turn. The cottage was slightly out of the village, so she needed to get back onto the opposite side of the road and go back up the hill. Glancing over Hannah's instructions again, she swung the car to the right — straight into the path of a motorcyclist.

The next few moments seemed to happen in slow motion. The rider tried to stop but couldn't do so in time, although he did manage to avoid hitting her car. As he turned his handlebars hard to the right, his tires lost grip on the wet road and he flew off, sliding some way before coming to a halt.

Layla sat motionless in her car, paralyzed temporarily by the shock. At last she managed to galvanize herself into action and fumbled for the door handle, her shaking hands making it hard to get a grip. When the door finally opened, another dilemma hit: What if she couldn't stand? Her legs felt like jelly; surely they wouldn't support her. Forcing herself upward, she was relieved to discover they held firm. Once she was sure they would continue to do so, she bolted over to where the biker lay, placed one hand on his soaked leather-clad shoulder, and said, "Are you okay?"

"No, I'm not bloody okay!" he replied, a pair of bright blue eyes meeting hers as he lifted his visor. "I'm a bit bruised and battered as it goes."

Despite his belligerent words, relief flooded through her: he wasn't dead!

"Oh, I'm so glad," she said, letting out a huge sigh.

"Glad?" he said, sitting up now and brushing the mud and leaves off his left arm. "Charming."

"Oh, no, no," she stuttered, realizing what she'd just said. "I'm not glad that I knocked you over. I'm glad you're alive."

"Only just, I think," he replied, needing a helping hand to stand up.

"Can I give you a lift somewhere, take you to the nearest hospital?"

"The nearest hospital? That would be in Bodmin, I think, about fifteen miles from here. I don't fancy driving fifteen miles with you behind the wheel."

Feeling a little indignant now, Layla replied, "I'm actually a very good driver, thank you. You're the first accident I've ever had."

"Lucky me," he replied sarcastically. "Look, I'm fine. Nothing appears to be broken. Just help me get my bike up, and I'll be on my way."

Both of them hurried over to the bike, lying abandoned on the road.

As they bent down to lift it, Layla said, "It doesn't look too damaged, does it?"

"It doesn't matter if it is," he replied, wincing at the effort it took to pick it up. "I'm not precious about it. It's just an old trail bike I muck around on. To be honest, the more battered it looks, the better."

Again she noticed him wincing with pain as he remounted the bike.

"Are you sure you're all right?"

"I'm fine," he replied. "Really, don't worry. Are you all right?"

Layla was surprised that he could feel concern for her after what she had done. "Yeah, yeah, I think so. Thanks for asking and sorry. Really, I am so sorry."

"There's no need to be. I'm okay," he said, and she could tell he was smiling, despite the fact his helmet covered almost all of his face.

She smiled back at him, but hesitantly so.

As he drove away, she got back into her car and leaned against the steering wheel, waiting for the shakes to subside.

Right, best get on, she thought before putting the car back into first gear and turning with exaggerated care up the hill, toward her new home.

There was the elusive turn-off—a tiny little lane just off the main road into the village, with quaint cottages on either side. On the right, in all its humble glory, stood Lenny Dryden's cottage.

The memory of the accident parceled up and put aside for now, she parked her car, stepped once more into the rain, and stood and stared at the cottage. Hannah had said it was lovely, and she was right. Painted white, its stucco walls were clean and bright with tiny window frames picked out in a fading shade of sage green. The door was sage green too and the roof traditional slate. Drawing nearer to it, she saw it had a name—The Outlook—etched in large letters on the glass panel above the door.

How charming, she thought, moving closer.

Opening the front door, she stepped into a tiny hallway, which in turn led through to the living room, a cluttered but cozy den with traditional oak beams and a cast iron wood burner in the fireplace. Bookshelves lined one wall, and walking over to them, she noted that some were by Lenny Dryden himself, books on plants and related matters. There were watercolors of flowers on the walls too, of Red Valerian, Tree Mallow, and Curled Dock, all painted by the owner. Hannah hadn't told her he was an artist, let alone a published writer. She was impressed.

At the back of the cottage was the kitchen, fairly largish with walls painted the color of buttermilk, flagstones on the floor, a black Rayburn oven, and an old-fashioned butler's sink. A sturdy old oak table dominated the room, and on it were the house keys, a big bunch of flowers, and a box of chocolates as well as a handwritten letter from Mr. Dryden, no doubt explaining all the cottage's ins and outs. Touched at his thoughtfulness, she stopped to sniff the lilies before making her way to the rear of the kitchen and another door, which she presumed led into the garden.

Layla opened the door, peered into the descending gloom, and noticed a long and narrow stretch of lawn lay before her. Lifting her eyes to gaze farther, she could make out the Atlantic Ocean in the distance. Squinting more, she gasped in surprise.

"Gull Rock," she cried out. "It's Gull Rock. I can see Gull Rock from my kitchen."

So that was her outlook, and what an outlook it was. She loved Gull Rock, remembered it well from childhood. How she and Angelica had stood on the shore before it and fantasized about making it their own, just the two of them, living there forevermore on their secret island. It had always remained tantalizingly out of reach, though. So near and yet so far.

A pang of longing for Angelica shot through her suddenly, so she parceled that up too and placed it in another box. Now was not the time for indulging in memories, good, bad, or indifferent. Now was the time to see what other delights the cottage held for her.

Venturing upstairs, she poked her head around the bathroom door. It was small but sufficient with a decent-looking shower and pretty blue and white tiles on the wall. The first bedroom she came to was sparsely furnished. There was a double bed in it, though, and a chest of drawers with a mirror hanging above it. More of Lenny's paintings graced the magnolia walls.

Saving the best for last—at least, she hoped so—she entered
the main bedroom, just above the kitchen. She was not disappointed.
It was pale blue in color with fresh white skirting, a picture rail (also
in white) wooden floorboards, and a black cast-iron fireplace. There
was an antique-looking walnut wardrobe with a full-length mirror
on the door and, the pièce de résistance, another vase of fresh flowers,
sitting atop a beautiful old chest of drawers. Clearly Lenny intended
for her to sleep in this room, and she wasn't going to argue. She could
see Gull Rock from here too and imagined lazy summer mornings
in bed, propped up with pillows, as she admired its majestic beauty.

She wrapped her arms around herself and smiled. This was perfect,
dust and all, a veritable haven in which to enjoy some much needed
time away from the rat race and the rats who inhabited it.

Going back downstairs, she found the kettle, filled it with water,
and switched it on, gasping for a cup of tea. Luckily, she had thought
to bring a few provisions with her and went to retrieve them from
the hallway. Whilst munching her way through a packet of salt and
vinegar crisps, her phone rang again.

"Where are you?" Hannah asked eagerly. "Have you arrived yet?"

"I have. I'm here and it's great. I love it."

"I knew you would!" cried Hannah. "So are you coming down?
Help me pull a pint or two?"

"Yeah, sure. Give me half an hour or so, and I'll be there."

"Brilliant. See you soon."

"Bye," Layla replied and hung up.

No time for eating, then, she'd better unpack the car, sort out
the bedraggled mess that she was, and get down to the pub. Start
learning the ropes.

She hauled one of the bags up the stairs, into her bedroom, and
plonked it on the bed. Before doing anything else, however, she
couldn't resist peering out of the window again, having to imagine
Gull Rock this time as dusk had now hidden it completely. *A year,* she
thought. *That's all I've got, a year. Enough time to get over anyone, surely?*

Taking in a deep breath then letting it slowly out, she bloody
hoped so.

chapter five

"Layla! Layla! Over here."

Pulling a pint with one hand and waving frantically with the other, Hannah handed the glass to its eager recipient and hurried round to the public side of the bar.

As she practically threw herself into Layla's outstretched arms, she felt the same surge of excitement at her friend's arrival as she'd had in childhood.

"I'm so happy you're here."

"Me, too," replied Layla, laughing along with her.

"You found us okay, then?"

"Yeah, it finally stopped raining, so I walked down. Needed to stretch my legs after being in the car all day. It's not that far at all, is it. It only took me about fifteen minutes. And you're right; nothing seems to have changed much out there. Just a few of the gift shops perhaps, but this pub is exactly how I remember it and, more to the point, *where* I remember it."

Hannah looked around fondly. "It's probably a bit more tired than it used to be. I might get Jim to repaint it soon, but it's got a good atmosphere, and the bar staff, of course, are amongst the best in Cornwall."

"I don't doubt it," Layla said with a smile. "I just hope I don't spoil things."

"No way. You'll be our finest asset, I'm sure. Now, let me look at you. Good, you're looking good. He's done no lasting damage, I can tell."

Hugging her close again, Hannah could actually tell he, whoever *he* was, had done quite a bit of damage. Layla had a look in her eyes that she'd never had before. Hannah was used to them being full of life and vitality. If she had to describe them now, she would say they were haunted.

"Come on." Hannah released her at last. "Come and meet the gang."

Leading Layla past the jukebox and over to a table in the furthest corner of the room, Hannah explained who the "gang" were.

"Jim, of course, you know, but sitting next to him are Curtis and Ryan. Do you remember meeting them briefly when we came down to Brighton? They're his band mates: Curtis on bass guitar, Ryan on drums. The redhead, that's Mick, our local fisherman, and still to come is Joseph, carpenter and cabinet maker extraordinaire. There's plenty of others too," she continued, "locals you'll get to know well over the coming months, especially as you'll be the one responsible for pouring them their favorite tipple. We're like one big family down here. We all look out for each other. You'll feel a part of it in no time."

As they neared the table, Jim jumped up. "Hey, Layla, how are you?"

"Fine, thanks," Layla answered, but Hannah could tell her friend was feeling overwhelmed at being the center of attention. A drink, that's what she needed.

"Glass of wine, Layla?"

"Oh, God, yes." Relief was evident in her voice. "White, please. Whatever you've got."

Hannah returned to the bar. Where was Joe? He knew Layla was arriving today, that they were getting together en masse to welcome her. Surely he'd turn up? Then she stopped herself. Why the heck was she worrying? Of course, he'd turn up. He always did. Eventually.

It wasn't overly busy in the pub, the winter weather still discouraging most people from leaving their firesides. But it would get steadily busy as the weather got warmer, as spring arrived and then summer, both seasons bringing with them the tourist hoards. She'd need to get several more paintings done by then to make the most of the influx and swell her coffers. She'd get Layla up and running in the pub as soon as possible, but despite joking about it earlier, she wouldn't do so tonight. Tonight Layla just needed to relax, get herself acquainted with everyone.

"There you go, Layla. It's a large one," said Hannah, seating herself beside her whilst simultaneously keeping an eye on the bar.

"Thanks, I need it." Layla took a few sips before turning back to chat to Mick.

Hannah looked across at Jim talking to Curtis and Ryan, no doubt about their next gig at the Admiral's Arms in Port Levin, further along the coast. His band had developed quite a cult following in these parts, and it was something he took very seriously. Along with his girlfriend, that is, she thought affectionately. Catching her watching him, he smiled — a cheeky smile, a smile that held a night full of promise.

They were a good bunch; she was sure Layla would grow as fond of them as she was. Curtis and Ryan were a few years younger than the rest of them, in their mid-twenties and just as laid-back as Jim, just as good-natured. Mick was a real laugh too, the joker of the pack with an eye for the ladies. Clearly, an eye for Layla, by the looks of it. Hannah would have to have a quiet word in his ear at some stage, tell him not to get his hopes up as Layla was off men at the moment. And then there was Joe. What would she think of Joe? What would he think of her? *Friends as well as neighbors,* she mused.

It was nearly an hour later when Joseph arrived, spotting them straightaway but going to the bar before joining them.

Hannah got up and went to serve him.

"Hey, you okay?" she asked as casually as she could muster.

"I'm fine thanks, Han," he replied. "How are you?"

"Yeah, good, good." She nodded. "What have you been doing? Working?"

"Yeah, sorry I'm late. It's all a bit frantic at the moment."

"Is that why we don't see so much of you lately?" she said, immediately annoyed with herself for asking.

"Er, I'm not sure." His eyebrows furrowed in confusion. "I didn't realize I was being elusive."

"I'm just saying," she mumbled, not quite able to meet his gaze. "Anyway, come on over and meet Trecastle's newest resident."

When they reached the table, Hannah started to introduce them. "Layla, this is Joe. Joe, this is—"

"We've already met," said Joseph, extending his hand and smiling.

"Have we?" asked Layla, baffled.

"Have you?" said Hannah. This was news to her.

"Yeah, we have," continued Joseph. "A couple of hours ago. On the road into the village. You tried to kill me, remember?"

"Kill you?" Layla gasped. "*You're* the biker? The one I knocked over?"

"You knocked him over?" repeated Hannah in horror.

"I didn't mean to," explained Layla quickly. "It was an accident. I was going to tell you about it. I just haven't had the chance yet."

Hannah turned to Joseph. "Are you okay? Are you hurt at all?"

"Well," he replied somberly, "apart from my right arm, which I'm not sure is ever going to work again, I'm fine."

Layla's jaw dropped open, and he added, "I'm joking. Really, it's just a joke. I'm fine."

"Right, well, in that case," Hannah continued, "as I was saying, Layla, this is Joseph Scott. Joe, this is Layla Lewis, your would-be killer, next-door neighbor, and my best friend. She's house-sitting whilst Lenny's in Scotland."

"Next-door neighbor, huh?" Joseph took a swig from his pint glass. "That could prove interesting."

"Really? Why?" said Hannah, unable to keep aloof.

"Why?" Joseph said, his gaze still firmly on Layla. "Because every time I step outside my front door, I'll be taking my life in my hands, that's why. Just as well my other vehicle is an armored tank. I'll have to get it out of retirement, make good use of it."

They all laughed at this, Layla, Jim, Curtis, Ryan, and Mick. Hannah laughed too, but not as hard as the rest of them. Since setting eyes on Layla, Joe had barely looked away. Come to think of it, the reverse could also be said. Was that a spark of something bursting into life between them or was she being paranoid? She didn't know. Pain, so familiar it was almost like a comfort blanket, flared up inside her. She tried hard to quash it. Too late. Jim had already noticed.

He was looking at her again, but this time the cheeky smile had gone. His face now showed concern, not for himself but for her.

Always for her. In the moment their eyes locked, she hated herself. Why couldn't she be happy with what she had? What was wrong with her? No man had ever loved her like Jim loved her. Which was, of course, part of the problem.

As much as she adored living in Trecastle, perhaps a move to the next village really would be a good idea when they finally got round to buying a house. Not too far. She didn't want to move too far, but far enough to avoid this daily torture. Smiling at Jim, she went over to him and ruffled his hair, hoping to silently reassure him before returning to the bar and the handful of customers that were waiting for her.

chapter six

So this was the man Layla had nearly killed. She should have known. His face may have been hidden by his helmet, but those eyes were unforgettable. She'd never seen a blue like it. They were as blue as the sky on a perfect summer's day.

After Hannah had introduced him to her, Joseph pulled up a chair beside her and joined in the fun and banter. Bantering mainly with her, she had to admit. She was surprised to see how quickly Hannah had retreated back behind the bar and wondered if she should go and help. But Hannah had told her not to just enjoy herself tonight. And she was; she really was. These were lovely people. Warm and welcoming. So different from the corporate types she was used to back home.

Jim was a real catch; Hannah must be very pleased with herself. He was good-looking in a thrown together kind of way with his shoulder length hair, loose jeans, and battered but oh-so-cool brown leather jacket. It was obvious from the way his eyes followed Hannah around that he adored her. Mick was also great. He trawled the high seas with his dad, his wind-reddened cheeks a clue to his profession and almost exactly the same shade as his unruly mop of hair. And then there was Joseph, tall and lean with dark blond hair that flopped every now and then over those eyes of his, those incredible blue eyes.

He was actually breathtaking if you liked that kind of man, which of course she didn't.

No, as she told him on their way home later that evening, the pair of them stopping every now and then to marvel at how brightly the stars glittered in the night sky (brighter than she'd ever seen them shine before), she wasn't into men at all. Nor was she into girls, she hastened to add, in case he got the wrong idea—she was from Brighton, after all.

"I just want to be on my own, to find myself." She hiccupped. "That's what this year is all about. Straightening myself out."

"Quite right, too," he said, rushing to grab her elbow, even though she was sure she wasn't staggering in the slightest.

"Indeed." She nodded, pleased he so readily agreed with her. "What about you? Do you like it here?" she continued merrily.

"I do, yes," Joseph replied, his voice suddenly thoughtful. "I didn't at first, wondered what the hell I was playing at, moving here from London. But gradually I came to like it, love it, in fact."

"Oh?" nudged Layla, intrigued.

"It's different than where I'm from—Hammersmith, by the way—but a good sort of different. The pace is slower, easier to live with. It changes you too, living in a place like this. Back in London, whatever I had never seemed enough. Like everyone else, I wanted bigger, better, more."

"Like what?" she asked, cursing the slur that had crept into her voice.

"Oh, I don't know." He laughed now—at the slur or the question she didn't know. "The latest LED-LCD HD TV, for example, with 3D kit and Blu-ray player. Back there, it would have been essential. Down here, I don't even own a TV!"

"Gosh." Layla was horrified and impressed at the same time. "No TV? I can't imagine."

They had reached her front door. Fumbling for the key in the pocket of her jeans, she made two attempts at inserting it in the lock before finally managing to open it. Before going inside, she swung back round to say goodnight to this newfound friend of hers. As she did so, something peculiar happened. Face-to-face, their eyes locked and the rest of the world vanished, just melted away, glittering stars and all, with absolutely no warning whatsoever, leaving the two of them alone and stranded in the universe, staring at each other.

As she stared and stared, the word *pheromones* popped into her head and floated tantalizingly around. Metaphorically grabbing hold of it as though it were the key to enlightenment, she decided, *That's it. That's all this is. An attack of pheromones, nothing more.*

She knew from past experience how much havoc a few stray pheromones could cause, particularly after one glass of wine too many. And she'd certainly had one glass of wine too many tonight, more like four or five in fact, with Hannah not exactly sticking to the rules regarding pub measures. She liked Joseph. He was nice. Funny and seemingly kind. But paramour material he was not. Probably around twenty-eight or twenty-nine, he was not in her preferred age bracket. She liked older men, men with character, men who had experienced something of life. *Men like Alex,* she thought, his name having the effect of several strong espressos. Coming to, she tore her gaze away, mumbled a flimsy excuse, flung the door shut, and rushed in to collapse at the kitchen table.

What the hell am I doing? she thought. *I've been here one night, and already I'm coming home drunk and making eyes at the boy next door.*

That was not why she'd come to Trecastle, as she had only been pointing out a few minutes ago. Getting friendly with the locals was okay; getting more than friendly was certainly not. Rebound action had never been her style, and that's all it would be. A bit of rebound action.

She was single, and single she would stay, until she'd worked Alex out of her system at least. Which didn't look likely to be happening anytime soon. No matter how much she'd enjoyed talking to Joseph tonight—to Mick, to Jim, to all of them—she craved Alex, as though he were a drug and she the addict. And little wonder, they'd only been apart three weeks. The wounds he'd inflicted were still suppurating.

Her head falling forward in her hands, the brave face she'd tried to wear ever since she found out about Sarah-Jane finally cracked. Now that she was hundreds of miles from Alex, she could admit how much she missed him. His soulful brown eyes, his impressive confidence, and, yes, she had to admit it, his incredibly sexy aura of power. He had made her feel special, like she was "the chosen one" or something. Now she just felt stupid. Alex didn't want her, perhaps had never wanted her. Taking off into the wild blue yonder with another (younger) member of staff and leaving nothing but a Post-It note by way of explanation pretty much told her that this was the case.

The tears began again, and instead of brushing them away, she let them fall, hoping they'd bring with them some kind of relief. They didn't.

Without Alex, without Penny, even without her mother, she felt lonely, perhaps the loneliest she had ever felt—which was saying something. She missed Brighton and wanted to wrap its familiarity around her like a cloak. Although she knew Trecastle from childhood, she was effectively a stranger in a strange land. Being here felt wrong. The edge of nowhere, as she'd called it, a stone's throw from oblivion. Perhaps Penny was right: running away was not the answer. She should have stayed, toughed it out. A thought, of course, which only made her cry harder.

chapter seven

"Hey, you're sounding brighter," Penny said. "Settling in at last?"

"Yeah, I think so," replied Layla. "It's taken a few weeks, but I'm getting used to life in the sticks. Even catch myself enjoying it at times."

Penny laughed. "And what about the job? Do you think you've found your calling in life?"

"That's going a bit far," Layla said, a smile in her voice, "but it's okay. It serves a purpose. It pays my way, at least."

"Good, glad to hear it. I'll be down tomorrow, late afternoon. Is that okay?"

"Okay?" yelled Layla, forcing Penny to hold the phone at a distance in order to safeguard her eardrums. "It's brilliant! I can't believe I've got you all to myself for a whole seven days. We've got so much to catch up on."

Quickly changing the subject, Penny asked, "Anyway, what are you up to tonight? Working?"

"No, I've got the week off in your honor, starting tonight, in fact. Joseph's coming round for a bite to eat."

"Again? That's becoming quite a habit, isn't it?"

"Not really." Layla's voice was prickly all of a sudden. "It just makes sense. He only lives next door, we get on well, and it's more fun cooking for two than one. It's only been a handful of times, anyway."

It's been a damn sight more than that, thought Penny. But not wanting to upset Layla's mood further, she said, "Have a good time tonight. Don't drink too much, and I'll see you tomorrow. Love you."

"Love you too, hun. Drive carefully, won't you?"

Assuring Layla she would, Penny hung up before shoving the phone back into her jacket pocket. As she crossed the road to the deli, intent on getting some lunch before rushing back to finish the day's work, she thought, *We certainly have got lots to catch up on.* But how much Penny was going to reveal, she hadn't yet decided.

Regarding Richard, there wasn't much to say. Things hadn't improved, although she had let him back into their bedroom. Not because she wanted sex or anything, far from it. Rather, she couldn't bear his constant moaning and groaning about how uncomfortable the bed in the spare room was. They hadn't had sex for ages—since she'd told him about Dylan, in fact. Sometimes she wondered if they ever would again.

After the incident with Diane Tyrrell, they hadn't spoken for over a week, although one heck of a lot of door banging had gone on during that time (mainly by her, she had to admit). After a while though, they had gradually softened from downright hostility to formal politeness, both of them realizing that if they were to continue living under the same roof, they had to at least pass the time of day every now and then. How much longer they'd carry on living under the same roof, though, was debatable. The thought of severing ties completely was too painful to contemplate, but neither could she bear the thought of living like this for weeks, months, or even years to come. She was still so angry with him. She couldn't help it, and certainly he was angry with her. Where had all this anger come from? It seemed to have crept up on them like some sort of comic book monster, ensnaring them in its vice-like hold. Why didn't they fight back instead of giving in to it? Join forces and banish the monster forever.

Regarding Alex, there was plenty to tell. When he had turned up on her doorstep last week, she'd nearly dropped down dead. She couldn't have been more surprised if she'd opened the door to find Queen Elizabeth II herself standing there, in full royal regalia with guards trooping the color behind her. For a while, they had stood and gawped at each other. Well, she had gawped at him, until at last he had broken the silence.

"Can I come in?" he had said, his agitation clear. "I need to talk to you."

Adopting what she'd hoped was a suitably haughty manner, she had replied, "I don't think so. We have nothing to talk about."

"Please," he had begged, and she'd been surprised to see a hint of vulnerability in those deep brown eyes of his, although whether it was as genuine as it looked, she couldn't tell. She had a sudden impression of the cat from *Shrek*, the one who could switch from being lethal to lovable with one glorious sweep of his eyelids.

Curious, she had let him in, but no further than the hallway.

"Be quick," she had snapped. "I'm busy."

"Where's Layla? I need to clarify something with her. It's important."

Clarify? What sort of a word was that? she remembered thinking. Did he think they were in a business meeting or something?

"She's gone, left Brighton. I'm afraid it's too late to *clarify* anything with Layla."

Her smugness at throwing such an inappropriate word back at him was swiftly replaced with shock when he bellowed back, "I know she's gone, for God's sake! That's why I'm here. I've been to her flat. Some bloody student answered the door, didn't know who the hell I was talking about. Where *is* she?"

Recovering quickly, she had yelled back, "As far away from you as she could possibly get, that's where!"

In the face of her spirited response, all fight had left him. He had just stood there, shoulders slumped. "This has all been a terrible mistake," he muttered pitifully. "All of it. I need to find her. Help me find her. *Please.*"

Penny had looked at him then—*really* looked at him. He was far from the confident figure he usually cut. In fact, he looked wretched. Heavy black rings encircled his eyes, his hair was unkempt, and his jaw was covered in stubble. Gray stubble, at that. He wouldn't look out of place down at the nightly soup run on the seafront, dejectedly shuffling his way to the front for a bowl of vegetable broth.

"Why?" she had asked, softening. "Why should I help you?"

Perhaps encouraged by her more gentle tone, he had leaned forward in an almost conspiratorial manner. "She needs to come clean about an email she wrote, an email she pretended was from me. Once Jack realizes I had nothing to do with it, nothing at all, I'll be able to get the merger back on track. Until then I'm stuffed."

Email? What email? It hadn't clicked at first. Then the memory of their drunken escapade had come flooding back. Of course! The email she'd sent to FarScapes' managing director telling him Easy Travel was no longer interested in joining forces with them, that they were, in fact, a bunch of losers. Clearly he thought Layla had written it and wanted her to absolve him.

Penny was about to tell him the truth, but she stopped. How much damage had that email actually caused? Was Easy Travel really in trouble because of it? If she did own up, could it impact on Richard in any way? Alex was a powerful man hereabouts, probably a member of the Rotary Club or even the Masons. He could jeopardize Richard's chances at a partnership even more so than she had done by insulting his client.

Rapidly she decided it was best to keep quiet, to feign complete and utter ignorance. What did she care about his company anyway? Let FarScapes think the worst. Besides which, was that all he cared about? What about the small matter of ripping her best friend's heart to shreds?

Her fury rising again, she had said as much to him.

"Of course I care about her," he had insisted, "but she left me in a real mess. My business is suffering because of her. I have to sort it out."

"How do you know she wrote that email, anyway?" she had dared to ask. "Anyone could have."

"Because of this," he'd replied, grabbing his wallet from his back pocket and pulling out a Post-It note before waving it in her face.

Snatching it from him, she'd read the message Layla had left on his desk that night back in January.

"And?" she'd asked. It seemed innocent enough.

"'Good luck with FarScapes. You'll need it,'" he'd read aloud, stabbing with his index finger at the words. "That proves she did it. It's my only evidence, but Jack Thomas won't have it. I've been trying to make him listen for weeks now. Layla needs to tell him herself; get me off the hook. He'll listen to her; he respected her. Don't get me wrong, I'm not angry with her. Not at all. I just want things to go back to the way they were. Everything."

"When you were top dog, you mean? Swanning around Easy Travel like some sort of Roman emperor. Working your way through your adoring but deluded minions. You needed taking down a peg or two. Whatever's happened with FarScapes, I'm glad. You deserve it."

"I know you think I'm only concerned with my company," he had replied, "but I'm not. I do have feelings for Layla. I realize that now. I miss her more than I thought I would. But I'm a business man. Layla appreciates that."

"She didn't appreciate your liaison with Sarah-Jane, though," she had growled back.

"That was a mistake. A moment of weakness. She'll understand."

"A moment of weakness?" she had practically screamed at him. "A pretty impressive moment, if you ask me! How long were you in Florida with her? Two weeks? And before that, you were shagging her in your office. Don't tell me you have feelings for Layla because I don't believe you. You're incapable of feeling anything for anybody but yourself."

He had looked downcast at that, as though she'd struck a nerve.

"I'll find her," he'd said finally, every word coated in determination. "I'll put things right. With Easy Travel and with Layla. Just watch me."

"I'd rather watch paint dry, thanks." Then she'd slammed the door in his face.

Going over it in her head now didn't make her dilemma any easier. How was she going to tell Layla about this, or more to the point, *what* was she going to tell her? Every last word that idiot had uttered, or a scaled-down version? Layla sounded much happier these days; the last thing Penny wanted was to unsettle her again. She knew she'd have to eventually, though. Keeping secrets wasn't her forte, as the current mess she was in with Richard proved. But the FarScapes fiasco she'd definitely keep quiet about. She knew what Layla was like: she'd feel responsible. Layla would rush back to Brighton, straight into his smug embrace, after publicly taking the blame, of course. And as much as she wanted Layla back in Brighton, she didn't want her to be hurt again. And Alex *would* hurt her again; his type couldn't help themselves.

As she left the deli to return to work, her phone beeped. Someone had left a message. Tingles ran up and down her spine as she skidded to a halt to read it.

Are we still on for a drink after work? D x

Unable to stop a big grin from spreading across her face, she quickly replied.

Okay, just a quick one. 6:30 at The Grenadier?

An obscure pub, out of the way. Surely they wouldn't bump into anyone they knew there?

Looking forward to it. D x

That was something else she wouldn't mention to Layla, either. That she had started seeing Dylan again. Strictly as friends, nothing more. She'd been absolutely clear with him about that. He was a laugh, though, and she could do with a laugh. Richard hadn't been exactly tickling her fancy lately.

As she reached New Britain House, a thought crossed her mind. *I'm not bad at keeping secrets, actually. In fact, I'm really rather good.* But it was a thought, she realized, that filled her with dismay, not pride.

chapter eight

After finishing her conversation with Penny, Layla wondered for a few moments whether to phone her mother next, before deciding against it. She needed to crack on with the cleaning as well as preparing tonight's meal.

When she had first told Angelica she had moved to Trecastle, the news had been greeted by a stunned silence at the other end of the line.

"Mum?" she had said, worried. "Are you still there?"

"Yes, darling, of course I am. I just can't quite believe what you're telling me, that you're living in Trecastle, of all places."

"You remember it, then?" she had asked, only half jokingly.

"I remember it well," had been Angelica's answer. "Very well, indeed."

There had been a wistful tone to her mother's voice that had surprised Layla, an echo of sadness. Soon after, Angelica had cut the conversation short: she had a lunch date and was running late. Same old Mum. Always busy. Always rushing to do something, see someone.

She'd been that way since Dad had died, when Layla was seven, filling her life with an almost endless stream of visitors coming and going at all hours. Rather than turn to her only child for solace, she had turned to them instead, their constant company, Layla suspected, some kind of coping mechanism. Unfortunately, most of these "friends" had regarded children as nothing but a nuisance, and so Layla had learned to avoid them, her mother included.

Before Greg's death, Layla remembered a happy family unit, the three of them together, close, always laughing. After he had gone, she had needed her remaining parent more than ever, but instead of pulling together, they had grown increasingly apart, unable to recapture what had once been.

Except in Trecastle. It was on holiday that Angelica relaxed, the years visibly falling from her as she allowed the demands of her hectic life and the people in it to retreat, for a short while at least, into the shadows. During this time, she seemed to look at her daughter with fresh eyes, remembering who she was and what to do with her. And that's when the fun would start!

Grabbing a duster and some all-purpose cleaner, Layla began wiping surfaces. As she worked, a favorite memory came to mind of her and Angelica, running along the beach, their feet splashing the cold Atlantic Ocean. They would cry out every time the icy foam washed over their bare toes. Normally it was daytime when they visited the beach, but this time it had been dusk and there was no one around, just the two of them, playing on what she would think of thereafter as "their beach." As the tide made its way back in, they had retreated to the rocks, and there Angelica had told her all about the smoke fairies who lived in the west country. Wispy, ethereal creatures, hidden in beachside caves and on the moors, their task to sprinkle magic into the humdrum lives of mere mortals. Pragmatic, even as a child, Layla had laughed, but Angelica had chided her, told her it was true, and to believe in them at all times. Listening to the gentle lilt of her mother's voice, Layla had found herself mesmerized by her storytelling, in the end, believing wholeheartedly in this mysterious and benevolent population. Certainly, the memory was magical. Whether it was for her mother too, she didn't know.

Having finished dusting and polishing, she turned her attention to the meal she was cooking for tonight: a Thai concoction she had managed to rustle up all by herself. Usually she stole from magazines or cookbooks, but this time she had devised a recipe of her own making. Joseph was a natural cook, an instinctive cook, often using ingredients she'd never heard of—such as samphire, a sea vegetable apparently, and gurnard, a type of fish—to create delicious dishes worthy of a Michelin-starred restaurant. She wanted to show that she, too, had an ounce of culinary flair. Although, if she were honest, she much preferred to eat than cook.

As she bruised lemongrass, peeled ginger, and tore up lime leaves (she'd had to make a special trip for such exotic ingredients to the supermarket in Bodmin), her mind drifted back to the short story she had recently written and sent off for possible publication.

Why she had been inspired to write again, she didn't know. Maybe living in a cottage that belonged to an artist and writer had encouraged her creative streak. What people didn't know—well, everyone except Mum and Hannah—was that she'd won a writing competition when she was sixteen. A potted rip-off of *Wuthering Heights,* it had nonetheless impressed the judges who had sent her a book voucher and a Parker pen for her efforts, along with a letter telling her she had definite talent and to hone it well over the coming years. She smiled as she remembered how proud she'd been of that letter, how she had kept it pinned to her bedside wall until it quite literally fell apart from too much reverential stroking. Despite the advice, the last time she had written anything creative had been when she was eighteen, just before starting City College and embarking on her marketing and business diploma. There just hadn't seemed the time after that to indulge in anything quite so frivolous.

Well, now she had finally made time, in between hanging out with Hannah and the gang and working at the pub. And she was pleased she had. It was really rather good, a tender mother-daughter story with Gull Rock featuring heavily. Flicking through the first edition of a new magazine called *Izabel,* she had seen an advert asking for contributions. And so, feeling vaguely hopeful, she had sent off her first story in years.

Content with how her Thai dish was shaping up, she rubbed the paste-like substance into some pollack—caught by Mick, of course—and left it to marinate while she went upstairs. Joseph would be here in a couple of hours. It was time to spring clean herself, instead of the cottage. Her hair could do with a really good condition, and a face pack wouldn't go amiss either, one of those deep-cleansing clay ones.

In the bedroom, putting away clothes fresh from the tumble dryer and changing the bedsheets, Layla marveled at how well she got on with Joseph. They'd actually become firm friends, despite their less than auspicious start. Penny had been surprised that they were spending so much time together, but as Layla had pointed out, they *were* next-door neighbors; it wasn't so strange. They had common ground too, and not only because she was Hannah's best friend and he Jim's. Once upon a time, he, too, had come to Trecastle to escape.

Hannah had told her that Joseph's ex-girlfriend was, in fact, a friend of Jim's. Tara and Jim hailed from the same village, not far from Trecastle, just along the coast. Tara made regular visits back home to visit parents and friends and had often brought Joseph along with her. Jim had usually been around on these occasions, and that was how the two boys had met.

Joseph and Tara had split when she'd decided she wanted to spend time backpacking in Australia with a view to settling there. She'd wanted Joseph to join her, but he had been hesitant, finally deciding against it. After she was gone, however, he'd confessed to Jim that he may have made a mistake. He'd felt lost in London without her.

Layla had quizzed further on this point.

"So was he, like, I don't know, heartbroken then?" she had asked Hannah.

"Heartbroken?" Hannah had pondered. "I don't know whether I'd go that far, but he was down about it, certainly. When I first met him, I could tell he was pining after her still."

Jim had been the one to persuade Joseph to move to Trecastle, a village he himself had only just moved to. Like Layla, Joseph had laughed at the idea initially, but the thought of sun, sea, and sand, as well as his best mate at hand had finally proved too tempting, and he'd arrived in Trecastle with little more than a couple of suitcases and high hopes. His profession as a carpenter meant he could pretty much work anywhere, and after finding a suitable workshop, business had boomed, enabling him to move off Jim's sofa and into a place of his own.

Joseph saw himself as one of the locals now, and he certainly knew his way around this neck of the woods, taking her to some very pretty villages. Each village had, at its heart, a pub, and many an evening they had whiled away in one of these charming hostelries, nestled beside the ocean, perhaps, or further inland, on the bleak but beautiful moor.

On one such evening outside The Anchor Inn—a gem of a place less than two miles away—they had sipped lazily at their respective drinks, watching the sun sink slowly behind Gull Rock. If she'd been with Alex, it would have counted as one of the most romantic nights of her life, with everything bathed in the soft golden glow of the setting sun, and the Rock deepening in shade as night encroached. Instead, she had sat cozily beside Joseph, hardly bothering to talk at all, she was so taken by the stunning view before her. They were lovely evenings, so different from the drink-fuelled, club-orientated nights she was used to in Brighton. Much more simple, carefree.

Looking at her watch, she was surprised to find another twenty minutes had passed. He'd be here in just over an hour and a half now. She'd have to skimp on pampering slightly, which was a shame. Although she must paint her nails that lovely shade of varnish — "Blue Lagoon" she thought it was called — purchased from Harvest Moon. Rapidly becoming her favorite shop in the village, it was filled with the kind of exotic lotions and potions she loved.

She also needed to sort out what she was going to wear. Usually she slung on a pair of jeans and a T-shirt, but tonight she wanted to look different, the warm spring day filling her with excitement at the prospect of a long, hot summer to come. Perhaps a dress would be nice, one of her long, floaty ones — floral and feminine, but also very trendy right now. She'd dress it up with some chunky jewelry and add a few tiny plaits to her hair like Hannah sometimes did, embracing that bohemian look.

Although pleased with her choice of outfit, she noticed a flutter of anxiety in the pit of her stomach. Quickly doubts came creeping in. What if Joseph thought she was dressing up for his benefit? To impress him? He might get the wrong idea. Perhaps she should stick to her tried-and-trusted uniform. Anxiety threatened to engulf her. It took a few minutes and a couple of deep breaths to calm down again. And when she did, she couldn't believe how worked up she'd become. She would wear what she liked; that was her prerogative. And he could think what he liked; that was his.

Sinking into the tub, filled to the brim with Celestial Dreams bubble bath, another Harvest Moon buy, she managed to laugh at herself for regressing fourteen years in as many seconds. *You're a grown woman,* she chided herself, *not a teenager. Stop acting like one.* After a while she dozed off, all things celestial on her mind. When she woke, her fingers and toes were as wrinkled as prunes and the facemask had set rigid, making her feel as though she were encased in stone.

Wincing at how the cold the water had become, she let the bath drain and rinsed off under a hot shower. *Damn, not enough time to smooth my hair into submission.* She was cross she'd fallen asleep and run out of time. Now she'd have to let her wavy hair dry naturally. It was a much softer look, though, less urban. Perhaps it would suit what she was going to wear better. Sitting at her dressing table, she applied mascara, a hint of blusher, and her favorite shade of lipstick—Rimmel's Amethyst Shimmer—which she'd worn since she was sixteen, then slipped into her dress, stepping back to check every angle of her appearance in the wardrobe mirror.

Not bad, she thought, unable to stop herself wondering if that would be Joseph's opinion too.

Layla opened the door and then looked pointedly at her watch. "And what time do you call this?" she teased. It was 7:18 p.m. "You're late!"

"Sorry," Joseph replied, following her through into the kitchen. "It's an old habit of mine, left over from London. Being late was all the rage back there, you know."

Still pretending she was put out, she took the bottle he handed her, a nicely chilled sauvignon blanc, one of the finest that May's, the village store, had to offer. Reminding herself not to drink too much (the last thing she wanted was to greet Penny tomorrow with a hangover), she poured herself a deliberately low measure, filled a second glass more generously, and handed it to him.

"You look nice," he commented before thanking her for the wine and making his way outside to the porch.

Grateful he had turned away and so couldn't see her blush, she fussed about in the kitchen for a while, preparing a dressing for the side salad, adding a few chopped herbs as an afterthought. Happy that all was well, she joined him, looking forward to another evening of lighthearted chat.

"I thought we'd eat out here tonight, if that's okay. It's a lovely evening. We should make the most of it," she said as she drew up a chair opposite him.

"Definitely," he replied, staring out toward Gull Rock.

"Beautiful," she sighed, realizing too late she was still looking at him as she spoke. Averting her eyes, she added, "The view, I mean."

"Oh, so not me?" he joked, one eyebrow raised in challenge.

Recovering quickly, she grinned back. "You're okay, I guess. Not my type, but I'm sure there's plenty out there who'll appreciate you."

"Thanks very much." He appeared somewhat crestfallen. "I don't know whether to be flattered or insulted."

"A bit of both, I think." She winked and then headed back to the kitchen to bring dinner out.

As they tucked into their food—Joseph suitably appreciative of her culinary efforts and topping up their glasses, she noticed, on an all-too-regular basis—the day began to draw to a close, leaving them bathed only in the light from the kitchen and a couple of candles working overtime on the table.

Finishing his last mouthful, Joseph leaned back in his chair and stretched out his long legs. "So are you getting used to our country ways?"

"Yeah," she replied, the wine making her feel blurred around the edges. "It helped to know something about the place before I pitched up, though. Unlike a friend of mine who moved to Canada recently. She'd never been there before, not even on holiday. Such a brave thing to do. I keep meaning to contact her on Facebook, see how she's getting on."

"Tara did the same," confided Joseph, a slight shadow crossing his face. "She'd never been to Australia before she moved there. Seems to love it, though."

Hoping it still wasn't a sensitive subject, she ventured, "Do you still hear from her?"

"Tara?" he said. "Not really. Just a postcard every now and then. She was stunned I moved to Cornwall a few months after she left, though. Probably thought I did it to be closer to her, in spirit, if not in body."

"And did you?"

"No," he replied. "I didn't. It was Jim I was after all along."

Because his delivery was so deadpan, it took a second or two for Layla to realize he was joking. When she did, she burst out laughing. That was the thing with Joseph: he made her laugh. More than Alex ever did, she realized with a start.

"So, come on, then," he said, leaning forward. "Tell me about you and your holidays here when you were younger. I want to hear all about it."

Feeling suddenly shy, she glanced at him to see if he really was interested in her childhood memories or whether he was simply being polite. He looked genuine enough, so she started to tell him, amazed that she hadn't really done so before. All about her mother and the good times they'd had in Trecastle. About how she had met Hannah on the beach. She touched upon her father's death, hoping he wouldn't push her to elaborate. But he didn't. He simply sat and listened, not interrupting, just nodding every now and again, soaking up her words.

"And now I'm here again," she finished. "For twelve months this time, instead of the usual two weeks — an extended holiday, like Hannah said."

"Maybe you won't go back at all?" he said, and unless she was very much mistaken, there was a hopeful note in his voice.

Blushing yet again, she started to stack plates on the table.

"Here, I'll do that." Joseph rose quickly, taking the cutlery from her hands.

He made his way into the kitchen, whilst she settled back down again, pouring them both another glass of wine. Just as she was about to take a sip, an almighty "Whoa" erupted from within. Startled, she sprang from her seat, nearly sending the glass flying as she rushed inside.

"What is it? What's the matter?"

He looked stricken, as white as a sheet.

She hurried over to him and gently pried the plates from his hands, placing them on the worktop instead. Firmly she repeated the question. It was a few seconds, however, before he answered.

"Over there," he managed at last, pointing.

She followed his finger with her eyes but couldn't see anything.

"What?" she urged. "What are you looking at?"

"There," he said again through gritted teeth.

And then she saw it: a spider. Impressively large, she had to admit, but a spider nonetheless. Sitting perfectly still on the kitchen counter, minding its own business.

She was relieved that this was all that seemed to be the problem, but also slightly bemused. "Is that it? Is that what's frightening you?"

"I am *not* frightened," he replied emphatically. "I just don't particularly like spiders. Can you get rid of it?"

Struggling to keep her amusement at bay, she grabbed a tumbler from the kitchen cupboard and a piece of card lying beside her laptop on the table. The offending creature sensed her approach and made a dash for it, its rapid movement eliciting a sharp intake of breath from behind her. Although it was quick, she was quicker, slamming the glass dome over it and sliding the card underneath.

"Ugh. Get it out of here," Joseph gasped, still rooted to the spot.

Chewing her lip to keep from laughing, Layla released it into the wild. As she made her way back to the kitchen, Joseph begged her to shut the door. And that did it. She couldn't hold back anymore. An image of the spider, indignant it had been unceremoniously evicted, doing an about turn and stomping back in to claim its rightful place caused her to practically double with convulsions.

"I fail to see what's funny." Clearly, he was not impressed by her reaction.

"I can't believe you're so frightened…" she began and then dissolved again into peals of laughter.

"I've told you I am not frightened of spiders," he continued haughtily. "I just don't like them. There's a difference."

"You're terrified," she managed in between giggles. "Absolutely terrified. Go on, admit it."

"I am *not* terrified," he persisted but then started smiling too.

After a few moments, Layla managed to speak again. "Sorry," she said, feigning contrition. "I shouldn't make fun. It's just that a big, strapping man like you and a tiny thing like that—"

"It was not tiny," he interrupted. "It was huge. Massive, in fact. God, they grow them big down here," he ended in almost pitiful despair.

"So you really can't bear them?" she asked, still unable to believe it.

"I think we've established that," he replied with more than a hint of sarcasm in his voice. "It's another reason I didn't move to Australia. They've got those bloody Huntsmans out there, as big as dinner plates, apparently."

Sidling up to him, Layla purred, "Well, I, for one, am glad you stayed. And if any of those nasty spiders frighten you again, call me. I'll save you."

Although he rolled his eyes at her, he was definitely sharing in her amusement. "So," he said, his voice husky all of a sudden, "I've got my very own spider catcher living just next door to me. That's good to know."

She was about to start laughing again, but instead she stood on tiptoe and kissed him, something in her unable to resist. Up close, he smelled so damn good. It wasn't aftershave, rather his natural scent. And the heat from his body seemed like a tangible thing, reaching out to envelope her. Although he was clearly startled at what she had done, he kissed her next—then again and again, harder each time.

Breaking away, her voice husky too, she whispered, "Let's go upstairs."

Leading him by the hand, she couldn't help but wonder who this wanton creature was that had possessed her—certainly she had never met her before. Once in the bedroom, they continued to kiss, those strong, capable hands of his removing her dress with deft skill and throwing it halfway across the room. Quickly she helped him remove his shirt, and before they knew it, they were on the bed, his hands running all over her body, her tongue seeking his.

Although the sex was urgent, she was surprised some part of her was able to commit every touch, every stroke to memory as though really they were moving in slow motion. When he temporarily broke away to smile at her, the only thing in the world she wanted was to feel him against her again, his lean body fit and hard against her softer one.

She pulled him to her, and this time he climbed on top, gently guiding her legs apart with his. As he entered her, she cried out. Hearing her gasp, he stopped to look at her again. At that exact moment, she was sure he could see into her very soul and she into his—an experience so powerful, so raw, it was frightening. Not wanting to think, only to feel, she cupped her hand behind his head and pulled his mouth toward her. As he moved back and forth, slowly at first but then more vigorously, Layla tried to hold on, desperate to make the moment last as long as possible. But she couldn't; her climax came fast and furious, followed swiftly by his.

Collapsing against her, it was some time before they were able to control their breathing. At last, he rolled off to lie by her side, one hand strewn casually across her stomach.

After a few relaxed moments, Layla turned to look at him. His eyes were closed, his face a perfect picture of contentedness. Staring at him, she suddenly sobered—what the hell had just happened?

It was as though she'd been caught up in some kind of a whirlwind, unable to resist the forces of nature. But it was wrong, completely and utterly wrong. Joseph was her friend, not her lover. Theirs was a lovely, uncomplicated relationship, one of the few she'd ever had with a man, and one she wanted to keep.

What she had just experienced, that fervor, she had read about in books and seen in films but didn't think happened in real life. Not to her, anyway. Where had those feelings come from? They had hit like a bolt from the blue and disappeared just as quickly. Where the hell to? She had never had an experience so intense before, not even with Alex. *Why not?*

As Joseph opened his eyes to look at her, a languid smile playing about the edges of his mouth, she couldn't help but groan.

"What is it?" he asked, slightly taken aback.

"This," she replied, clutching at the duvet, embarrassed now by her nakedness. "This is the matter. It's a mistake."

Also sitting up, but not bothering to cover himself, he replied, "Not for me, it wasn't."

"I'm sorry. I didn't mean it like that. It's just that…this isn't why I came to Trecastle. To get involved with someone else. I wanted a break from all that." And then hesitating slightly, she added, "Besides, I still love Alex."

If she had punched him in the face, he couldn't have looked more shocked. But why, she couldn't fathom. He knew the reason she had come here. She had told him, the bare bones of it, anyway. What did he expect? One shag and she'd change allegiance?

Without another word, he rose from the bed to find his clothes.

Alarm bells went off in her head, and she quickly grabbed his arm. "I'm sorry, Joseph," she repeated. "Really I am."

"It's fine," he replied, brushing her off gently, but brushing her off nonetheless.

As he started to dress, she got out of bed too, grabbing her dressing gown from the back of the door and wrapping it tight around herself.

He buttoned up his jeans and left the room to go downstairs. Smoothing down her hair, she followed him.

"Joseph," she implored as he strode toward the front door. "Please don't let what's happened affect our friendship. I love what we've got."

His hand on the door handle, she once again grabbed his arm. "Please."

He turned round to face her at last. "You still want to be friends?" he asked.

"Of course, I do," she replied, shrinking slightly from the hardness in his eyes. She had never seen that steely glint in them before.

"Okay," he said, nodding his head in acquiescence before turning to go.

As she watched him make his way next door, she shouted, "Perhaps I'll see you tomorrow, with Penny, for a drink in the pub?"

"Uh-huh," was his distant reply.

She waited until he had disappeared from sight and then went back inside, closed the door, and slumped against it. Reaching her hand up to smooth her hair once again, she couldn't believe how her lovely lighthearted evening had turned out. Certainly not the way she'd envisaged.

Congratulations, Layla, she thought, angry beyond belief with herself. *You really know how to mess things up.* Then she headed to the lounge to spend the rest of the night awake on the sofa.

chapter nine

"Layla, it's me!" yelled Penny as she thumped on the oak door.

Thank heavens, thought Layla, practically tearing the door off its hinges and hurling herself into Penny's arms.

"Wow!" said Penny, clearly taken aback. "You really have missed me, haven't you?"

Not wanting to linger on the doorstep, Layla quickly pulled her inside. "I'm so glad you're here," she said before hugging her once again.

"Steady on." Penny was laughing now. "It's only been a few weeks since we've seen each other, you know, not decades!"

Layla started laughing too, realizing how extreme she was being. But she was just so relieved to see Penny, the first time she'd felt anything other than confusion and upset since last night. *Do NOT think about last night,* she reminded herself for the millionth time. In truth though, she could think of nothing else, which was why seeing Penny was even more fantastic than anticipated. If anyone could take her mind off the whole Joseph debacle, Penny could. Not that she would tell her what had happened; that was best kept under wraps. Penny would tell her to make the most of having such a hunky neighbor, that a fling with him would do her bruised heart the world of good. She'd be wrong, though, and Layla could prove it. Her bruised heart, instead of feeling lighter, felt heavier than ever.

She would keep it quiet from Hannah, too. That way the whole thing might blow over quicker.

The first thing Penny wanted after her long drive was a hot soak in the bath and a decent cup of tea. After that, she declared, they could catch up properly at their leisure. This suited Layla fine. She still needed time to collect herself. She hurried to Penny's car—a brand new Qashqai in that purple-black color they had both admired in the showroom prior to Penny buying it—and started lugging bags inside as Penny sauntered upstairs to check out the sleeping arrangements. After her third trip, Layla had to exercise all her powers of self-restraint not to comment sarcastically on her friend's complete and utter inability to travel light. Everything but the kitchen sink was in the boot of that car, she was sure of it.

Having hauled in the last bag, Layla went in search of Penny. As she neared the landing, she heard Penny call out, "This isn't as bad as I thought. In fact, it's not bad at all."

"I'm glad you approve," Layla called back, a little put out that she thought it might have been bad in the first place.

Walking into "Penny's Room," as Layla had dubbed it from the start, she said, "Right, there's plenty of hot water. Why don't you relax in the bath whilst I pop down to May's to stock up. I've only got one bottle of wine left. I think we'll need more than that."

"One bottle of wine?" said Penny in mock outrage. "Layla! You'd never have allowed stocks to run so low in Brighton. This country air, it must be addling your brain."

"You could say that," mumbled Layla before plastering a big smile on her face. "Is pasta okay tonight?"

"Pasta is perfect, and don't forget to grab a ton of chocolate as well. I'm on holiday. The diet can go to hell."

The light was just beginning to fade as Layla walked down to the village, although complete darkness, that strangely still Cornish darkness that she was still getting used to, was some way off yet. Buoyed by Penny's arrival, she was feeling slightly more optimistic. She and Joseph were adults; surely they'd be able to put what had happened behind them. Yes, it had been intense, she couldn't deny it, but it had been a fleeting intensity, and she'd probably exaggerated the whole thing in her mind afterward anyway, her newly-revived creative streak going into overdrive.

They hadn't parted on the best of terms, though, that was the problem. He'd seemed distinctly pissed off, but hopefully he wouldn't be for long. He had told her several times being single suited him. Why change his mind now? Being single suited her too. If she couldn't have Alex, she didn't want anyone.

Passing the local primary school on her right, its tiny playground silenced by the weekend, she entered the village proper, turning left toward May's. In the air, the smell of fish and chips reigned supreme, Uncle Davy's Cabin gearing up for the supper-time rush. As she walked along the narrow pavement, she was unable to resist, yet again, mulling over the previous night's events. What had possessed her to kiss him? She hadn't even known she was going to do so until she found her lips locked on his. She'd also been the one to drag him to the bedroom, having her wicked way with him before promptly declaring the whole episode one big mistake. Even by the most liberal of standards, she'd behaved badly. And she couldn't even blame the drink; she hadn't consumed so much as to warrant her brazen behavior. But *why* had she behaved so badly? That was the question. A question she had asked herself hundreds of time since but still had no answer to.

Completely lost in thought, it took a while to register someone was calling her name from outside the shop. It was Jim, a carrier bag of groceries cradled in his arms. Always happy to see him, she started to wave, her hand freezing in midair when she noticed someone else coming out of May's and falling into step behind him. Joseph!

"Layla, hey, how are you?" cried Jim as he rushed up to greet her.

"Fine," she managed to croak.

Seeing Joseph had thrown her into turmoil. She knew she had to see him again—of course she did—but this was too soon. Way too soon. She could feel his eyes on her, searing her, but try as she might, she could not meet them, memories of their encounter last night too vivid in her mind. Praying she was the only one to notice she was shaking like an alcoholic denied his life's blood, she honed in on Jim instead.

"So where are you off to?" she asked, attempting nonchalance.

"Just grabbing a few beers and heading back to the flat. Fancy joining us?"

"No," she replied far too quickly and far too loudly. Forcing herself to remain calm, she endeavored to explain. "My friend Penny's just arrived. I'm picking up a few things from the shop, and then I need to get home. She's waiting for me."

"Oh, right, Penny's here at last," drawled Jim. "We'll probably be moving off the sofa later, going to the pub. Hannah's working tonight. Bring her down. We'll all be there."

She had intended to do that very thing, take Penny to the pub on her first night and introduce her to everyone. Not now, though. Now she wanted to get as far away as possible from the pub and everyone in it.

"No, we can't, not tonight," Layla said, desperation building up inside her again at his persistence. "We haven't seen each other in ages. We need to catch up. Soon, though."

"You bet. We're having a bit of a gathering tomorrow night. Has Hannah told you? Herald the start of summer, that sort of thing. Bring her then. It'll be good to meet her at last."

Layla realized resistance would be futile. "Yeah, Hannah did mention something about it. That would be great. Tomorrow night is great." Remembering her manners, she added, "She's looking forward to meeting you too, of course."

"About nine, then, round at ours?"

"About nine," she agreed, defeated.

Satisfied, Jim continued on his way, but Joseph didn't move. He simply stood where he was, blocking her escape route into the suddenly comforting depths of May's. Knowing she couldn't stare at his chest any longer, she managed, with monumental effort, to lift her head and acknowledge him. "Hi," fell rather pitifully out of her mouth.

"Strange," he said. "I thought you wanted to remain friends."

"I do," she replied, hoping she sounded suitably earnest.

"Act like it, then," he said, pushing past her, but not before she had time to notice the hurt in his eyes and disappointment too, she was sure of it.

As he continued walking, the word *damn* played on repeat in her head. She swung round to look at him, wondering whether to rush after him and try to make amends, but decided against it. She doubted anything she had to say at this precise moment in time would be constructive; she would probably just dig herself into an even deeper hole.

She switched to autopilot and rushed round the store, throwing pasta, tinned tomatoes, a few motley looking vegetables, and a couple of bottles of wine into her basket before paying for them and sprinting home, the need for sanctuary more frantic with every step. Entering the cottage, she was relieved to find that Penny was still upstairs, snatches of the latest Kelly Clarkson song floating down from the direction of the bathroom.

Placing the carrier bag on the kitchen table, she leaned against it, wondering what on earth she was going to do. He had seemed appalled by how she had reacted to him, and rightly so. Being ignored was horrid at the best of times, let alone the worst. She knew that.

The party, she thought, an idea forming. *I can explain then.* She would seek him out as soon as she arrived and apologize profusely. Hopefully he'd understand, although understand what, she didn't know. She understood none of this herself.

Her mind made up, she filled two glasses of wine and took them upstairs. She'd make some excuse as to why they weren't going out tonight, say everyone was busy or something. Maybe Penny wouldn't mind too much. Quickly she'd announce Hannah was holding a party tomorrow, which would go some way to appeasing her. Penny had never met Hannah before, or Jim. She hadn't been around the week they came to Brighton; she had been in the Maldives with Richard or perhaps it was Mauritius, somewhere exotic, anyway. Penny was always saying how much she wanted to meet them, but it could wait. Just another twenty-four hours. That's all she needed. Another twenty-four hours to plan what she was going to say to Joseph, to rehearse it in her mind and then deliver it to him pitch perfect.

chapter ten

"Liebfraumilch?" Penny looked at the bottle in horror. "What the bloody hell are you doing buying Liebfraumilch?"

"Did I?" replied Layla, surprised. "Sorry, I wasn't concentrating."

Quickly downing the first glass of wine, she advised Layla to do the same. "The next one will be better," she promised. "By the time we're on our third, it'll taste as good as Chablis."

Penny gulped whilst Layla sipped.

Muttering almost to herself as much as Layla, she added, "Never mind, at least we've got plenty of chocolate."

"Oh, chocolate!" Layla's hand flew to her mouth. "I forgot."

Forgotten chocolate? Crikey, things were bad.

Penny had been at the cottage a mere couple of hours, but already she could tell something was wrong with Layla. It was as though she were only half present, the other half trapped in a dark and distant place. Penny had asked if everything was okay, and Layla assured her it was, but Penny could tell she was lying. She always could with Layla.

Strange, she thought, taking another gulp. *Layla seemed really happy when I spoke to her yesterday.*

Penny knew Layla had taken the split with Alex badly; it was why she was here. Because of that idiot, she had to travel nearly three hundred miles just to see her best friend. But lately, it had seemed as though Layla were on the mend. She was starting to sound increasingly upbeat during their phone calls; it seemed country life suited her. But something had happened in between speaking to her on the phone yesterday and seeing her today. What, though? And why wouldn't she say?

Penny stared surreptitiously at her friend. She really did seem to be lost in a world of her own, sipping at her wine and looking really quite despondent. Was it Alex? Was he on her mind? Was he ever *not* on her mind? How would she react to what Penny had to tell her? She'd keep quiet about FarScapes, that much was decided. But what about Alex's insistence he cared for Layla. Should she labor the point or gloss over it?

Penny wasn't even sure she believed him. She still thought he seemed far more concerned with his company than Layla. Maybe his fancy words were just a ploy, to get himself back in Layla's good books so she could dig him out of whatever trouble he was in with Jack Thomas. And once Layla had fulfilled her function, he might very well abandon her again. Then what? How would Layla react a second time? Three hundred miles might not cut the mustard then. She might move three thousand miles away, maybe more.

Then again, Penny admonished herself, perhaps she was being overprotective. Layla was a big girl, capable of making her own decisions. She really shouldn't take it upon herself to decide her future. Trouble was, there was a vulnerable streak in Layla. A vulnerability that brought out Penny's otherwise dormant maternal side. Oh, God, what should she say?

"What is it, Penny? What's the matter? Is it Richard?"

Bugger, thought Penny, *here goes.*

Pushing her wine glass aside, she answered, "No. No, it's got nothing to do with Richard. Nothing at all." After a brief pause, she continued, "Guess who came to see me a few days ago?"

Layla shrugged her shoulders nonchalantly. "Who?"

"Mr. Big Boss Man himself, that's who. Alex Kline."

Splattering a mouthful of wine everywhere, Layla demanded, "Alex came to see you? Why?"

"To find out where you'd gone, of course," she replied. "Why else?"

"You didn't tell him, did you?" squealed Layla in alarm.

"Of course not," countered Penny. "What do you take me for?" Nervously, she asked, "That was the right thing to do, wasn't it?"

"Absolutely." Layla banged her glass down on the table, wasting yet more of its contents. "I want nothing more to do with him."

"My thoughts exactly," said Penny, relieved she had guessed right.

Layla dragged the back of her hand across her mouth and looked at Penny, her green eyes intent and a slight catch in her voice as she said, "So, come on, then, what did he say?"

Fiddling with her rings, Penny hesitated once more. She really didn't want to be the one to stir things up between them again. Alex was no good for her, but it was obvious Layla's love for him hadn't diminished, judging by her dramatic reaction. Love was a strange thing; Penny didn't need telling that. Never black and white, it came in so many shades of gray, something making itself crystal clear to her lately.

Richard and she hardly talked any more. Sometimes "pass the salt" was the only communication between them for days. Their relationship was at an all-time low. Which was why she had been stunned when, last night, he had woken her in the middle of the night, like he used to do so often once upon a time, and they had made love, sweet and tender, without words or the need for them. She had been going to refuse him at first, push him away, say something like *I don't bloody think so*, but changed her mind as his arms wrapped round her, the need to hold him close a surprisingly desperate one. When she had woken the next morning, he had already left for work, leaving her wondering if she had dreamed the entire thing.

Soon after, she had left for Trecastle, which was just as well. It would give them breathing space. Clearly he still felt something for her, deep down, under layers and layers of anger and resentment. That had been the first time they had come together since Dylan. Was he finally beginning to forgive her? More to the point, could she forgive him? Not for Diane Tyrrell—she didn't believe he was having an affair with her any more than she believed England could ever win the World Cup, but for making her suffer so badly for one mistake, one really-not-that-big-in-the-whole-scheme-of-things mistake.

Taking a deep breath, she started to reiterate to Layla what had happened, being careful to leave out any references whatsoever to Easy Travel and FarScapes. She told her Alex had split with Sarah-Jane Johnson, that it had been a "moment of weakness"—his words, not hers—and that he missed Layla dreadfully. That one day soon he would find her, he had been adamant about it, to explain his behavior, saying that "she would understand." Again his words, she pointed out, not hers.

By the end of Penny's account, Layla's face was the color of milk. When she finally spoke, all she said was, "He's got cheek!"

"So what are you going to do about it?" prompted Penny gently.

"Nothing. Absolutely nothing. Let's see if he's man enough to turn up on my doorstep. He certainly didn't bother when I was in Brighton. Until then, I'm not going to waste another minute thinking about him."

Although Penny knew, just as Layla did, that this was a complete lie, they drank to it anyway. After finishing both bottles, they went upstairs. While she was getting ready for bed, Penny's mobile beeped.

"Is that Richard?" called Layla, slipping into her pajamas.

"Er, yeah," replied Penny quickly. "Just saying goodnight."

It wasn't Richard at all, though to be fair he had texted earlier to make sure she'd arrived safely. Another sign he still cared. It was Dylan.

Nite, sexy. Can't wait to see you again. D x

Penny texted back, a little uneasy.

Nite.

She had meant it when she'd told him she only wanted to be friends, no more kisses. He had seemed happy enough about it. She especially meant it since last night with Richard. Was "Nite, sexy" just a throwaway comment, typical of his cheeky personality, or did it signify he didn't believe her, that he had intentions she didn't want him to have?

"Why don't you sleep in my room tonight?" suggested Layla, coming up behind her and interrupting her train of thought. "There's plenty of room."

Choosing the throwaway comment option, she smiled in agreement, and they climbed into the king-size bed with its antique metal frame.

"Hey," Layla said with a giggle, "the room's spinning."

"Just like old times," agreed Penny, giggling too.

chapter eleven

It was just after eleven when Layla woke the next day. Penny was snoring softly beside her until she received a friendly dig in her ribs and awakened. They chatted a bit before heading downstairs, launching straight into lunch as breakfast was long gone.

"I'm really excited about tonight," Penny said as she munched happily on a cheese and pickle sandwich. "Getting to meet everyone at last."

"Yeah, great," replied Layla, her lack of enthusiasm blatant.

Wrapped up in her own thoughts, Penny was oblivious to her mood. "Are you going to eat that or just push it round your plate forever?"

"Take it if you want it. I'm not hungry."

"Lovely, thanks. I'm starving." Penny leaned over and grabbed it before Layla had a chance to change her mind.

Penny needn't have worried, though. There was no way Layla could eat a thing. If she did, she'd be sick, she was sure of it. The thought of facing Joseph again was making her want to run and hide, take refuge in one of those endless caverns down at the beach, emerging weeks later when the memory of what they'd done had faded into history. But, of course, she'd do no such thing. She would face him like the grown-up she was, keeping her troublesome inner teenager firmly under wraps.

It was raining heavily outside, so they decided to spend the rest of the day lolling around. Later that afternoon, Layla showed

Penny the short story she had sent to *Izabel*, shyly explaining it was for a magazine seeking to publish new talent. Penny had duly read it, making all the right noises in all the right places, but Layla could tell she wasn't interested, her mind preoccupied with what she was going to wear later.

"Jeans will be fine," sighed Layla eventually, even though Penny hadn't asked her. "No one dresses up around here."

"All the more reason to do so, then." Penny smiled mischievously. "I want to make an impression."

"Oh, you'll do that all right, Pen. It doesn't matter what you wear," replied Layla with a roll of her eyes.

Evening arrived far too quickly as far as Layla was concerned, and Penny had spent well over her allotted time in the bathroom. Whilst Penny was soaking herself at leisure, Layla sat patiently in the kitchen, letting a mug of tea go cold as she belatedly replied to a few emails.

Deciding enough was enough, she shut her laptop, poured the tea down the sink, and went upstairs.

As she passed the bathroom door, she shouted, "Hurry up, Pen. I need to get ready too, you know."

"Just a few more minutes. This bubble bath you've got—Celestial something—it smells divine," Penny shouted back.

Layla shook her head and went into her bedroom—or the scene of the crime as she now regarded it—and studied her reflection in the mirror. To her dismay, her face was as gray as an old bed sheet. Not surprising really, considering how nervous she felt. She longed for a glass of wine to instill some bravado in her, false or otherwise, it didn't matter, but decided against it. She needed complete control of her faculties tonight.

Joseph wasn't the only reason she was in turmoil, however. Penny's news about Alex had also knocked her for six. She had described how down at heel he had looked, how dejected, which wasn't like him at all. Maybe he really was feeling terrible about Sarah-Jane.

She wondered again if she had been too hasty in leaving Brighton. Perhaps she should have given him a chance to explain. Then again, explain what? If he could do such a thing once—and she presumed it had only been the once—what was to stop him doing it again? He was away on business so much, she would perpetually wonder just what sort of business he was away on. Because of his good looks, his charm, and his status, he was never short of admirers; she had witnessed that many times over the years. He could take his pick of the bunch, which was why she couldn't believe it when finally he had noticed her after several years of stopping only briefly at her desk to push papers at her before rushing off to some meeting or other. She had been elated.

Whomever Alex dallied with, it never lasted long. Having reached the almost-year mark with him therefore had given her reason to think he was as serious about her as she was about him. And maybe he was, maybe he did love her, after all. Perhaps Sarah-Jane was just a blip. But what about Joseph? Where had those feelings come from? Feelings she had never experienced with Alex before, feelings she had never known existed. If she were so in love with Alex, how was it possible to feel that way, albeit briefly, with another man? It didn't make sense.

She pressed her palms to her eyes and rubbed hard as though trying to erase the contents of her mind. *Enough*, she told herself. A few days ago everything had been crystal clear: she was busy suffering from a broken heart courtesy of Alex Kline. She wanted him; he didn't want her, simple. Now, not only was Alex apparently regretting the end of their affair, but Joseph was involved too, stirring up several kinds of chaos within her.

Struggling to come to grips with the situation, she reminded herself yet again that Joseph was just a friend, and a friend he would stay—fingers crossed. If Alex did find her, which was doubtful, she would give him what for, the memory of that hateful Post-It note indelible in her mind. If he turned up on her doorstep, she would tell him to turn right back round again and be on his way—but would she? Would she really?

Graduating from sitting head-in-hand to pacing the room, she finally forced herself to come to a stop. She had a plan of action, and she would stick to it. Tonight she would apologize to Joseph, and that would put an end to that. Alex and his philandering ways, meanwhile, could go to hell.

"Penny, get out of the bath!" she yelled, any lingering vestige of patience deserting her.

"All right, all right. No need to shout," said Penny, choosing that exact minute to emerge from within, a pink fluffy towel wrapped round her and a big grin on her face.

Penny made a great show of peering at the clock as she walked into the bedroom. "Oh, Layla, look at the time. Don't be long, will you? I don't want to be late."

Making a strangling gesture with her hands, Layla took her turn in the bathroom, silently thankful that Penny was there to lighten the mood.

It was Jim who opened the door to them, greeting them enthusiastically. "And you must be Penny," he said, enfolding her in a hug.

"Well deduced," said Penny, flashing her best smile at him upon release.

"Hey, Layla." This time it was Hannah, beckoning them down the hallway and into the already packed kitchen. From the living room, ambient music filled the air.

"You look amazing," Layla said to Hannah, and indeed she did, clad in a colorful tie-dyed dress that barely covered the essentials but did show off her figure — petite and voluptuous — to perfection.

Sworn off flirty dresses forever, Layla was back in her uniform: an old but comfortable pair of jeans, a plain white T-shirt, and boots. Her hair was swept up in a scruffy bun, and her makeup barely there. Penny had raised an eyebrow at her appearance, but then again, Layla had done the same to her. Looking like a reject from a punk rock band, Penny was clad in black jeans, skin-tight to say the least, a pair of black high-heeled lace-up boots that ended just below her knee, and a clingy blouse emblazoned with a sequin-encrusted skulls and crossbones. Her blond hair was backcombed for that "wild child" look, and her eyes were dark and dramatic, lined with liquid eyeliner and lashings of mascara.

"Hannah, this is Penny. Penny, this is Hannah."

"Hi." Hannah extended her hand. "I've heard so much about you."

"All good, I hope. But then again, not too good — that would be misleading," Penny replied with a laugh.

Penny and Hannah continued chatting while Layla scanned the room to see where Joseph was. There were various people gossiping and drinking, including Mick holding court with one of his famous "peril at sea" stories, but Joseph was nowhere to be seen.

Desperate to get her apology over and done with so she could start enjoying herself, she decided to leave Penny in Hannah's capable hands and go search the living room. Although well proportioned, it looked small because of the amount of people packed into it. Usually, it was minimal in style, with a huge white sofa for lolling about on, a stereo for Jim's impressive vinyl collection—he preferred them to CDs—and a large flat screen TV, monopolized for Hannah's soap operas. The smell of oil paints often hung in the air, and Hannah's own pictures, when you could see them, lent color to the walls. She looked toward the French doors, noticing they were open with people spilling out into the night.

Layla quickly made her way toward them. Perhaps he was outside. Before she could reach them, however, she was spun round. Not by Joseph, unfortunately, but by Mick. He must have followed her in from the kitchen.

"Hey, Layla," he yelled above the noise. "Good to see you."

Knowing she couldn't just cut and run, continue her desperate search, she stayed and talked with him, unable to see much of anything past his broad frame. After what seemed like an age, she pleaded a need to go and check on Penny. Luckily Mick didn't seem to mind, turning his attentions to a group of people standing close by.

Alone again, she continued looking, peering through the thick sea of shoulders and heads. At last she spotted him. Not outside as she had previously thought, but leaning up against the far corner of the living room wall, a bottle of Bud in hand, and chatting to a man she'd never seen before. Unexpectedly, she felt her breath catch in her throat. The other man, who was about average height with a hooked nose and skinny frame, seemed like a prop, set in place solely to highlight the golden good looks of his counterpart.

Steeling herself, she placed one foot in front of the other, willing herself on and on until she stood before him. At her arrival, the other man looked inquiringly at her.

"Hi, I'm Dave," he said affably.

"Oh, hi, I'm Layla," she replied, looking from Dave to Joseph, who had no such smile of welcome on his face. Taking a deep breath, she said to Dave, "Is it possible to have a few words with Joseph, please?"

"Sure," he replied, standing stock still.

"Um, I meant in private."

"Oh, right, yeah, of course," he flustered, finally getting the message. "Gotta catch up with a few of the others anyway."

To Joseph, he said, "See you soon," before disappearing into the crowd.

Joseph nodded at him before turning his attention back to Layla, his face still distinctly unwelcome.

"Sorry to interrupt you," she began.

"What did you want?"

Thrown by his somewhat blunt manner, she continued nonetheless. "I wanted to say sorry. You know, about yesterday."

"Okay," he replied, expectant.

Quickly she endeavored to recall her avidly rehearsed speech. Not one word of it had the good grace to come to mind.

"Erm," she began after a moment. "Erm, I was a bit taken aback. Yesterday, I mean. Seeing you so soon after we'd…erm, after we'd…"

"Made love?" he finished for her, a definite challenge in his voice.

Just as her breath had unexpectedly caught in her throat earlier, her stomach somersaulted at his choice of words. She hadn't thought of what they'd done in those terms, but yes, she supposed he had a point. They *had* made love. It wasn't just sex. "Just sex" never felt *that* good.

Feeling the heat start in her toes, creep up her legs, and reach her upper torso before it suffused her face entirely, she spluttered, "Yes, that's it. That's exactly what I was going to say. I don't know why I acted the way I did, really I don't. I've never behaved that way before. So stupidly, I mean. I didn't mean to ignore you. I won't do it again. Can we just put it all behind us and move on?"

His reaction to her babble of words, kind or otherwise, was lost, because at that moment Penny appeared, pointing at Joseph and yelling, "Joseph? You must be Joseph. Layla never stops talking about you!"

"Penny," hissed Layla, mortified.

Lurching forward, Penny grabbed Joseph's hand in hers and shook it enthusiastically. "I am *so* pleased to meet you. I'm Penny, by the way, but I expect you'd guessed that."

Although annoyed that Penny had interrupted her at such a critical moment, Layla took small comfort in the fact that Joseph's infuriatingly cool demeanor had, at last, been broken.

"Er, hi, Penny," he said, closely resembling a rabbit caught in the headlights. "Nice to meet you too."

Layla noticed an attempt on Joseph's part to extract his hand from Penny's vice-like grip, but she was having none of it. She held firm, stopping just short of a wolf whistle as she looked him up and down.

"Yep, you're quite a looker. Layla said you were."

At this point, Penny gave Joseph a knowing wink, and if Layla hadn't quite wished the ground would open up and swallow her before, she did now.

"I said no such thing," she protested.

"You did too, and you know it." Penny chuckled, finally letting go of Joseph's hand but only so she could link arms with him instead.

"Come on," she whispered in his ear. "Let's get out of here."

At that, Penny yanked him through the French doors, leaving Layla staring open-mouthed after them.

"That was quite an introduction," Hannah said, materializing out of nowhere, a similar look of shock on her face. "Penny's very, erm, effervescent, isn't she?"

"She can be." Layla was trying hard not to cringe.

She wondered briefly just how much Penny had drunk during their time apart. Not enough to turn her from a fairly reasonable human being into one that's certifiable, surely?

"Is everything okay between you and Joe?" asked Hannah.

"Yeah, of course. Of course it is," Layla replied, feigning innocence at the question.

"It's just the atmosphere seemed a bit tense between you."

Layla was surprised. Had it been that obvious?

"No, we're fine," she insisted. "I just needed to sort something out with him, that's all. And I almost did before Penny barged in."

"He's been a bit down these past couple of days," Hannah continued. "I wondered if you knew why?"

The protective tone in Hannah's voice was not lost on Layla. It was also, she thought, slightly accusatory. For a moment, she had an almost overwhelming urge to grab Hannah as Penny had grabbed Joseph and take her somewhere quiet to explain all. Keeping everything under wraps was proving nothing short of excruciating. But she resisted; it would only add fuel to a fire she was hoping would soon burn itself out.

Wishing afterward she hadn't sounded so defensive, she replied, "No, I don't know why he's been down. Why should I?"

Hannah looked intently at her for a few more seconds before saying brightly, "Come on, then. Let's go and find Jim, see what he's up to."

Layla would rather have found Penny and Joseph and seen what they were up to, but she duly obliged. Back in the kitchen, Jim and his bandmates, Curtis and Ryan, had joined forces, delighting their audience with an impromptu song. As soon as Jim saw Hannah, however, he made his excuses and came over to hug her. Such devotion made Layla smile.

An attractive couple, Hannah fit Jim like a glove, nestling into the groove of his chest, her head resting just below his shoulder. As Layla stood there admiring them, she locked eyes briefly with Hannah. As she did so, she detected a deep core of sadness within her and was surprised. What on earth did Hannah have to be sad about? She was happy with Jim, wasn't she? She always said she was.

Layla would have pondered it further, but Joseph and Penny were occupying her thoughts. She should go and find them, stop Penny from telling him any more ridiculous untruths. She certainly did *not* talk about him all the time as Penny had insisted. She spoke about everyone equally, she was sure of it. And then something else occurred to her: what if Penny gave Joseph the impression that she knew about their night together? That the pair of them had cackled together like old witches about it? He could quite easily come to that conclusion, given the type of innuendoes Penny was fond of dishing up.

She decided there was no time to waste; she left Jim and Hannah to it and went in search of the missing duo.

Making her way through the crowd proved just as difficult as before. Not Mick this time, but several others determined to engage her in conversation. After responding with as few words as she could politely get away with, she had managed to escape, dismayed again at how much time had passed.

Layla peered anxiously into the darkness. It was raucous laughter, courtesy of Penny, that finally provided the clue to their whereabouts. They were in a secluded spot, just beyond the paved barbeque area, sitting on some kind of makeshift bench with Penny snuggled so close to Joseph she was practically on his lap. Much to Layla's consternation, he no longer looked terrified. Rather, he looked amused, lifting his eyes only briefly to acknowledge Layla before turning his attention back to Penny.

"There you are," said Layla, forcing brightness into her voice. "We were wondering where you'd got to."

Of course, *we* weren't wondering at all. Even Hannah had lost interest a while ago.

"Layla, hi," Penny slurred. "You needn't have worried. We've been perfectly happy getting to know each other, haven't we, Joe?"

"We have indeed." Joseph smiled—far too indulgently, she thought.

At Penny's feet lay an empty wine bottle, rolling back and forth every time she inadvertently kicked it as her legs swung to and fro.

"I'm glad you've had a good time," said Layla, looking pointedly at the wine bottle. "But it's getting late. We need to make a move."

"Late?" Penny held up her wrist in an exaggerated attempt to tell the time. "It's hardly late. It's not even midnight yet."

Her irritation rising, Layla continued, "It is, almost. Come on, let's go."

"Blimey, Layla," declared Penny with dramatic flourish, "this isn't like you!" Turning to Joseph, she said, "She's usually the last one standing, you know. Comes home with the milk cart and, more often than not, the milk man himself." Penny burst out laughing at her own joke, inflaming Layla even more.

"That is *not* true," Layla began, but Penny was unrelenting.

"Oh, I know. I know why she wants to go home," she continued, leaning even further into Joseph, if such a thing were possible, and whispering in an annoyingly conspiratorial fashion. "She's bored. That's what it is. There's no one here that takes her fancy. She hasn't got a playmate."

At this, Layla screamed at Penny to move her backside.

When Penny still cheerfully refused, it was Joseph who broke the tension, saying to Penny in a gentle and appeasing manner, "Come on, I'll walk with you. I've got an early start in the morning. I could do with getting home too."

As Penny rose unsteadily to her feet, she turned to Layla and, on a hiccup, boomed, "Layla Lewis, country living is turning you into a bore. And I can't think why, it's brilliant down here!"

Deep down, Layla knew Penny's comments were tongue-in-cheek, but she could find no humor in them. She tried to tell herself Penny wasn't being deliberately mean; her friend didn't know what had happened between her and Joseph and so couldn't possibly be aware of the impact her words were having. But it didn't do much good; Layla was still furious.

Eager to shake Joseph off, Layla turned to him and said firmly, "You don't need to walk back with us, thanks. We're fine."

"He most certainly does," Penny contradicted as she tripped over the empty bottle and fell into Joseph's arms.

Effortlessly catching her, he replied just as firmly, "It's not a problem. I do happen to be going your way, after all."

Layla bristled at his insistence, but she knew it would be useless to protest further. Penny would shoot her down in flames if she did. Flouncing around, she walked back toward the living room, the two of them following close behind. As they pushed their way to the front door, they said their goodbyes to various revelers, only managing to wave at Jim and Hannah who were in the kitchen, swamped by friends.

It was less than a fifteen-minute walk from Jim and Hannah's flat to the cottage, but Layla knew it would seem one hell of a lot longer than that. Penny had linked her arm with Joseph's, and the two of them walked slightly ahead, leaving her trailing behind.

Shivering from the night air, she pulled her biker-style jacket closed. As she did so, chatter and laughter floated back to taunt her. *Thanks a lot, Penny,* she thought miserably.

Because of her so-called best friend, Joseph could be forgiven for thinking she was some sort of man-eating monster, jumping into bed with any man that had a pulse before packing them off with some convenient story about suffering from a broken heart. But it hadn't been like that. She hadn't meant to jump into bed with him, and she certainly hadn't meant to enjoy it so much! She hadn't meant to act like such an idiot afterward, either. *And it's true,* she sniffed. *I do have a broken heart.*

Why was Penny flirting so outrageously with him, anyway? Hadn't she learned her lesson with Dylan? The girl was married, for God's sake. Did she keep forgetting that, or was she just plain greedy? Layla would give anything to be loved the way Penny was. Richard adored her; it was obvious. Well, obvious to everyone but Penny. Yes, they'd hit a glitch, it couldn't be denied, but with a bit of effort on both their parts, they could clamber onto safe ground again. She had hurt him because of Dylan, and she ran the risk of hurting him again if she took things too far with Joseph. On holiday she might be, but she wasn't at liberty to have a holiday romance. Layla would have to remind her of that. As for Joseph, he knew Penny was married; she had mentioned it several times. What was he doing encouraging her? It didn't say much for his sense of honor either.

As they reached the cottage, Layla's anger was at boiling point. Joseph and Penny were still linked together and looking unbearably smug.

"Come on," Layla said. "Let's get you inside."

"Okay, come on, Joe. I think we've still got some wine left from earlier."

"No," interrupted Layla. "I meant just you and me, Penny. It's time to call it a night."

"Oh, come on," Penny moaned. "The night is young, and so are we."

"It's okay," said Joseph, gently disentangling himself before Penny could say anymore. "I need to get back. I've got a busy day tomorrow."

"You can spare another hour at least," implored Penny. "If Layla insists on being a bore, that's up to her. We'll go back to yours."

"Another time you'd be welcome, but not right now. I've got to get some sleep."

"When can we meet again, though?" she asked, her voice petulant like a small child's. Nodding at Layla, she continued, "I need to have fun with someone around here."

"Whenever you like." He laughed. "Pop down to the workshop tomorrow, say hello. Layla will tell you where it is."

Oh, will I indeed! thought Layla, grabbing onto Penny's arm, bidding Joseph a terse goodnight and pushing her through the door, all in one swift move.

As the door banged shut behind them, Penny rubbed at her arm. "Crikey, Layla, take it easy, will you? What's your problem?"

"My problem?" roared Layla in disbelief. "I'm not the one with the problem. You're the one making a fool of yourself."

"Hey," countered Penny, "I am not. I'm just having a good time. You remember that, don't you, what it's like to have a good time?"

"Of course I do, but you don't need to get quite so drunk to have a good time, you know. I don't know what everyone must have thought."

"If by everyone, you're referring to Joe, he thought I was great, actually. He told me so. In fact, we were getting on really well until you showed up and spoilt things."

"He was probably making the best of a bad situation," snapped Layla. "After all, you launched yourself at him like a space missile. He couldn't exactly escape."

Penny looked visibly hurt at this. Her brow furrowed in confusion. "What's the matter, Layla? Why are you so angry? I haven't done anything wrong."

"You're married, Penny," Layla continued, deep inside hating how self-righteous she sounded. "You seem to forget that. I'm sure Richard would be ecstatic to know you're throwing yourself at another man." Then, almost against her will, she heard herself say, "Again."

Penny stared at her, her blue eyes glittering dangerously. There was no trace of drunkenness in her voice now. "How dare you! I was *not* throwing myself at him. I was being friendly. He understood that, even if you can't. As for Dylan, you know why that happened, how lonely I felt."

"All I'm saying," replied Layla, more warily now, "is that acting the way you do after a couple of drinks around the male half of the human race won't improve your situation. If you even hint to Richard you've spent the evening with someone else, he'll fly off the handle. Trust is a big issue between you now. Face up to it."

"Face up to it? Me? What about you?" Penny yelled. "You ran away from your job, your home, and your friends because you couldn't face up to things. You didn't have the balls to stay and make Alex pay for what he did."

"I didn't just leave because of Alex—"

"Yes, you did! You liar," interrupted Penny. "You've got a bloody cheek, standing there preaching to me. But, hang on…this isn't all about Alex, is it?"

"What are you talking about?" snorted Layla derisively.

"Has something happened between you and Joe?"

"Me and Joe? Don't be ridiculous."

"It has, hasn't it? Something's happened. And you're jealous, jealous he spent time with me tonight instead of you. Have you got some kind of crush on him? You never stop talking about him, after all."

"No, I have not. He is not my type, and you know it."

"Oh, yeah, what am I thinking? Of course, he's not your type. If he's not old enough to be your father, you're not interested."

"What!" Layla exploded. "What has my father got to do with this?"

"That's what you're looking for, isn't it? A sugar daddy, someone to take care of you, because you don't think you can take care of yourself? Guys your age don't stand a chance."

Rendered speechless at her words, Layla could only stare at Penny in complete amazement. The look on her face brought Penny to a halt, too. The girls rarely argued, and if they did, it was just over petty things, like why Layla hadn't saved enough money for a taxi home when it was her turn to pay or why had Penny swiped Layla's best sparkly top when she knew she was planning on wearing it herself—minor misdemeanors that could be resolved in minutes, if not seconds. This time, however, harsh truths had hit home and in the most brutal of ways.

"I think you're right," said Penny at last, her voice catching in her throat. "I have had too much to drink."

"And I probably haven't had enough." Layla tried to smile but couldn't.

"Look, it's late. Let's talk about it in the morning. I think we both need to get some sleep, to calm down."

"Okay." Layla felt tears running down her cheeks as she watched Penny leave, going to her own room no doubt. There'd be no sharing of beds tonight.

Slumping into a chair, she made great attempts to keep her sobbing quiet, even though she felt like wailing from the rafters. She couldn't believe what they had said to each other, how they had used each other's private sufferings to inflict pain. Besides, it wasn't true what Penny had said: Layla wasn't looking for a sugar daddy. She'd never heard anything so ridiculous. There'd been Adam briefly a couple of years ago, in case she'd forgotten. He was only six years older than her and had worked as a postman—hardly "sugar daddy" material. God, she missed her father, though; he seemed such a distant figure now, kept alive only by a few well-thumbed photographs and cherished memories. He had been so loving, so strong and capable. A rock. As strong and permanent as Gull Rock. Although not so permanent as it had turned out. It was a tragedy that he had been killed in his prime, taken out by some young and reckless driver.

In the bleak months and years that followed, it had been him Layla had longed for whenever she was feeling down, not her mother, and her mother knew it. And now was no different. Sitting in her kitchen, all alone, she wanted him and only him. She wanted him to wrap his arms around her as he used to so often once upon a time and tell her everything was going to be okay. No, Penny was wrong; she didn't want to replace her father. Nobody could. She just wanted to be loved as he had loved her—unconditionally. She wanted to feel special again.

chapter twelve

"Hey, girls, ready for a bit of sightseeing?"

Hannah looked at the two swollen and miserable faces in front of her. *Hmm, maybe not.* Realizing she needed to buy herself time in order to assess the situation, she shifted her focus from Penny and Layla to the kettle instead, staring at its tarnished silver exterior as though it were the most fascinating thing in the world whilst waiting for it to boil.

Yep, definitely a frost in the air, she decided as she rummaged around the cupboards for a mug. *What the hell's gone on here?*

She took a few sips of her herbal tea, swiveled round on her heel, and endeavored to inject some lightheartedness into the atmosphere.

"I thought Port Isaac for lunch and Boscastle for a cream tea?" she ventured. "With a walk over the headland in between to burn off any excess calories. Is that okay?"

Penny gave an almost imperceptible nod of her head, whilst Layla merely grunted in reply. Clearly whatever had happened had been serious.

She had seen them leave the party early last night, with Joe in tow. As she'd waved goodbye to them from the kitchen — not even sure if they'd seen her — she had wondered why they were leaving so soon. It hadn't even been midnight, for heaven's sake. And why had Layla looked so thoroughly pissed off? Two questions she still had no answer to.

She had noticed the tension between Joe and Layla earlier in the evening too, but Layla had insisted all was well. It wasn't though; she could tell. Joe had been off color these past couple of days, sitting morosely round at their flat the night before the party, beer can in hand, looking like he'd been hit with the news that his favorite aunt had died.

Jim hadn't noticed, of course. He and Curtis had been busy working on lyrics for a new song, but she most certainly had. When it came to Joe, she noticed everything.

Had the girls fallen out because of him? Layla had looked less than pleased when Penny carted him outside last night. Perhaps she was jealous? After all, she and Joe had been spending quite a bit of time together lately, another thing that hadn't gone unnoticed. And why had Penny monopolized him, anyway? She was married, wasn't she?

Starting to feel pissed off too, she swiftly halted her train of thought. Adding to the sulk-off was not going to help. Today was meant to be a good day, a fun day, and fun they would have. She placed her mug on the counter, clapped her hands, and said in a voice she hoped emulated the no-nonsense tone of her old Brownie leader, "Right, girls, chop, chop. Let's get going."

Incredibly, it worked. Layla and Penny stood up, albeit rather reluctantly, scraping their chairs loudly against the flagstone floor. Then, with eyes downcast, they obediently followed her to the door.

Outside, Hannah threw a surreptitious glance at Joe's cottage, wondering if she might catch a glimpse of him. What she hadn't bargained for, though, was the others doing exactly the same and looking just as furtive about it as she felt.

Slightly miffed but striving to keep her voice neutral, she turned to Penny and asked, "Is it still okay to go in your car? I don't think you'll appreciate a ride in my old banger when you're used to such luxury."

"Of course," muttered Penny, climbing into the driving seat.

Layla immediately got into the back, pointedly so, leaving Hannah no option but to occupy the seat beside Penny.

"Right," she said as brightly as she dared under the circumstances. "Let's head south."

"Pull in over there," said Hannah, pointing to Silvershell Road. "It's easier to park up here. The harbor's not far away, just down the hill."

It had been an awful journey, every one of its twenty minutes painful. As Penny had never been to Cornwall before, Hannah had tried pointing out various landmarks to start up conversation. But nothing, not even the famous Delabole Quarry or the Butterfly Farm, had elicited more than a few mumbled words in response. She had even resorted to saying how nice the weather was, more like a day in June than early April, but that too had been met with zero enthusiasm. Eventually she had conceded defeat and turned the radio up, listening to a rockumentary on bands from the eighties as they sped along.

Beginning the descent into Port Isaac, Hannah was dying to say something— *Okay, girls, I realize something's up between you two, but whatever it is, let's put it behind us and enjoy the day*— but she couldn't. Maybe over lunch she'd pluck up the courage.

As they walked into the village proper— one of the most beautiful in North Cornwall— Penny cracked at last.

"This really is lovely, isn't it? Like on that program, Doc something? You know, the one with Martin Clunes."

"Hardly surprising," said Hannah, hugely relieved that one of the silent duo had spoken properly at last. "*Doc Martin* is filmed here."

"Really?" Penny said in astonishment. "I love that series."

And with that she was off, wanting to explore every narrow, winding street, marveling at how tiny the ice-cream-colored cottages were, and popping into every last gift shop to wade through acres and acres of souvenirs. Her enthusiasm was catching; even Layla ummed and aahed at various junctures. Maybe lunch wouldn't be so bad after all.

After an hour or so of admiring just about everything Port Isaac had to offer, they settled themselves at The Galleon for lunch. A delightful sixteenth-century pub right on the harbor's edge, it had once been the haunt of smugglers and big buxom serving wenches. They were lucky enough to be able to eat outside, bagging one of only two tables on the terrace, their view of the harbor itself dotted with colorful fishing boats and young families searching amongst the rocks for creature the sea had left behind.

Penny opted for the crab salad, Layla for Atlantic prawns, and Hannah for the smoked fish platter—all wonderfully fresh ingredients from the fish cellars just opposite the pub. A fish cellar Mick and his father often provided for, Hannah told them. Lots of home-baked crusty bread accompanied their meal, with a glass of chilled wine for the non-drivers and a Diet Coke for Penny.

As they tucked in, Hannah noticed both girls were looking slightly more relaxed. Well, mainly Penny who seemed truly knocked out by her beautiful surroundings. Layla was definitely still not her usual self.

Attempting to re-start the conversation which had stalled again, Hannah asked, "Has Layla taken you to visit the castle in our humble village yet?"

"No, she hasn't." Penny was amicable enough. "Can we do that today?"

"Yeah, sure after lunch, we could—"

"It's hardly a castle," Layla interrupted. "It's just a few tumbled down walls dotted here and there."

"Ah, but it's the history that counts," continued Hannah, undaunted. "It dates back to ancient times, you know. Back to the Dark Ages, they think."

"Wow!" said Penny, impressed again. "Let's go and see it. I love anything historical."

Making eye contact with Layla for the first time that day, she added, "And so do you, Layla. Don't lie."

"Humph," replied Layla, slathering butter on a hunk of bread and shoving it in her mouth.

"Right, that's settled. We'll head back to Trecastle to see the sights before pushing on to Boscastle." And with that, Hannah finished her glass of wine, glad of its slightly fuzzy effect.

The sun continued to shine upon them as they explored the castle and coastline, Hannah explaining to Penny how she played amongst the ruins as a child.

"But it's so precarious," said Penny, referring to its cliff-top location. "Even dangerous, I'd say."

"I know what you mean," Hannah conceded, "but when you grow up with this type of landscape, you quickly learn every one of its pitfalls and how to avoid them."

"Not everyone," Layla pointed out. "What about that man on the news yesterday? The one from Bude. Lived all his life in Cornwall but still got caught out by the tide. He drowned."

"True." Hannah nodded her head in grave agreement. "Mostly learn to avoid them, I should say." At least Layla was talking again, even if it was about a drowning man.

"Speaking of the tide," said Hannah, pointing to the beach below, "it's out. Let's go and explore."

The pathway down to the beach from the cliff top was steep in places, and Penny tripped over rocks and stones a couple of times, her much-loved pink Converse boots not lending themselves too well to the terrain. Layla was just as bad, letting out a squeal every now and then as she lunged forward. Both girls expressed disbelief at Hannah's effortless negotiation of the path, running on ahead as though she were part of the landscape itself.

"I told you," she called back happily. "I'm used to it."

The tide was far out and looked as though it were still receding. All three ran up to the water's edge and immediately started splashing each other with ice-cold water, thoroughly soaking themselves but laughing all the while, laughter that was music to Hannah's ears.

Deciding she was wet enough, Hannah started running back toward the cliffs, both girls following in her sandy footsteps.

"You ready for this, Penny?" she teased as they ventured closer.

"You bet," replied Penny excitedly. "Lead the way."

This was the deepest cave on the beach, known locally as Merlin's Cave, although there were Merlin's Caves aplenty in these parts, some on the coast, some on the moors. Dark Age history was everywhere. Hannah had never been all the way in, not even when armed with a flashlight. It got decidedly murkier and scarier the further you retreated from civilization.

They were only at what she considered the halfway mark when Penny piped up, "It stinks in here. Can we leave now?"

"Just a few steps more," said Hannah, noticing that Penny was holding onto Layla's arm and that Layla was letting her.

Passing the halfway mark, they heard a big boom. Penny had clearly had enough. She let out an ear-piercing scream before turning round and beating a hasty retreat, followed swiftly by Layla and Hannah.

Back in the sunshine, it took a while for the giggles to subside.

"This reminds me of being a kid," said Layla, no trace of grumpiness on her face now.

"Me, too. Remember how we used to dare each other to go further and further in?"

"I do," Layla replied happily. "I always won, didn't I?"

"Yeah, right," said Hannah, chucking a handful of sand at her.

"Guys, guys," interrupted Penny, able to speak now her laughter had subsided. "What was that noise in there? It was deafening."

"Well," said Hannah, winking at Layla, "you know Loch Ness has its very own monster? So do we. It's a cave monster, and that's his lair."

"Whatever." Penny grinned good-naturedly. "Anyway, enough of monsters, caves, and freezing cold water. You mentioned something about a cream tea?"

"I did indeed," said Hannah. "Off to Boscastle we go. They do the best cream tea in the world there!"

"With lots of that gorgeous clotted cream?" Penny's eyes were as wide as saucers as she rose to her feet.

"And lashings of strawberry jam," Layla added, licking her lips.

The trip to Boscastle went well, Penny's newfound love for quaint Cornish villages infectious. After eating their fill, all three declared themselves stuffed to the gills. When Hannah suggested an early evening drink in the Trecastle Inn, however, they didn't disagree.

Singing along to Katy Perry's "Firework" at the top of their voices on the return journey, they parked outside The Outlook and walked back to the village, Penny gushing about stunning sea views all the way.

Just outside the pub, Hannah spotted Joe's Land Rover further along the road.

"Is that Joe's car?" asked Penny.

"Yeah. Why?" Layla replied before Hannah had a chance to.

"Does that mean he's at his workshop?"

"Erm, yeah, he must be," Hannah quickly interjected.

"I might pop in and say hello. Join you girls later," Penny said breezily.

"But he'll be busy, I'm sure," Hannah insisted. "He's got a truck load of work on at the moment."

"I won't be long. I said I'd pop in, so I should really. It's only polite." And with that she was gone.

Uh-oh, back to square one, thought Hannah, glancing at Layla, who looked decidedly pissed off again.

"Drink?" she suggested tentatively.

"A bloody big one," said Layla, stomping over to the pub and disappearing inside.

chapter thirteen

Flicking idly though her post, Layla's heart leapt as she noticed an envelope with the logo for *Izabel* magazine on its left hand corner. She stopped short and stared at it for a few moments before tearing it open, trembling fingers making a simple task hard.

Dear Miss Lewis,

Thank you for sending us your short story "Gull Rock" for inclusion in our magazine.

We have read it, loved it, and would be delighted to include it. We pay £150 per story and have therefore enclosed a cheque for £150.

We would also like to see more of your short stories. We publish a wide range of titles, of which *Izabel* is the latest, and your writing style is eminently suitable for several of them. Current women's issues and romance are our preferred topics, but we are open to persuasion.

Please email anything else you think would be suitable to me at the address below.

Thank you and I look forward to hearing from you soon.

Rachel Aitkins
Editor
Izabel Magazine

"Oh, God," she kept saying to herself as she read the letter over and over again. "Rachel Aitkins, the editor of *Izabel* magazine, loved my story. Not only that, she wants more of them."

As that thought sank in, *oh, no* replaced *oh, God*. She didn't have any more of them! Something she'd have to remedy, and fast.

Whispering a silent thank-you to Lenny Dryden, the man she credited for reminding her to write again, she bounded out of the kitchen and up the stairs, the letter clutched firmly in her hand.

"Penny, Penny!" she screamed, bursting into her room.

"Ugh? What's the matter? Is the house on fire or something?"

"Better than that," cried Layla. "*Izabel* wants to publish my short story."

"Good for her, but tell me about it later. I'm actually asleep right now."

With that, Penny pulled her pillow over her head and turned back on her side. Her enthusiasm still intact, Layla raced back downstairs, grabbed her jacket from the hook beside the front door and flew out into the sunshine. She noticed Joseph's Land Rover wasn't parked out front. He and Penny had eventually joined them at the pub last night, coming in about an hour behind them. What had taken them so long, she didn't know. Layla and Hannah had been behind the bar by then, helping the occasional barman, Tom, with his shift, the good weather ensuring a steady flow of customers. She'd been glad about having to help, as Hannah had started asking questions about the argument she'd had with Penny, and it was getting increasingly awkward trying to deflect them.

Penny had wandered up to her and cheerily asked for a bottle of merlot and two glasses—one for her, one for Joseph. Sincerely hoping it was corked, Layla handed the wine over to her, watching disgruntledly as Penny sashayed away. The drinking had gone on long after-hours with Jim's band, 96 Tears, giving an impromptu performance to a very appreciative crowd. They were good too, really good, relaxed but with a bit of an edge to them. No wonder they'd bagged a spot in the Brighton Fringe Festival. She was only surprised they weren't more successful.

"They will be," Hannah had said. "They will be."

Layla really admired arty people, musicians like Jim, artists like Hannah, even craftsmen like Joseph, whose work was so skilled, so precise. She had always wanted to be arty, and now she was. Well, she had a way with words, she supposed. That must count for something.

She really must get some more stories written and soon, send them to Rachel Aitkins and other publishers, too. Maybe even enter another competition, see if she could win again. After several short stories, she might attempt a novel. Right now anything felt possible.

Breathing in great gulps of salty sea air and clutching her letter to her chest, she arrived at Jim and Hannah's flat and knocked on the door. There was no reply. Disappointed, she made her way to the pub instead. She knew Hannah was working today; maybe Hannah had put in an early appearance in order to clear the debris from last night. If that was so, she'd get stuck in too—after first sharing her news, of course.

She hurried along the high street and came to the pub where all hope at finding Hannah deserted her. The pub looked suspiciously empty, and a few bangs on the door proved it. Impatient now, she wondered whether she should pop into May's. Hilda behind the counter was always game for a chat; perhaps Layla could regale her with her stellar achievement.

Layla was just starting to cross the road, when she spied Joseph's Land Rover. *Hmm,* she thought, *I wonder…*

Deciding to take a chance, she stepped back onto the pavement and made her way there instead.

Nestled between New Age Encounters and Cornish Dreams stood a tiny two-story building with whitewashed walls, a sloping slate roof, and a slightly dilapidated waist-high slate wall surrounding it. Obviously someone's home in a former life, it had since been converted into Joseph's workshop. She remembered him telling her it had lain empty for ages before he rescued it, knocking through the two rooms downstairs to create a spacious workspace and using upstairs primarily for storage.

Walking up the short pathway, weeds poking through the paving here and there, she arrived at the front door. Painted British Racing Green, it looked for a moment almost forbidding. Beside it, fixed to the wall, was a shiny metal sign embellished with the words: *Joseph Scott, Carpenter and Cabinet Maker.* She took another big gulp of air, pushed the door open, and went inside. She realized this was the first time she had set foot in his workshop and was surprised; after all, she passed it almost every day. The fact that Penny had been here already irked her somewhat, but she let it go. She didn't want to spoil her mood.

As she expected, the interior was packed with tools, some hung neatly on the wall, others strewn across a huge workbench that dominated the center of the room. There were rows and rows of books too, plenty of titles with the words *Antique* and *Restoration* in almost all of them. A wonderful smell of freshly-sawn wood filled the air, mixed in with rich undertones of linseed oil. And in the midst of it all stood Joseph, leaning over a piece of wood, saw in hand. Thoroughly engrossed in what he was doing, he neither saw nor heard Layla enter.

Time stopped momentarily as she drank him in, his white linen shirt only half tucked in, his black jeans a regular fit, and his work boots scuffed. He looked so intent, so content, like an artist at work, the master of his universe, able to create from beautiful materials something even more beautiful. Feeling a bit guilty she was staring, as though she were some kind of Peeping Tom, she coughed slightly to announce her presence.

Immediately, he looked up. "Layla, what are you doing here?"

"I was just passing," she lied. "Thought I'd pop in and see you."

She was relieved to note he looked really quite pleased to see her. Placing his saw on the bench, he walked toward her, his smile widening as he approached. They hadn't spoken since Hannah and Jim's party, not even last night at the pub. Penny had either commandeered him or he had peeled away to spend time with Jim and Mick instead.

"This is some place you've got here," said Layla, "and it's packed to the rafters."

"Yep, but everything's needed," he replied amicably. "I know it looks like chaos, but it's organized chaos, believe me."

"Oh, I do," she said, lost for a moment in his smile.

Recalling just why she had "popped" in as she had put it, she waved the letter from Rachel in front of her and said almost shyly, "I've had some good news."

"Really?" said Joseph. "Let's hear it."

"I sent a short story off to a magazine a little while ago. I never expected to hear back, not really. But I have, and they're going to publish it. They even paid me for it. Not only that, they want more from me."

"Fantastic," he enthused, coming closer.

After a moment's hesitation, he hugged her. Although it was a brief hug, almost perfunctory in nature, Layla had time enough to register how nice it was to be back in his arms.

Upon release, she said, "I know. I'm in shock. I can't believe it."

"I can. I'm proud of you."

Basking in his kind words, she realized how much she missed him. How much she wanted "the old Joseph" back in her life.

"I suppose I'd better get going," she said almost regretfully. "Let you get on with your work."

"I suppose," he replied, a hint of regret in his voice too, she was certain. "Thanks for coming to tell me, though. I'm really touched that you did."

"Oh, that's okay," she said in a happy rush. "Penny's still asleep and Hannah's not in, so it was a toss-up between you or Hilda."

She had meant it as a joke, but giving voice to the words, they didn't seem funny at all. Cringing, she looked up at him. His face, so friendly, so welcoming just seconds before, now looked anything but.

"Right, well, thanks for that. I'm glad I'm good for something. Now, if you don't mind, I've got to get on."

"Joseph…" she beseeched, but it was too late. He had turned away, clearly not interested in any further exchange.

Again she stared at him, feeling an urge to grab him, to spin him round to face her, to tell him that she hadn't meant what she had said, that she was just trying to be funny. She would admit that, okay, he hadn't been the first person she thought about telling, but she was pleased it had turned out that way. Really pleased. It made the whole thing seem more special somehow. But she couldn't say a word. Her throat had closed tight.

Feeling increasingly hard done by, she stood for a few seconds more before turning abruptly on her heel and leaving, only just resisting the temptation to slam the door behind her.

On the street again, she squinted in the bright daylight, moving her Wayfarers, currently perched on top of her head, to their rightful position. Fed up, she thought, *To hell with you*, before retracing her footsteps home.

She knew her words had been tactless, hurtful even, but he hadn't given her a chance to redeem herself. *It's like one strike and you're out with him,* she thought bitterly. She had been fooling herself they could be friends. They couldn't. They'd crossed a line; there was no going back.

Despite the warmth of the beautiful spring day, she felt bleak inside. As bleak as she had felt during her first evening here, more so even. She passed a field of daffodils to her left and forced herself to slow down, to admire their cheerful beauty, but even they failed to lift her spirits. *Damn him,* she thought, continuing her journey.

If she had expected life to be less complicated in the sticks, she couldn't have been more wrong. It was getting more complicated by the minute. *Why couldn't he see I was joking?*

It was almost as though he were a different person since they had slept together. As though he were continually angry with her, not on the surface, but underneath, ready to fire up at the slightest excuse. She had been different too, she knew that, but she was trying not to be. And why was he angry, anyway? Most men would be delighted they'd had a one night stand or brief encounter or whatever you wanted to call it. But he hadn't called it that, had he? He had called it *love, making love.*

If only that night hadn't happened, she thought, losing count of how many times she had wished that. For a moment there, back in his workshop, it had been like it used to be between them: easygoing and relaxed. If only it could be that way again. If she had hurt him with her careless words, she was sorry, but was it her fault he took her so seriously? Would she always have to mind her P's and Q's around him? Well, she wouldn't. She had neither the inclination nor the energy to do so. She needed to forget him and focus entirely on *Izabel* magazine, keep them champing at the bit for more. She would email Rachel when she got in, thank her for the check and for publishing "Gull Rock," and tell her another story would be winging its way to her soon.

Once again excitement surged within her, and Joseph was consigned determinedly and ferociously to the furthest corner of her mind.

"I'm sorry I've got to work whilst you're down here. I feel so mean."

"Don't worry," insisted Penny. "You need to whip up another story and fast. I understand that. Just keep the evening free, that's all."

Promising she would, Layla said, "So what's on the agenda for today?"

"I spoke to Joe this morning, and he said he could knock off around lunchtime, so we're going to see some sacred waterfall or something. St. Nectan's Glen, I think he called it. It's stunning, apparently."

Indeed it was. Layla had been there several times as a kid with Hannah and their respective mothers. She had talked about revisiting it with Joseph too, but they'd never got round to it and probably wouldn't now. Not that he cared, obviously, having arranged to go with Penny.

"Oh, right." Layla was unable to stop an edge from creeping into her voice. "I thought Hannah said he was busy with work."

"He probably is." Penny laughed. "But unlike Richard, he's not all-consumed by it."

"Good. Lucky you. Have a nice time."

"We will," continued Penny cheerily. "You could join us, you know. Strictly speaking, you're not working to a deadline."

"I am, actually," replied Layla stonily. "Rachel's expecting more from me, and soon. They paid me over a hundred pounds for that story. I could do with a few more checks like that, I can tell you. There isn't a moment to waste."

"Okay, okay." Penny held her hands up in mock surrender and backed away. "Good luck. I'll see you back here around five, okay?"

"Yep," said Layla, turning back to her laptop. "See you at five."

A story was starting to take shape in her head. "The Castle Ruins" it was called, and it had a parallel time dimension to it. Typing out a few notes, she decided the heroine would be a troubled soul called Katherine, a tourist mysteriously drawn to Trecastle's ancient headland, whereupon she found herself tuning into her past life, reaching out to a love she lost long ago but who was still waiting for her in the mists of time.

As she was tapping away, Layla couldn't help wonder if Alex was still waiting for her in the mists of time, and if he was, what the hell he was still doing there. He had told Penny he would track her down, but there was no sign of him yet. More than likely it was all talk. He wouldn't come looking for her, she was sure of it.

Coming to an abrupt halt, she thought, *Bugger*.

It was no good. She couldn't concentrate. It should be her showing Penny St. Nectan's Glen, not Joseph. Why had she insisted on writing, anyway? As Penny said, she wasn't beholden to a deadline. There was no need to panic. Too late now, though. Penny had skipped off into the sunlight with Joseph and seemed more than happy to be doing so.

After another hour of staring into space, she realized she was fighting a losing battle. As far as "The Castle Ruins" was concerned, she had lost momentum. She decided to go for a walk instead, taking her pen and paper with her in case the muse struck whilst she was out. She decided to take a picnic too and packed a small wicker basket she'd purchased from the Saturday morning market in Camelford with a cheese sandwich, a packet of crisps, and a bottle of sparkling mineral water, locally sourced, of course.

It was still relatively early in the holiday season, and there were few people on the beach. A mum, dad, and their two children—a toddler boy and slightly older girl—played on the fringes of the surf, whilst a much older couple, in their late sixties perhaps, strolled contentedly arm in arm into the distance. The older couple, particularly, held her attention. She wondered if they'd been together since they were young, and if they had, she envied them, able to weather life's storms together and remain strong.

Wrapping her cardigan around her, as it was slightly cooler than the clear skies suggested, she walked along the water's edge, too. Salt spray stung her lips, and gulls circled round or rested on the rock named after them. As usual, childhood memories engulfed her. She had walked this route so many times with her mother, the two of them holding hands or pushing playfully at one another.

Despite the sadness that had shrouded her heart since her father's death, she had felt happy on those occasions, close to her mother. Away from here, though, back in the real world, back in Brighton, she had felt anything but. Angelica spread herself too thinly amongst too many people to be truly close to anyone. Being widowed so young seemed to have only temporarily taken the wind out of her sails. She had picked herself up with a vengeance, her suddenly massive appetite for life attracting the hordes, all eager to bask in her warm and inviting glow.

Even now, coming up to her fiftieth birthday, she hadn't slowed down, living it up in Milan with Giorgio, her paramour (as she dubbed him) of nearly three years. Angelica loved Milan, the ebb and flow of it, the sheer dynamism of the place. It suited her perfectly.

Layla had flown out to visit her once, when her mother had first moved there, but the trip hadn't been entirely successful, not for her anyway. New to Milan, Angelica had dazzled all Giorgio's friends and family, her diary quickly becoming filled with social engagements. When Layla arrived, Angelica had barely a window left, and so, by and large, she was left to her own devices, a repeat performance of childhood. One afternoon, though, whilst her mother was busy lunching with some wives of Giorgio's business associates, Layla at least had the chance to spend time with him. He, too, seemed slightly exasperated by how much Angelica managed to pack into a day, but fondly so; it was clear he adored her.

A merchant banker, he was well off, and the apartment they lived in was wonderful, right in the heart of the city, just steps from the famous Piazza del Duomo, with cool marble floors, pristine white walls, and opulent furnishings. She had enjoyed her stay there but had come home having barely spent an hour alone with her mother in a week.

They had spoken several times since, on the telephone, but they were only ever snatched, unsatisfactory conversations—Angelica was always en route to some function or other. The only time Layla had managed to garner her mother's full attention was when she mentioned the move to Trecastle and even then, only for a few short seconds. Staring at the endless sea, Layla wished the mother that populated her holiday memories was here with her now. She missed her mum, but more than that she missed the relationship they could have had. She felt like an orphan and had done so for a long time. But she *wasn't* an orphan. She had a mother, and she must remember that. Perhaps invite her to stay for a few days. Envisaging her mother dressed in clothes made for her by some young Italian designer and strutting down the streets of Trecastle made her smile. The village might never recover! Angelica would probably balk at the idea of coming back, but then again, she might not. It wouldn't hurt to ask.

Layla returned home just after five to find Joseph and Penny pulling up in his Land Rover.

"Hey, Layla," Penny yelled, winding down the window. "Have you finished working yet?"

"Er, yeah. Yeah, I've been down at the beach, scribbling away," Layla replied, her eyes slightly averted.

Although the sandwich and crisps had made it out of the basket, the notebook and pen certainly hadn't.

"Great, 'cause I've got plans for tonight. We went for lunch after the waterfall, and it was okay, but the portions were miniscule. We're starving, so I'm cooking dinner."

"What, for all of us?" inquired Layla, her heart sinking. Not at the prospect of Penny's cooking, although that was bad enough, but of being in such close proximity to Joseph.

"Absolutely," laughed Penny, hopping down from the car. Turning to Joseph, she said, "You're not busy tonight, are you?" It was more of a statement than a question, and before he could answer, Penny said, "Right, that's settled. Let's go inside, open some wine, and let the evening begin."

Layla entered her cottage first, followed by a reluctant Joseph and an exuberant Penny. Once inside, Penny went straight to the fridge, took out a bottle of white wine, opened it, poured two large glasses, and handed one to Joseph and one to Layla.

"Aren't you having one?" inquired Layla.

"I most definitely am, but I need to pop down to the village first and get some ingredients."

And with that, she was off, leaving Layla in a state of abandoned horror. Whilst Joseph stared fixedly at the floor, she flicked through a magazine she had already read cover-to-cover, both of them keenly aware that the last time he'd been in this cottage one thing had led to another. After a while though, she couldn't stand it; she had to speak.

"So did you have a nice day?" she said, pleased at how nonchalant she sounded.

"Yeah, it was good, thanks. And you?" he replied, also impressively casual considering the atmosphere was as taut as a stretched rubber band.

"Yeah, I got quite a bit of work done," she lied. "Almost finished another story for *Izabel*. Then I went for a walk along the beach. It was nice."

"Sounds good. Hopefully the sun will stick around for a while longer. There's nowhere else in the world I'd rather be when the weather's good."

"Me neither," she agreed, their shared view easing the tension slightly. Taking advantage of the moment, Layla said, "Erm, look, if you're busy working at the moment and Penny's stopping you, just say, won't you?"

"It's fine. She isn't. I deserve some time off anyway."

"Yes, but if it's a problem, let me know, and I'll have a quiet word with her," Layla insisted. "She won't mind, not in the slightest."

"Like I said, it isn't a problem," he replied, equally as insistent. "I like spending time with Penny. She's fun, uncomplicated."

Drawing out the last word of his sentence more than she thought was strictly necessary, Layla was incensed. She turned away, suddenly glad she had left some dishes in the sink earlier that she could attend to now. If he meant that in contrast to Penny she was complicated, she felt very insulted indeed. She wasn't, not really. He didn't know her well enough to imply such a thing. Besides which, he was hardly a walk in the park.

Having finished the washing-up, she turned back to him and said, "Penny's very friendly by nature, but that's all she's being: friendly."

"If you say so," said Joseph, his manner irritatingly cool.

Riled further, she continued, "And she's married. You'd do well to remember that, too."

Looking directly at her, he said, "I know, but for how long?"

Layla was stunned. Obviously Penny had wasted no time at all in telling her newfound confidante all about her problems with Richard.

"She's confused, that's all. She and Richard are going through a bad patch, but they'll make it. I know they will. He's a lovely guy, perfect for her," she emphasized. "She doesn't need any more distractions."

"I think Penny should be the judge of that, don't you?"

Layla stared at him, the fury in her eyes more than a match for the defiance in his. Some part of her said he was baiting her, testing her reaction. There was no way he could be serious about hitting on Penny. But another part of her just wasn't sure. Whatever his game was, she wanted none of it. She wished she could evict him, tell him to leave, but if she did, she would have to explain why to Penny, and that could prove problematic. Instead, she turned away again, banging and crashing pots around her, making it obvious she didn't appreciate his remarks.

Penny arrived back shortly after, out of puff from hurrying up the hill. "Right, pour me a glass of *vino*, Layla. I'm in dire need."

Without a word, Layla did as she was asked, pouring some more into her own glass whilst she was at it but pointedly ignoring Joseph's. Her head was starting to hurt, and she wished she could go and lie down, leave the pair of them to it, but that was the last thing she should do and she knew it. The frustrating thing was, deep down, Penny did love Richard and vice versa; they were just having trouble admitting it. And one good thing, he had been texting an awful lot lately. Her phone beeped almost relentlessly. If Joseph contributed in any way, no matter how small, to their marital problems, Layla would never forgive him.

Penny busied herself, announcing with great flourish she was making spaghetti carbonara. Layla had no desire to tuck into a hearty bowl of pasta, but she'd have to make a token effort, keep Penny happy. And happy Penny was, laughing and cracking jokes, completely oblivious to the fact that neither of her friends were responding in kind.

Halfway through dinner, which was surprisingly good, the telephone rang. Layla went to hunt down the cordless phone, eventually located it, said hello and came back into the kitchen, holding it out to Penny.

"It's Richard," she said solemnly.

Clearly surprised, Penny took the phone from Layla and went into the living room. Whilst she was talking, Joseph and Layla sat once again in uncomfortable silence. Penny returned a few minutes later.

"I'm really sorry, Layla, but I've got to leave in the morning. Richard wants me to come home."

"Why? What's the matter?"

"It's his father. He's been taken into hospital. Suspected heart attack. Richard sounds upset. I think he's been drinking. He said he missed me."

"Of course, he misses you." Layla got up and hugged her. "He loves you. He's lost without you, you know that."

She had directed her words as much toward Joseph as to Penny, but if they had any impact on him, it didn't show.

"Maybe," said Penny, her voice quiet at first as though contemplating. Brightening after a few moments, she continued, "Still, there's nothing I can do tonight. I've been drinking, I can't drive. Let's finish dinner, and then I'll pack."

With that, she picked up her glass, shouted cheers, and loudly clicked her glass against Joseph's and Layla's, both of them mumbling less than heartfelt "cheers" in return. Although she was going to miss Penny—and she would—a part of her couldn't help but feel relieved she was going, a feeling she held Joseph wholly responsible for.

chapter fourteen

It was a shame she had to cut her holiday short by a few days, especially since she was enjoying herself so much, but there was no choice: she had to make her way back to Brighton and to Richard.

He had sounded really upset on the phone. She prayed it wasn't terminal with Bill. The powers that be had said "suspected heart attack," not "heart attack." Fingers crossed they'd got it right.

Bill had been taken into the Queen Alexandra in Cosham, near Portsmouth, which was en route home, so she told Richard she would meet him there. His two brothers would be there also, traveling from the north of the country and the east, respectively. She had only met them once, at their wedding, and neither was as handsome as their eldest brother, one short and squat, the other with Richard's features but more exaggerated somehow. She'd hardly met his father either, again at her wedding and once on his seventieth birthday. He seemed okay, chatty enough, a bit of a drinker she'd guessed from his reddened face and rheumy eyes. Richard had been awkward in his company, practically itching to get away. She knew he hated being quizzed about his childhood, but she couldn't resist asking him on their second visit why they didn't see Bill more than they did.

"We just don't get on," Richard had replied curtly.

"Do you mean you don't get on lately or you've never got on?"

"Never got on. Now leave it," he had said, staring fixedly at the road ahead and holding on tight to the steering wheel.

If they'd never got on, though, why was he so upset now? The news of his father's illness had caused him to reach for the whisky, something he hardly ever did. Unlike his father, Richard didn't drink much at all, the odd glass of red wine perhaps, a pint or two of beer on occasions. And on the nights she came home steaming, you could tell it riled him.

As she joined the motorway at Southampton, Penny's thoughts turned from Richard and his family to her days spent in Trecastle. It was a quaint but lively village, almost forgotten by time, although they had Internet access in the pub Layla worked in, at least. Her mobile signal had held up pretty well considering they were so rural, which was a mixed blessing. Dylan had literally bombarded her with texts.

Hey, how's the holiday going? Is it sunny down there? Done any surfing yet? etc., etc. One good thing: there had been no more mention of how sexy she was. They were more general texts, but it was a nuisance, having to give a running commentary of her daily activities. Eventually she had ignored him, but he still kept on sending, unable to take a hint.

Layla had commented a couple of times on how often she received messages but believed her readily enough when she said it was Richard or a friend from work asking how she was. She'd have to have a word with Dylan when she got home, though, tell him to back off. If Richard found out, it really would be the end; she had no doubt about that.

She was now just minutes from the hospital. Her stomach began to flutter at the thought of seeing her husband again, something it hadn't done in a while. He had said he missed her on the phone, a sentiment which had sounded genuine enough, not merely whisky-induced. She had missed him too, but then she had done for ages—it was nothing new. Not that she had time to dwell on it. Joe had kept her too busy for that. What a lovely guy! So open and friendly, not to mention good looking. Shame Layla didn't go for men like him, instead of idiots like Alex. Someone grounded and decent. That was the thing that amazed her about Layla: her taste in men was awful. For somebody so down-to-earth, she was easily dazzled by a bit of glitz and glamour, failing to see the falseness that usually lurked behind it. Those romantic books she favored didn't help, filling her head with all sorts of nonsense.

That argument they'd had, it had been dreadful, really bad. They had never argued like that in the entire ten years they had known each other. Thank heavens Hannah had managed to chivvy them up the next day, pulling them out of their respective sulks with her determined cheerfulness. If it wasn't for her, they might still be ignoring each other.

She was lovely, Hannah. A gentle, arty soul, the kind of person a village like Trecastle was made for. Jim matched her perfectly in temperament. And as for Mick, he was hilarious. She'd have to go back down again before Layla's year was up, spend some more time with them.

Parking her car, she rushed into the hospital foyer, looking around for Richard. There he was, buying himself a cup of coffee from a small kiosk and looking, she had to admit, even in stark hospital lighting, gorgeous in dark gray chinos and a slightly lighter gray cashmere pullover—every inch the off-duty professional. He must have sensed her staring at him as he looked up, straight into her eyes. Smiling, she rushed over and hugged him.

"How's your dad?" she asked. "Have you seen him?"

"Yes." He smiled back at her, relief evident on his face. "He's going to be okay, apparently. This was more of a warning than a full-on heart attack. He needs to quit smoking, though, or he won't be so lucky next time."

"And what about you?" she asked gently. "Are you okay?"

"I'm fine," he replied. Then almost shyly, he added, "Better for seeing you."

She squeezed his hand. "Come on. Let's go and say hello."

Their hands entwined, they made their way to the lift that would whizz them up to the second floor and her father-in-law. As the doors closed, she felt her phone vibrating in her pocket. Thankfully she had remembered to put it on silent, resolving to sort Dylan out as soon as she possibly could. The future was beginning to look brighter with Richard; she mustn't allow anyone or anything to derail them again.

chapter fifteen

The Outlook seemed quiet and empty without Penny. Layla had her work at the pub to occupy her, though, as well as her writing, which would keep her busy until Penny returned, maybe even with Richard in tow. If anyone could use a holiday, he could. Hopefully his father would be okay. Hopefully *they* would be okay. For Richard to have rung and say he missed her, even if he needed a few stiff drinks beforehand, was quite something. If they did manage to patch things up, how would Joseph feel? Not that she cared, of course. He had shown his true colors last night as far as she was concerned, proving himself to be about as deep as a puddle. One minute he was disappointed because she didn't want to be in a relationship with him, the next he was all over Penny! He had seemed like such a nice guy at first, but it just went to show, you never could tell.

In fact, Layla was seriously beginning to question her judgment of men in general. She had thought Alex was a nice guy too, underneath his sometimes flash exterior, but she couldn't have been more wrong. She didn't think of herself as gullible, but the evidence to support that notion was mounting steadily.

At least the sunshine was something to smile about. So many people went abroad in search of hotter climes, but the weather on these western shores had been more than kind lately, lifting her mood with it.

She had stuck the Nike slogan "Just Do It" onto the cover of her laptop, hoping it would inspire her to, well, just do it, she supposed. Get on with crafting more short stories and earning herself a bit extra in the process.

Every night she charged her laptop, and in the morning, if the rain held off, she strode purposefully down to the castle to pound away at the keyboard, glad touch-typing was one of those "extra" skills she had opted to learn at college. Settling beside a favorite crumbling wall, a wall that once enclosed the Great Hall apparently, she would take a few minutes to drink in the view before firing up the computer. On the headland, yellow gorse vied with green tufts of grass for complete coverage, and seabirds swooped high and low in their endless quest for food. The sea was always the star of the show, though, a shimmering azure blue, hugging the ragged coastline.

Day after day, she wrote until she fell into a kind of rhythm, the weeks passing peacefully by as spring melted into summer. During this time, she produced not just one or two but several stories to send off to various publications, scoring a few successes along the way. She had grown more confident about writing a novel too, certain that as soon as a good enough plot hit her, peopled with characters she could believe in, she'd be unstoppable. Working outdoors by day, she was developing a nice tan, her skin, an olive tone in the first place, darkening to a deeper hue. In contrast her hair was lightening in the sun, strands of golden brown a pleasing contrast to her natural, much darker, shade. She looked well and felt even better. Her job at the pub was enjoyable too, more so now they were busy. A far cry from her coveted position as marketing executive, she actually preferred it, unsure she could ever stomach an office environment again. She felt freer somehow, less restricted. Joseph had mentioned that living in Trecastle changed people, made them less concerned about material things, and he was right. Having the latest high-heeled wedges from Kurt Geiger or a show-off handbag didn't matter here. Nobody cared. Mind you, that was one of the few things he had been right about.

Since Penny had left, she'd only seen him a handful of times, and each one of those had been at a distance. If he came into the pub, which wasn't often, he'd simply order his drink and walk away, as though he barely knew her. It hurt, if she was honest, but two could play at that game, and she had. If others noticed their coldness toward one another, they didn't say anything, although Hannah cocked her head thoughtfully at her from time to time. And dying as Layla was to say, "What? Why are you looking at me like that?" she didn't. She let it pass.

Today, Layla was down at the beach. She smoothed flat a wicker mat on the sand, rolled her cardigan into a makeshift pillow and thought she'd rest for a while in preparation for a burst of creativity. She was actually fast asleep when Hannah sat down beside her and gently touched her arm, startling her into wakefulness.

"Sorry," laughed Hannah, her nose wrinkling in amusement. "I didn't realize you were asleep."

"I wasn't," insisted Layla, quickly pushing herself up into a sitting position. "I was thinking, that's all."

"You were snoring," Hannah pointed out.

"Oh, God, was I?" asked Layla in horror.

"Of course not. I was just joking. But you were asleep, admit it."

After sheepishly agreeing, she and Hannah sat in congenial silence for a while, soaking up the beautiful day and their equally beautiful surroundings. The village was heaving now as high summer approached. It seemed everywhere you looked there were young couples in love, strolling hand in hand to the castle or the beach. Although schools hadn't yet broken up, there were plenty of young families too, kids trailing behind their parents, buckets and spades in hand, intent on some serious digging. "No Vacancies" signs were hanging in almost all the B&B's, and even Trecastle's one and only hotel, perched slightly out of the village in a spectacular spot on the headland, was packed to the rafters. Layla enjoyed the lively vibe. It reminded her of Brighton, and although she hardly missed Brighton, she had grown up there, so a bit of hustle and bustle was in the blood.

"For such a small village, it packs in the visitors, doesn't it?"

"It's the history of the place, and the beach…plus the fact that two of the most gorgeous barmaids in Cornwall happen to live here!" Hannah joked. More seriously, she added, "And it's magical. Whether you believe in magic or not, it's what draws people back here year after year."

"Yeah, yeah, you're right," said Layla, wistfully recalling that long ago tale of the smoke fairies. "There's definitely magic in the air."

Layla had first been touched by that magic as a child. As soon as she and her mother arrived, the world would seem all right again, if just for a short while. Mind you, Trecastle's particular brand of magic could affect you in surprising ways, make you act a bit crazy, as she had done that night with Joseph. You had to watch it at times.

"Anyway, what are you up to?" Hannah asked, idly picking up a smooth shiny pebble and throwing it slightly ahead of her.

"Just getting another story ready to send off whilst waiting for inspiration to hit me so I can start a novel. Nothing new."

"I can't believe you're a famous writer, Layla. I'm so impressed."

"I'm hardly famous," scoffed Layla. "I've been lucky enough to get a few short stories published, that's all. But Rachel's hoping to include me in an anthology she's putting together. I'm really excited about that."

"Do you think you would have started writing again if you'd stayed in Brighton?"

Layla thought for a few moments. "Do you know, I don't think I would have. Life was so hectic there; I barely had time to think most days. I'm busy here, but it's in a different way, a good way." Smiling at Hannah, she continued, "I actually think Lenny's creative spirit has rubbed off on me. It's him I've got to thank for finding my muse again."

"See, I told you it was a good idea to come and housesit. At this rate you won't be going anywhere in January."

"I'll have to. I won't have a place to stay."

"You don't have a place to stay in Brighton," Hannah pointed out.

"Don't remind me," said Layla grimly.

Changing the subject, Hannah said, "You working in the pub tonight?"

"Yes, I am. I'm doing Tom's shift. He's got a hot date with a girl from Bodmin, so I said I'd cover."

"Okay, it's probably going to be busy, judging by the amount of people around. I've got a meeting with the owner of an art gallery in Bude at five. I shouldn't be long. We're just finalizing which pictures of mine he wants to show. I'll be back to give you a hand as soon as I've finished."

"Yeah, no worries. Kate is working too, so we'll manage until you get there." Standing up and gathering her belongings, she continued, "I think I'll go home now, finish that nap I was having, and grab a shower."

"You do that," laughed Hannah, also standing up. "Catch you later."

It was busy in the pub, but manageable between herself and Kate, a summer-time-only member of staff. Mainly families grabbing a drink on their way home from the beach. The more adult crowd would arrive later on.

A young man with spectacles perched on the tip of his sunburned nose had just ordered two Cokes for his children, a pint of shandy for him, and a glass of white wine for his wife. He also wanted two packets of cheese and onion crisps. Layla knelt down to locate the crisps, situated in a box just below the Pride of Cornwall beer pump, grabbed two bags, and stood up. She was just about to say *That'll be nine pounds and eighty pence, please*, when her voice shriveled in her throat and died.

There standing before her, in all his glory, was Alex Kline.

"Layla!" he said. "At last I've found you."

As she stood there staring, she was aware of another pair of eyes burning into her. As if in a dream, she shifted her gaze from Alex to the other man at the bar, who was still brandishing a ten-pound note at her.

"Sorry," she spluttered. "Em, er, nine pounds, eighty, please."

Somehow managing to calculate the change she owed, she handed it over with trembling hands before turning back to Alex. "What do you want?" she managed at last.

"I'd have thought that was obvious," he replied, his voice as soft as the silk ties he liked to wear. "But meanwhile, a pint of ale will do."

Glad to be issued an instruction, even if it was by him, she forced her limbs to cooperate as she grabbed a glass and lowered the pump, keeping her eyes firmly on the flowing dark liquid at all times. As the glass filled, she endeavored to come to terms with what was happening. Alex had found her! He had told Penny he would, and he had.

As she handed him the pint, his fingers brushed hers, causing the trembling to escalate into violent jolting. If he noticed, though, he didn't say. Instead he took a leisurely sip of his drink before speaking again.

"You look well, Layla. Beautiful, in fact." As his eyes roamed appreciatively over her, she struggled to keep cool, calm, and collected.

Next he asked if there was somewhere private they could talk.

"I'm working. You'll have to wait," she croaked, a far from cool sound.

"What time do you knock off?"

"Not until eleven."

"That's okay. I'm not going anywhere," he said, moving to one side so she could continue to serve the increasing number of customers.

How she was keeping her mind on the job she didn't know. Alex was standing opposite her, just staring at her. She felt disorientated, nauseous, but still she managed to pull pints, serve wine, and hand out packets of crisps and nuts, all without so much as a glitch.

It was an hour later and Alex was on his second pint when Jim and Joseph came into the pub, followed swiftly by Mick.

Oh, great, she thought. *Just when I thought it couldn't get any worse.*

"Hey, Layla," Jim drawled, "Hannah's running late, but she shouldn't be too long. She says sorry and that she'll be here as soon as possible."

"Okay," she replied, wishing Hannah was already here so she could take Alex and go hear whatever pathetic excuses for his behavior he intended to ply her with and send him on his way.

"Are you all right?" asked Jim, rather perceptively, she thought.

"I'm fine," she lied.

"Are you sure?" It was Joseph this time, and the genuine concern in his eyes and voice nearly undid her.

"Yes," she said, attempting to smile but feeling her eyes well up instead.

He was about to say something else, she was sure of it, when Alex came over and interrupted. "Friends of Layla's?" he asked, offering his hand.

Jim and Joseph looked confused. Mick, however, offered his hand readily. "We most certainly are," he said affably. "You too?"

"You could say that. I'm Alex."

Layla watched Joseph's face as the penny dropped. The gentle look he had given her when he realized she was upset fell away, replaced by a stoniness instead. He offered his hand too, as did Jim, but then turned away, taking the pint she had pulled with him and retreating to the furthest corner of the pub. Only Mick stayed.

During the hour before Hannah arrived, Mick and Alex got on like a house on fire, their mutual love of the sea providing opportunity aplenty for bonding. Not that fishing was Alex's style. Rather he liked to take his fancy speedboat, *The Molly McGuire,* moored at Brighton's marina, out for long trips on the ocean, round the coastline to Plymouth, down to France even, Cannes and Nice. He had once referred to it as *The Love Boat,* the namesake of a seventies show he used to love when he was younger apparently. Layla had wondered at the time whether he nicknamed it that for another reason. Certainly he had once tried to woo her on-board, to no avail, however; the sea always gave her such terrible motion sickness.

In between enduring snatches of their conversation, she found the courage to glance over at Joseph. Whatever topic he was discussing with Jim must be equally as fascinating, because not once did he tear his gaze away from his friend. After finishing his pint, he got up and left, without so much as a backward glance, leaving her feeling surprisingly bereft.

Thank God! There was Hannah, scurrying through the door, dressed not in her usual uniform of leggings, mini-skirt, and top but a smart skirt and blouse.

"Hannah, Hannah," Layla called urgently, "can you cope without me? Alex is here. I've got to go."

"Hang on," said Hannah, reeling from the flurry of words thrown at her. "What do you mean? Alex is here? Where?"

"Over there," replied Layla, indicating with her eyes.

With embarrassing indiscretion, Hannah turned and looked directly at him before saying far too loudly, "What, him?"

"Yes, him," Layla hissed.

"Cor blimey, Layla, he's getting on a bit, isn't he?"

Getting on a bit? He most certainly was not. He was forty-three, still positively kittenish by today's standards. Looking at him again, she tried to see what Hannah saw, but couldn't. If he had looked disheveled when he'd gone to see Penny, he didn't now. He looked chic and debonair, totally at odds, in fact, with his rustic surroundings.

"*Please,* Hannah," implored Layla. "This is excruciating."

"Yeah, of course, fine, go. Kate and I can manage."

As Layla hurried round to the other side of the bar, Hannah spoke again. "But don't just fall back into his arms, Layla. He really hurt you. Remember that."

As if she were likely to forget.

chapter sixteen

They barely talked on the way back home, the impressive pace Layla was setting more than a match for the thoughts that careered through her mind.

Six months she'd been in Trecastle, six whole months! And now he turned up, just like that, out of the blue, with no warning whatsoever. What had he been doing all this time? Pining for her as he had insisted to Penny, or carrying on with a succession of other naïve young lovelies? And just what excuse was he going to come up with regarding Sarah-Jane? Was it even possible to excuse an affair? Question after question flung themselves at her, relentless in their succession. By the time they reached the cottage, she thought her head might explode.

Shoving her way inside, she threw her keys on the kitchen table before turning round, hands on hips and shouting, "Well?"

"Layla," he said, a kind of wonderment in his eyes, "I can't tell you how good it is to see you."

"Don't, then," she spat back, nostrils flaring. "What do you want from me? Why are you here?"

"I want you, Layla," he smoldered. "That's why I'm here. God, I want you. Do you realize how sexy you look when you're angry?"

She was stunned. He was coming on to her. She hadn't seen him for six months, and the first thing he does is come on to her. Where the hell was his humility, his heartfelt apology?

"Drop the smooth talk," she said, her voice menacingly low. "It doesn't work with me, not anymore. You drop me for that, that… flake, Sarah-Jane Johnson, rip my heart in two, then walk back into my life thinking flattery is going to get you everywhere. It won't. Do you have any idea how much you've hurt me?"

He stepped closer, too close in fact. "I do know how much I've hurt you. I'm not a fool. The fact you ran away told me everything I needed to know. And I'm sorry, I really am. But if it's any consolation, I hurt myself, too. I didn't realize how much I cared until it was too late."

He looked earnest now. Instead of carnal, his eyes shone almost dutifully with unshed tears, but it wasn't enough. No amount of pretty words that fell from his mouth would ever be enough.

"I didn't run away." She wanted to get that fact straight at least. "An opportunity came up elsewhere. That's why I left."

"Of course," he replied, trying to appease.

"I'm hungry," she said, needing to change the subject, to buy herself time to think. "Do you want toast?"

"Toast?" he asked, taken aback. "Okay, if you want. I don't mind."

Turning from him, she walked over to the bread bin, relieved it of two slices of wholemeal bread, and threw them in the toaster. She hadn't eaten since midday; she was ravenous. Her blood sugar levels were dropping and confusing her further, she was sure of it. When the toast popped up, she quickly buttered it before taking it to the table, sitting down, and devouring it completely, not bothering to offer any in the end.

Alex sank down into the chair next to her, looking nonplussed. As he did so, she noticed a slight paunch above his trousers. That hadn't been there before. Wasn't he going to the gym anymore? He used to be obsessed, practically an everyday man. His hair was still the same: expensively cut but with a few strands of gray at the temples. It was also slightly thinner on top. Was that a recent occurrence or had it been like that for a while?

Making a show of looking around, Alex said, "So this is where I find you. Not some far flung country, as I feared. This is your refuge."

"It's not my refuge," she flashed back. "It's my home."

"Yes, yes, of course. That's what I meant, your home. It's very nice, erm, rustic but not without charm. A change from Brighton."

"You know what they say, Alex: a change is as good as a rest," she answered. "A maxim you tend to live by."

It was the prompt he needed. He reached across to grab her hands. "Layla, please, listen to me. That thing with Sarah-Jane, it was a mistake. The biggest I've ever made. I've been so miserable without you."

Hastily reclaiming her hands, she was surprised at how passionate his voice sounded, as though he truly believed the words he was saying. She had dreamed this so often: Alex telling her what a terrible mistake he had made, how he had realized it straightaway, and that he loved her above everything. And now, with the exception of the bit about loving her above everything, her dream was coming true. So how come she felt so flat?

"How did you find me?" was all she could think to say.

"It wasn't easy, believe me. I searched everywhere for you, Layla, at home and abroad. I was desperate."

"When did you realize you'd made a mistake?" she inquired further.

"In Florida," he replied quickly. "The very first day."

"Oh? If you realized so soon, why didn't you call me from America or come and see me the minute you got back? I didn't leave straightaway; I was around for a few days…waiting."

"Erm, well," he faltered, the smugness on his face suddenly replaced by a growing unease. "It was a busy week; I had a lot to catch up on."

"A lot to catch up on?" she repeated scathingly. "And that's your excuse, is it? You didn't come to see me because you were busy. You liar. Penny was right; you don't give a damn about anyone but yourself."

"No, Layla, no," he replied, lunging for her hands again, "that's not true. I did care, I do care. I was confused, scared even. I've never felt about another woman the way I feel about you. I am not a liar."

Shaking him off, she said, "Okay, come on then, tell me. How do you feel about me?"

"Well, you know," he said, faltering again.

"Do you love me?" she interjected, amazed at her boldness.

"Love you? Yes, of course. Of course, I love you."

It was the first time he had ever said those words to her but only after being prompted. That wasn't right, surely.

"Alex, I think you'd better go. I don't want you here."

Bewildered by her rejection, it took a few moments for him to rally. "Layla, please, give me a second chance. I deserve that much at least. You've made your point. I get it, I understand. Someone like you doesn't belong in this rural backwater. It will kill you, with boredom, if nothing else. Come back with me, to Brighton, where you belong. We'll start again. We'll make it work. I promise."

Incensed, she stood abruptly up, sending her chair crashing to the ground behind her, an almighty bang against the flagstone tiles.

"How dare you?" she shouted, all the pain and fury of the last few months exploding. "All of this, it's not about making a point, not to you anyway. It's about me, about trying to be happy again, a happiness you took from me in the first place because I wasn't enough for you. And as for deserving a second chance, you deserve nothing. You left me, and the first I know about it is that hateful Post-It note. Well, that and Hazel shouting it from the rooftops. If you were bored of me, Alex, you should have been a man about it. You should have told me face-to-face. And in private."

Alex jumped up too and grabbed her by the shoulders. "But that's just it. I never wanted to finish things between us. Don't you see? Commitment and me, we've never been the best of friends, I admit it. The fact that I was falling in love with you, that I couldn't see a future without you, terrified me. And that's why I did what I did. It wasn't because of lust. I didn't even fancy Sarah-Jane. It was because of fear. I was frightened."

"What, and suddenly that fear's just gone, has it? Or will it rear its ugly head time and time again, every time you decide to have an affair?"

"There won't be any more affairs, I promise. If you come back to me, I won't let you down again. All that philandering, it disgusts me as much as it disgusts you. I want no more of it. I'm sick and tired of it. I've changed, Layla. I've grown up. All I want is you. I've tried, but I can't live without you."

"Rubbish," said Layla, quickly turning from him, hoping to hide the tears that were starting to fall.

"It's not rubbish. It's not. Look," he insisted, fishing about in his jacket pocket for something.

Curious, she turned back to see what he was doing. Dangling in his hand was the diamond bracelet he had given her for Christmas.

"As soon as we get back to Brighton, we'll buy an engagement ring to match, an antique one from those shops you love so much in the Lanes. I'll marry you. You'd like that, wouldn't you? To get married?"

Staring at it, she took it from him, unable to believe it had found its way to her again. It was still a merry little thing. Still sparkling away. After a while, she took his hand, placed it back in his palm, and closed his fingers over it. She was not a donkey, and the carrot did not tempt her.

"You know what?" She was more sad than angry now. "You make it sound as though you'd be doing me a favor, marrying me."

"Of course not," he blustered. "Nothing could be further from the truth. I want to marry you. I'd do it right now, right this minute, if I could."

"Just as well you can't, then," she whispered. "Just as well you can't."

"Layla," he continued desperately. "I want nothing more than to marry you, to have children with you. We can have a great life together. We belong together. I'm just sorry it took me longer than you to realize it."

His hands were on her shoulders again, and she let them rest there this time. She was tired of fighting. Earlier that day she had said to Hannah she couldn't stay in Trecastle when the year was up because she wouldn't have anywhere to live. As Hannah had pointed out, she didn't have anywhere to live in Brighton, either. It was true: she was, to all intents and purposes, a vagrant or would be in a matter of months. And now here was Alex, offering her the world. Not just a place to live but marriage too, a family. Everything she had wanted not so long ago.

Looking into his face, she searched for signs of sincerity. Unless he had developed a talent for acting, he looked genuine enough. Whilst scrutinizing him, she noticed how deep set the lines around his eyes were, his slightly saggy jowls, and it took her by surprise. He seemed to have aged since Christmas. Is that what missing her had done to him?

Not wanting to even utter her name but knowing she must, she asked, "What about Sarah-Jane? What's happened to her?"

"She's long gone. I fired her. The last thing I needed was a daily reminder of where I'd gone wrong."

"You fired her?" Layla was stunned. "Because of me?"

"Yeah, no, not just because of you. Look, I've had to make all sorts of cutbacks. She was last in, so of course she'd be first out," Alex replied hastily. "But never mind that. All you need to know is Sarah-Jane has gone. It's you I want. It always was."

Feeling like a battered opponent in a boxing ring, Layla tried to make sense of everything Alex was saying to her. It was hard, though. Her mind, heart, and soul were reeling from the onslaught.

"I'm getting rid of Hazel, too," Alex continued. "Her people skills are appalling. You can have her job. You'd be brilliant at it."

So not only a place to live, marriage, and children, but a promotion, too. Was there anything this man wasn't prepared to offer her?

"I don't know," she said, shaking her head in confusion. "I just don't know."

"But I do," replied Alex, the certainty in his voice impressive. "I know for both of us. What we have is special, too special to lose. We owe it to ourselves to try again, to learn from our mistakes, to move forward."

Our mistakes? she was about to say, amazed at the cheek of him, but then she faltered. Maybe he had a point; maybe she had made mistakes too. He had never mentioned love or marriage to her when they had been together. Those had been her dreams. Not yet his. Could he really be accused of leading her on? More likely she had led herself on. Read too much into a pretty trinket.

"Layla?" he prompted, agitated now.

"I, Alex, I don't know…maybe."

"Maybe?" he said, his eyes brightening endearingly. "Is that a yes?"

"Don't push it, Alex. It's a maybe. I can't be more specific than that."

A huge grin spread across his face. For such a powerful man, he had a little boy look about him sometimes. A look, she found, that still tugged at her heart.

"If I do decide it's a yes," she continued tentatively, "if I do come back, it's zero tolerance, I warn you. Another affair and I'm gone for good."

"It's irrelevant," he said, still grinning. "It's never going to happen."

He pulled her to him and hugged her, his arms so tight around her she could barely breathe. She hugged him back but limply in comparison, unable to inject much energy into it.

After a few moments, he pulled away. Staring at her intently, he said, "Could that maybe be more of a yes than a no?"

"Alex," she warned again but she couldn't help it, she started smiling too. "Maybe, yes."

He lifted his hand to stroke her face. As he did so, she thought, *This is it, the big reunion kiss, the kiss you've been waiting for.* She braced herself as his lips found hers, his breath slightly sour, she noted, from the beer he had been drinking earlier. As he continued to kiss her, she wondered where the fanfare was: the trumpets, the drumroll. Surely her internal orchestra should be going into overdrive as they attempted to put the past behind them and move on? Instead, the only sound she heard was the lonely ticking of Lenny Dryden's wall clock.

Pulling apart, his voice was husky as he whispered, "Layla, it's been so long, too long."

"And it's going to be a bit longer," she replied, pushing him away. "Don't think I'm sleeping with you, Alex. Not tonight, tomorrow night, or the night after. Maybe doesn't warrant that."

"Oh," he said, clearly pissed off, "what am I going to do with this, then?"

Refusing to look where his eyes indicated, she retorted, "You're going to have to save it for another time."

"Layla," he whined, but she stopped him.

"Don't, Alex. I mean it. I'm still angry with you for what you did. Just…give me time, that's all."

"Okay," he replied, looking petulant, a little boy look of his that was not so endearing. "So where do I sleep tonight?"

"On the couch. It's comfy; I'm always falling asleep on it. I'll get you a blanket."

"Fine," he said, a heavy sigh indicating it was anything but.

She was about to turn away, to go and get a blanket and a pillow, when he started speaking again.

"Er, Layla, there's one more thing we need to sort out whilst we're at it," he said, rather cautiously, she thought.

"Oh?" Layla tilted her head expectantly.

"Yeah, yeah, come and sit down for a minute. It's just a small thing. We can chat about it over a cup of tea. It's to do with FarScapes…"

chapter seventeen

Just a small thing, he had said, as though he really believed the potential demise of his empire was just a small thing. Layla had been furious. Not only with him for believing she could do such a thing, but with Penny for doing the bloody thing in the first place! Go easy, she had said to Penny that night they had crept back in the office and she'd emailed FarScapes. She should have known better. A bull in a china shop sometimes, Penny wasn't renowned for taking things easy.

Layla was tired; she had barely slept, about an hour or two at most. It had taken Alex a while to calm her down, to appease her, again. Was she too easily appeased, she wondered? Perhaps, when it came to him.

"I'm not accusing you of anything," he had insisted. "All I'm saying is that if you didn't do it, who the hell did?"

She could enlighten him, of course, but she wouldn't. She wouldn't drag Penny into this.

"Okay," she had said finally, through gritted teeth. "It was me. I did it. I never meant to cause any trouble, though."

"I can tell you didn't," he had said, reaching out to smooth her hair, "but unfortunately it has caused serious trouble. Jack refuses to have anything more to do with me because of it. And I need him,

Layla. I wish I didn't, but I do. People just haven't got the money they once had to spend on holidays; business is sliding. Talk to him, make him see sense."

What had been in the email anyway? She'd have to phone Penny to find out, once she'd torn her off a strip or two. And why did Alex think anything she had to say to Jack would make a difference? She was, or had been at least, a lowly marketing executive. Jack wouldn't take a blind bit of notice.

"But he will," Alex had disagreed. "He liked you. I could tell. Please, Layla, help me."

She had a sneaking suspicion he had just stopped himself from adding, *It's the least you can do*, which was just as well. She would have lost it if he had, big time. But he had a point: it *was* the least she could do. She couldn't let an entire company sink because of her, add to the already alarming number of people unemployed in this country. Many that worked for him had families too, kept photos of them on their desks. Often she'd stopped to admire beautiful Byron or darling Delphi. If it was in her power to ensure their parent's livelihood, she had to do it.

"Just call him," he had urged, "in the morning, first thing. Tell him that email had nothing to do with me."

It had nothing to do with her either, but she had agreed to do so. And now it was morning, and she was exhausted. Lying in bed, staring at the ceiling, wondering what she was going to say to Jack Thomas.

She forced herself to push back the duvet, stood up, stretched, then hurried to the bathroom, showering quickly before scrubbing at her teeth. Catching sight of herself in the mirror, she thought how dreadful she looked, her complexion too pale, her expression lifeless.

Is this what you want? To marry Alex? she asked herself. Of course she got no reply. Dead eyes just stared back at her, unnerving somehow.

It used to be what she wanted; whether it still was, she didn't know, not really, not deep down. But did she have a choice? Life was hard nowadays. It wasn't easy to get by on your own. Rents were enormous, and wages barely covered them. So many of her single friends struggled. She had struggled too. It was no joke. With Alex she had a shot at a decent life, a life she had once vividly imagined, but a life far removed from the one she lived now. A life without Hannah, without her newfound friends, without Joseph.

At his name, she started. Of course it would be a life without Joseph. Even if she stayed, it would be a life without Joseph. She'd do well to remember that.

And what about her writing? As marketing manager of Easy Travel, there would be no time for literary pursuits. Any hopes of penning a novel would have to be shelved, permanently, most likely. Which was a shame. She loved writing, and finally she was getting somewhere. Mind you, a hundred pounds here, two hundred pounds there didn't constitute a living wage — another thing worth remembering.

Pulling on her denim miniskirt and favorite dusky pink T-shirt, which had molded itself nicely to her frame over the two years she'd had it, she ventured downstairs, expecting to find Alex still asleep. He wasn't. He was up, looking slightly rumpled but happy enough.

"Hey, babe," he said, grabbing her by the waist as she passed by, "you look gorgeous. Fancy some breakfast?"

She quickly extricated herself. "Not really. Just a cup of tea, please."

Whilst he searched for mugs and tea bags, she wandered over to the kitchen window to look at Gull Rock, a view she would miss when she left. And then it hit her. She was under no obligation to leave. Not straight away. She had said maybe, not yes, even if it was a maybe yes.

It was another six months before Lenny was due back. She could stay until then. She owed it to Lenny to stay. Although she'd never met him, he had rescued her in her hour of need, offered her a place to live when she needed one. She couldn't just abandon their agreement. And staying would test how serious Alex was. If he could wait that long for her — celibately, of course — it would lend weight to his ardent words.

She looked at him frying several rashers of bacon, cracking an egg into the saucepan, cooking the full works. "Alex, I'm not coming back to Brighton with you. Not yet."

Spatula in hand, he swung round. "What do you mean 'not yet'?"

"Exactly that," she replied determinedly. "I promised Lenny, who owns this cottage, I'd look after it until he returns in January, see that all running costs are paid, keep it neat and tidy, that sort of thing. I can't break my side of the bargain. I *won't* break my side of the bargain. It wouldn't be fair."

Laughing, as though with relief, Alex said, "Oh, don't be silly, Layla. You're under no obligation to this Lenny chap. I'll leave enough money to settle the bills for the rest of the year and just get that friend of yours, Hannah or whatever she's called, to look in every now and again. It'll be fine."

"No, Alex." She could feel her anger rising. "You can't just buy your way out of every situation. I said I'd look after his cottage whilst he was away, and that's what I'm going to do. I'm not asking you to stay with me. I don't want you to stay with me. I said last night I need time; well, I do, time *and* space. I want you to go back to Brighton and wait for me there."

"Wait for you? But it's such a long time."

"It isn't. It's no time at all. You said you wanted to marry me, which means spending the rest of your life with me, up against which six months is a drop in the ocean. I'm sure you'll manage it."

"But I want you *now*," he said, looking shell-shocked to say the least.

"It doesn't matter what you want. It's what *I* want that counts," she replied. "If we're going to get back together again, you'd better keep that in mind. I'm staying until Lenny returns, and sadly for you, I don't think he'd be best pleased if I entertained houseguests."

"Fine, terrific, have it your way," he said at last, hardly bothering to conceal his anger. "But by Christmas, you're mine, okay? Mine."

We'll see, she thought, before deliberately replying, "Maybe."

"Here's Jack's number," he said, snatching up a piece of paper he must have scrawled on earlier and almost throwing it at her. "That's something that won't wait, at least."

chapter eighteen

"He's not in, I'm afraid," said a curt voice on the other end of the line — Jack's secretary, she presumed. "Can I get him to call you back?"

"Er, yeah, that'll be great. Thanks."

"Damn," said Alex. He stood over her, looking as if he were about to weep tears of frustration. "I can't believe he's not in."

Layla rolled her eyes. "Well, he isn't. We'll just have to wait."

"You're right. There's nothing we can do." Looking at her lasciviously, he swiftly changed his mind. "Actually there is, there's plenty we can do."

"No," she replied crossly. "I've told you, I'm not doing that. Not yet. If you're really itching for something to do, go and have a shower — a cold one, I think by the looks of it, and then you can pack what little you've brought with you. After that, it's time to leave."

"Layla," he said imploringly.

"Alex," she replied sternly.

"But you will speak to Jack, won't you? Call him if he doesn't call you?"

"I promised I would, and I will. I'll let you know what happens."

"I suppose I'll have to keep Hazel on for a few more months, then?"

"I suppose you will," she said, smiling at him for the first time since last night.

After he had gone, she thought she would miss him, regret that she had sent him away. Instead, she relished having the cottage to herself, the silence like balm to her frazzled nerves.

Alex had threatened to come down again soon, but she told him not to, that talking on the phone would have to suffice for now. He had made her wait for six months; she would make him wait the same length of time. Not for malicious reasons, far from it, but because she needed every hour of that time to contemplate becoming Mrs. Kline.

As soon as she had waved him off, she'd phoned Penny. Another phone call she was dreading. She could guess Penny's reaction, and she was right.

"Have you completely lost your mind?" Penny shouted down the phone.

"No, I have not," Layla countered. "I know exactly what I'm doing."

"He had an affair, Layla," Penny emphasized. "That's unforgivable."

But is it? Is it really? There were many reasons for having an affair: Penny had kissed Dylan because she was lonely, Alex had had a so-called "final" fling with Sarah-Jane because he was afraid of commitment. If you understood the reasons why, maybe it wasn't *that* unforgivable.

Suspecting Penny was in no mood to agree with her, however, she said instead, "Look, Penny, I haven't said an outright yes. I've said maybe. I can change my mind at any time. The ball is in my court, not his."

"Until you're married, that is, then he's back in control again."

"It's not like that. *He's* not like that, not anymore. He's changed."

"Men like him never change."

They do, she wanted to shout back at her, frustration building, but she knew it was no good. Alex would never top Penny's Christmas card list.

"You haven't slept with him, have you?" said Penny after a pause.

"No, of course I haven't. What do you take me for?"

"Good, that's one thing you've managed to get right."

Annoyed, Layla said, "Anyway, enough of Alex. Back to FarScapes. You still haven't told me what you wrote in that blasted email."

"It was nothing." Penny was sheepish now, Layla was pleased to note. "Not really. All I said was Easy Travel wasn't interested in the merger with FarScapes anymore and to go and take a running jump."

"That's not exactly taking it easy, is it?"

"He deserved it after what he did."

"Yeah, but what you did doesn't just affect Alex; it affects everyone. A lot of people count on him paying them a wage, you know."

"Ah," said Penny contritely, "I didn't think about that. In which case, I'm sorry. I can't believe FarScapes took my email that seriously in the first place, though."

"Well, they did. Jack was furious, apparently, and now it's up to me to try to rectify matters, talk him round."

"You?" Penny was clearly surprised. "Why you?"

"I'm not exactly sure. According to Alex, Jack likes me. I mean, I know we got on well, but I didn't think we got on that well. At any rate, I'm the last chance saloon; he refuses to have anything to do with Alex."

"He likes you?" Penny said, sounding wary now. "In what way does he like you? He's not another Alex, is he?"

"No," said Layla. "At least, I don't think so. Oh, God, I hope not."

"Don't agree to meet up with him or anything, just in case. You should be able to say everything you need to say over the phone. The last thing you need is another old letch making passes at you."

Bridling at yet another dig at Alex, Layla changed the subject entirely. "How are things with you and Richard?" she asked. "Better?"

"Yeah, they are actually, much better."

"That's a relief," said Layla. "I'm glad."

"Yeah, me too…but Layla, there is something I need to talk to you about."

At which point Layla's mobile rang. Walking over to it, the other phone still pressed to her ear, she checked the caller ID.

"Oh, crikey, Penny, it's him. It's Jack. I've got to answer it."

"Of course, Layla, that's fine. We'll speak later."

"What were you going to say, though? Anything important?"

"No," replied Penny quickly, "nothing important. Now hurry up, answer the phone or you'll miss him."

"Okay, speak later. Love you."

"Yeah, I know," said Penny. "I love you too, despite Alex."

Answering her mobile on what was probably the final ring, she said hello, her whole body tense with nerves.

"Layla, is that you? My secretary said you called."

"I did, Jack. Hi, how are you?"

"Good, thanks. Long time no speak. How can I help you?"

"Well…" she said, wondering where to start.

Oh, Christ, Jack wanted to meet up. Worse than that and despite Penny's advice, she had agreed. FarScapes' head office was in Bristol. When she said she couldn't possibly travel that far, thinking it a perfectly reasonable excuse, he had quickly outwitted her.

"No worries. Launceston's a sort of midway point. We can meet there."

A town less than twenty miles from Trecastle, she had no option but to agree. And he had sounded pleased to hear from her, really pleased. Alex was right: Jack did like her, although in what way she couldn't tell. Alex had told him already that she'd written the email (*thanks, Alex*), but Jack hadn't believed him. Now Jack wanted to know why she'd written it. After all, it had caused him to pull out of a deal which would have brought FarScapes and Easy Travel a lot of business. If she was convincing, it might still be a do-able deal. Stuttering and spluttering, she had tried to conjure up a reason, but although she knew she was speaking, no sense would come out of her mouth. That's when he had suggested they meet; it would be easier to talk face to face than on the phone. It was the last thing she wanted, but she made herself remember all the people that were relying on Alex, people who could lose their jobs unless she pulled this off, and so she gave in. At the end of the week they would meet for lunch in a little restaurant he knew; she couldn't help sighing with relief at his suggestion to meet somewhere public. Apparently, he visited North Cornwall quite often, and he knew the best places to eat. Praying the venue wasn't too posh — she had nothing suitable to wear — she agreed to meet him at midday at a restaurant called The Olive Tree.

Ringing off, she supposed she'd better call Alex next and tell him the good news.

The next day, Layla had gone round to Hannah's flat. To her dismay, Hannah had practically mirrored Penny word for word when she had revealed what had happened with Alex. With one exception: she had asked Layla if she loved him.

"I think so," Layla had replied before abruptly stopping.

Think? What had thinking got to do with anything? Why had she even uttered such a word? Hannah hadn't looked impressed at all.

God, she was confused. She loved Alex, had done from afar for several years and up close and personal for nearly one. She knew she loved him as surely as she knew night followed day. She didn't need to *think* about anything.

"Isn't he a bit old for you?"

That's another thing Hannah had asked. It annoyed Layla. Why did she have a problem with the age gap? Both she and Penny. It wasn't that outrageous, fifteen years. It was nothing. Well, practically nothing.

On Thursday they met again, this time to work the lunchtime shift at the pub. Hannah didn't mention a thing about Alex this time, obviously sensing it was a sensitive subject. Instead, she informed Layla that there was going to be a barbeque at Shipwreck Cove that very night, quite a few people were going, and did she fancy it?

"I'm not sure," said Layla, knowing she had to meet Jack the next morning and plead for the future of Easy Travel.

Joseph might be at the barbeque, too. She didn't know if she could deal with the inner conflict his presence always engendered in her. Not on top of the already broiling emotions Alex had dredged up.

"Come on," Hannah had urged. "It's a beautiful day. Looks like it's going to be a beautiful evening, too. It would be a shame to waste it."

Launceston wasn't that far away. If she did go, she wouldn't have to get up too early, she supposed. She could still enjoy a bit of a lie-in. As for Joseph, if he ignored her, she'd ignore him too, continue the game they were playing.

"Okay," she said at last. "I'll see you tonight."

Saying goodbye to Hannah, Layla went home to pamper herself in a relaxing bath, using more aromatherapy products from Harvest

Moon, the same shop she had bought the Celestial bubble bath from and the Blue Lagoon nail polish. The bubble bath she used this time was called Heavenly Spheres, and as she cocooned herself in the scented water, she did indeed feel calm and clarified, just as the label on the bottle had promised.

After drying herself off, she brushed her hair until it shone, marveling at how long it had grown since the winter, the sunshine sending her follicles into overdrive. She opted for a slightly cropped olive green vest, sitting atop a long, black, floaty skirt—both items recently purchased in Bude, a big town further north along the coast with quite a few decent clothes shops in it. Pleased with how she looked, she set off.

The sun was just beginning to sink when she reached Shipwreck Cove, the nickname for a small secluded bay less than a mile from the village center. Because you had to descend a rather precarious path to get to it, it was largely left alone by the tourists, who preferred to keep to the larger, more easily accessible beaches. Hannah had said it should be deserted, and it was, except for Hannah, of course, and her friends sitting round the fireside close to the water's edge in the distance.

Hitching up her skirt, she negotiated her way down the steep rocky path, praying she wouldn't fall and break her neck as she did so. Upon reaching the flat golden sand, she brushed her skirt smooth, flicked her hair over her shoulders, and breathed a huge sigh of relief that she had made it intact before heading toward the crowd. She strained her eyes in the increasing gloom, just about able to make out Mick sitting tight with a group of people she didn't recognize. Curtis and Ryan were there too, doing what they always did, strumming their guitars, whilst Jim had opted for the role of head cook this time rather than lead singer, pushing every now and then at items on the grill. Hannah was sitting beside him, hugging her legs as she swigged from a bottle of beer, but Joseph was nowhere to be seen. Instead of feeling relieved, disappointment rose up in her.

As she drew closer, someone she didn't recognize moved slightly, and she spotted Joseph's blond head. He was there, after all! Maybe she'd plonk herself down beside him and force him to talk to her, she thought, feeling brave all of a sudden. That approach always seemed to work wonders for Penny; it might for her, too. With renewed vigor, she walked faster, slowing down again when she saw the stranger sitting beside him—a girl with long auburn hair and what looked like dozens of Indian bangles on her wrist—lean in to kiss him on the mouth.

As though encountering an invisible brick wall, she came to an abrupt halt. Her mouth wide open, it took a few seconds to realize what a strange figure she must cut, standing there, stock still, staring like a demented fool. Luckily, she seemed to have escaped detection. Clamping her jaw shut, she moved quickly forward again. *He's got a girlfriend. How come I didn't know that?* Layla lived next door to him; surely she would have seen them coming and going? But she hadn't. Not one single sighting.

"Hey, Layla, how you doing? Come on over and grab a beer," Jim said, his voice as usual a lazy drawl. Hannah looked up too, and Mick waved. Joseph took his time acknowledging her, waiting for the redhead to finish whatever it was she was saying before making only very brief eye contact.

Sitting beside Joseph no longer an option, she sat next to Hannah instead, first handing over the wine she'd brought to Jim and gratefully taking a bottle of beer.

Furtively, she studied Joseph's companion. She was pretty, in a hippy kind of way, quite young, early twenties possibly, with pale skin that flickered almost ethereally in the firelight.

Hannah must have noticed Layla sizing up the stranger in their midst as she proclaimed loudly, "Wondering who Joe's friend is, Layla? Join the club. So did we. It's Clare—a bit more than a friend as it turns out and the main reason we haven't seen him much in the last few weeks."

Surprised at the slightly aggressive tone in Hannah's voice, Layla nonetheless smiled at Clare who smiled back briefly before resuming her conversation with Joseph. Clearly, she was interested in nothing but him, this girlfriend of his.

Lost in thought, it was another few seconds before Layla realized Hannah was speaking again. "He's a dark horse, isn't he? No one knew anything about her until tonight. You have to hand it to him; Joe must be the only man who, in a village like Trecastle, can keep his private life exactly that—private."

Joseph glanced up at this comment, a look of discomfort crossing his face. He appeared far from pleased at being the center of attention.

Sensing it was probably a good idea to change the subject, Layla asked Jim for a rundown of the menu. She was starving, having barely eaten anything since breakfast.

Jim looked grateful she had done so. "Mick brought a load of fish, fresh from the sea today," he replied. "It'll be ready soon."

"Lovely," replied Layla. She was just about to ask what kind of fish it was when Hannah cut in again.

"So, come on, Joe, why all the mystery? How come you haven't introduced Clare to us before now?"

Even Jim looked embarrassed at Hannah's strident quizzing. He kept his eyes determinedly on the barbeque, turning the fish over a few times more than was strictly necessary, risking its flesh falling from the bones.

"There's no great mystery," Joseph said at last. "We've been busy, that's all."

"Too busy to waste time with us?" Hannah almost spat.

"Okay," said Mick, taking his turn to change the subject. "I can't wait anymore. I have to eat." He clapped his hands very loudly together. "Jim, my man, plate up."

There were hearty murmurs of agreement as people moved toward the fire and started helping themselves to food. Baffled by what had just taken place, Layla didn't feel particularly hungry anymore but joined the queue nonetheless.

Joseph and Clare hung back, clearly not interested in eating. In fact, casting another furtive glance at them, Layla thought Joseph looked as though he'd rather be anywhere else in the world but here. Clare seemed almost to be disappearing into him too, maybe in a bid to protect herself against any more abrasive comments from Hannah, or maybe just because she could. She really did look in awe.

Why was Hannah making such a big deal of Joseph being with Clare, anyway? Layla presumed the girl wasn't married; she looked too young. Besides, there was no wedding ring on her finger, an improvement on his last flirtation at least. Layla flinched at this thought, knowing she was being deliberately mean. Part of her actually felt glad he had a girlfriend; at least there'd be no more flirting with Penny when she came down. And they looked good together, he and Clare, easy on the eye.

Still, it was a shame Layla wouldn't have a chance to build bridges with him tonight, or any other night probably. But maybe that was for the best. She would just have to savor what they had once and leave it at that.

Layla was feeling a bit concerned that Hannah was knocking back the beers at lightning speed and becoming more and more sullen. She was about to ask if her friend was okay when Mick came and sat down beside her, effectively quashing that idea.

"Hello, gorgeous," he said, putting his arm around her.

"Hiya, Mick," she replied. "This fish is delicious. You've obviously had a good day's catch."

"Sure did." He chuckled, his arm remaining firmly in place. "I'm hoping for a bit of a catch tonight, too."

Layla laughed at his joke but out of courtesy rather than amusement. She was fond of Mick, but she didn't feel up to their usual banter right now. Instead, she wished she was home alone, chilling on the sofa, watching something mindless on the telly or reading a good book. She was surprised to find herself aching for The Outlook, but then again perhaps not. Fending off Mick whilst staring at love's young dream across the campfire was not really her idea of a good night out. It would look odd if she left now, though; she'd barely arrived. So not really hearing anything Mick was saying, she stared at the inky ocean, feeling strangely lost inside.

Her reverie was rudely interrupted minutes later by Hannah lurching toward them on unsteady legs. "You okay, Layla," she asked, her voice slurred, "or is Mick pestering you again?"

Alarmed at her attitude and concerned for Mick, who had extracted his arm rather hastily from her shoulder at Hannah's words, Layla replied, "We're fine, thanks. We're just talking. What about you? Are you okay?"

"Oh, yeah, I'm great." She laughed, but it was not a happy sound. "Never better. Can't you tell?"

She directed her words at Joseph as much as Layla. Upon hearing them, he leaned over to Clare and whispered something in her ear. She nodded in eager agreement, and they started gathering their things to leave.

"You off, then?" Hannah sneered. "Had enough of us, have you? Better things to do?"

Joseph ignored her, said goodbye to Jim, then disappeared with Clare into the darkness, back toward the steep path that would lead them home. Mick had separated himself from Layla and moved toward Jim, who sat there, a determined smile etched on his face. Curtis and Ryan were still softly strumming away, lost in the music, but a few others started drifting, perhaps driven away by the awkward atmosphere or simply wanting to swap the campfire for a more private part of the cove.

"Hannah, come on. Come with me. Let's go for a walk."

Layla needed to get Hannah away from here and fast, find out what was making her behave so out of character. She would never have thought her capable of such rude behavior, never in a million years. She seemed to dislike Clare, but why? Had they known each other previously and had some kind of falling out? Clare gave no indication of knowing anyone other than Joseph, hadn't even spoken to anyone else as far as Layla knew. In fact, she'd barely looked at anyone else. If only Layla could entice Hannah somewhere quiet, somewhere where it was just the two of them, she could try to get to the bottom of it.

Hannah hesitated before replying, but then said, "Yeah, yeah, okay, I'll come for a walk."

As they linked arms, Hannah pointed at the route Joseph and Clare had taken and said angrily, "Not that way, though. Let's go this way. We don't want to bump into any courting couples, do we?"

Jim looked up at this, and Layla caught his eye. Despite his fixed smile, his eyes were sad.

Gently she asked, "Is that okay, Jim? I think us girls could do with some fresh air."

"Yeah, sure, Layla…look after her, though, won't you?"

"I will," promised Layla, touched by his enduring sweetness. And with that she steered Hannah along the water's edge and into the distance.

chapter nineteen

The tide was far out now, and the moon shone brightly in the sky, lighting their path perfectly. Hannah broke free of Layla and started running along the water's edge, faster and faster as though her very life depended on it, trying to leave the past and everything in it as far behind as possible.

Layla caught up with her after a while and grabbed her arm, the movement causing Hannah to stumble and in stumbling bring them both down. As they toppled to the ground, the water lapped against her bare legs, causing an involuntary intake of breath, it was so cold. It also brought her to her senses.

Quickly backing away from the tide before she got any wetter, Hannah pointed to a collection of rocks some meters away. They made their way toward them and flopped down, fighting hard to catch their breath.

It was Layla who spoke first. "So, come on," she said, her chest still heaving, "what was all that about?"

Layla, of course, didn't know a thing. Was it better to keep it that way? Fairer on everyone concerned? Or should she confide in her? She so wanted to confide in her.

"Hannah." Layla was clearly becoming impatient. "I'm your friend, hopefully your best friend. Something's upset you, and I want to help."

Help? That would be nice. But she couldn't help, no one could help. Still, there may be some relief in sharing.

Unable to hold back any longer, she said, "Have you ever loved someone who didn't love you?"

Layla looked stunned. Whatever she'd expected Hannah to say, it clearly wasn't that. She rallied quickly, though, replying, "I thought Alex didn't love me. When he ran off to Florida, I mean. Turns out he does, or at least he says he does, but for a while I didn't think so. So, yeah, I suppose I qualify, in a way."

"Oh, Layla," said Hannah on a sob. "I wish I could control my feelings. I wish I didn't feel the way I do. I wish I could be happy with what I've got."

"That's one heck of a lot of wishes, Hannah," replied Layla, her voice spilling over with concern.

"Tell me about it," sighed Hannah.

Layla ran her hand through her hair. "I suppose we've all got a tendency to think the grass is greener on the other side. But I don't think it is usually."

"But what if you *know* it is?" beseeched Hannah. "What if you had everything you ever wanted, only to find out it didn't want you?"

"Hannah, I don't understand. I thought you were happy with Jim."

"I am. I am happy with Jim," Hannah insisted. "Who wouldn't be? He's funny, kind, and generous to a fault. He's also bloody good in bed." She laughed but despairingly so.

"What is it, then? What's the problem? He worships you."

Fighting back the tears, Hannah said, "I know, and I love that he does. But there's something else or rather someone else. Someone else I've loved more than Jim, and although I've tried to, I can't seem to forget it."

"Anyone I know?" prompted Layla, her brows furrowed in confusion.

"Oh, yeah, you know him well." She wondered how long it would take for Layla to guess. Not too long as it turned out, realization widening her eyes after just a few moments.

"Joseph?" she said at last.

"Joseph," Hannah confirmed.

"Crikey."

Crikey, indeed.

It was a few moments more before Layla spoke again, and then it was one long string of questions. What? When? Where? How?

"Slow down," Hannah urged. "I'll tell you if you'll let me."

Immediately, Layla fell silent.

"You had no way of knowing," Hannah began. "We'd lost touch at the time, but Joe and I, well, we were a couple for quite a while before Jim. For nearly eight months, in fact."

"A couple?" Layla gasped. "You and Joseph? When?"

"About three years ago. I'd already met Jim when he moved to Trecastle. He had the hots for me straight away. Jim, I mean, I could tell." She smiled. "But I wasn't sure. Just when I decided I liked him too, Joe turns up — fresh from London and sexy as hell — to crash on Jim's sofa. And that was it, I was lost. Jim quickly realized and took a back seat." The memory pricked tears of guilt and caused her to pause for a moment.

"Go on," said Layla gently.

"Joe took a bit of persuasion at first, said he still missed his ex, but finally we got it together, and it was magical, honestly. The best summer I'd ever had in my life. I didn't realize it was possible to be so happy. You know that saying 'walking on air'? Well, I was. I truly was. As time went by, though, I began to realize he wasn't quite as in love with me as I was with him."

As Hannah's tears started flowing freely, Layla leaned across and reached for her hand, squeezing it tight.

"We started going out in March of that year, and he ended it in November. He was worried I was getting too serious. He wanted to nip it in the bud before I got hurt. Too late, though. It was too late from the moment I set eyes on him, to be honest. I was devastated."

"Oh, Hannah, I'm so sorry," said Layla, welling up.

"Yeah, me too," she whispered.

"What about Jim? Does he know how you feel?"

"Of course, he does. Jim knows everything. He picked up the pieces, and in his own way, tried to fix me. He's been trying to fix me ever since, and most of the time he does a pretty good job." She took a deep breath and then continued. "Jim's always been there for me. He knows I still have feelings for Joe. He said he'd rather have a part of me than nothing at all. We don't talk about it much, and usually everything's okay. It's just sometimes it gets to me, you know? It's hard seeing him around all the time and knowing I can't have him."

"It all makes sense now," said Layla after Hannah had finished. "A couple of times I've noticed a kind of sadness about you, but I couldn't figure out why. I thought I was imagining it. You couldn't be unhappy. You had it all. Now I know I wasn't imagining anything."

"Now you know," agreed Hannah forlornly.

For a while the two girls sat on the rocks, Layla's head resting on Hannah's shoulder, each of them staring blindly into space.

"I know it's over between me and Joe," said Hannah eventually. "We're history, well and truly, but I'm worried about Jim. I'm worried if I can't find a way to switch off these feelings, he'll tire of me. Tire of being second best. Everyone's got their breaking point."

"Not Jim," Layla disagreed. "He loves you. I've never seen a guy so in love. Not even Richard with Penny, and that's saying something."

This made Hannah cry harder, but after a minute she stopped, sniffling slightly. "How do you get on with Joe? You two seemed close at one point. There was a definite spark between you. I thought something might happen; you might get it together."

"He's just a friend, that's all," Layla replied quickly. "I don't see him much. He's either at his workshop or with Clare, as we've just found out."

"So," Hannah persisted, "nothing's ever happened between you?"

"Good God, no. Nothing at all. Why?"

"I just wondered, that's all, about the spark."

"There's no spark. None at all. Barely even a friendship between us at the moment."

Was that a slight crack in her voice? Hannah wondered. Turning to face her, Hannah said, "I've confided in you. You'd do the same, wouldn't you? Confide in me if you needed to? Don't let what I've said stop you. Joe and me, we'll never be together again. I know that. You and him, well, you'd make a pretty hot couple, actually."

"I'm with Alex, remember?" said Layla, her voice barely audible. "And Joseph's got Clare."

"For now," replied Hannah, briefly touching Layla's cheek.

Although Layla had denied it, Hannah had been serious about the spark between her best friend and Joseph. She had seen it strike into life the very first night they had met. Lately, though, things had been different. The atmosphere awkward when they were together, even cringe-worthy on occasions, the reasons why, she didn't know. Layla wasn't ready to say. Not yet. And maybe that was okay. There'd been enough revelations for one night. Another time she'd probe deeper. Right now, her priority was Jim. She needed to apologize to him for her behavior. If he was still waiting for her, that is. If he hadn't reached breaking point.

Panicked at the thought, she rose from the rocks, pulling Layla to her feet too.

Before turning to go, however, she said, "Thanks for listening, Layla. You're a good friend."

"So are you. The best." Layla smiled and hugged her tightly. "Life, love, and all its problems, huh?"

"You know what they say: what doesn't kill you makes you stronger," replied Hannah, not sure whether she really believed in the old saying.

"Come on. Let's go."

As they walked arm in arm toward the campfire, Hannah whispered, "You won't say anything about what I told you, will you, to Joe or Jim?"

"Of course not. I won't say a word."

"It's just that I don't think it would help matters."

"I know. I'm not daft. I realize that."

Trusting her friend implicitly, Hannah started running again, her laughter matching Layla's as they raced toward the campfire. Jim was there, still waiting for her.

"So what have you been up to?" he asked clearly relieved to see Hannah in better spirits and kissing her hair as she snuggled into him.

"Girl talk," said Hannah, winking at Layla before turning to kiss Jim on the cheek.

Playful now, they fell back onto the sand, Jim tickling her into submission as she pretended to fight him off. Finally, when she stopped wriggling, he leaned over and kissed her on the lips, stroking her hair all the while, wrapping her in his particular brand of love. And it was a good brand of love, she had to admit, obliterating all other brands of love at times, or rather, one particular brand.

Sometimes that seemed possible, at other times impossible. Happily, this was one of those possible times.

Standing beside them, Layla declared loudly that Mick could walk her home. Hannah would have to say sorry to Mick too, tell him she didn't mean to accuse him of pestering Layla. She had meant no such thing. But right now, it was Jim she needed to make amends with, and considering the way he was looking at her right now, she had a feeling it was going to be fun.

chapter twenty

That night, Layla lay awake in bed, completely unable to believe what Hannah had told her. She and Joseph had been a couple? Really? She had been in love with him — still was — and more so than with Jim? It was hard to get her head around. Hannah had never so much as hinted at any of this prior to tonight, and certainly Joseph had never mentioned anything, back in the days when they had spent time together, that was. He had talked about Tara a few times but never Hannah, and perhaps she could understand why. Jim was his best friend, she was Hannah's; it was an awkward situation all round.

And then Hannah had asked about her and Joseph, insisted she confide in her if she needed to. How could she possibly confide in her? What she had to say would hurt her; she knew it would, despite Hannah protesting otherwise. Besides, telling Hannah would breathe new life into that whole "sleeping with Joseph" issue, undo all the hard work she'd done to date trying to repress it. It was best not talked about, not thought about, best completely and utterly forgotten about. It had destroyed her friendship with Joseph; she couldn't bear losing Hannah over it too.

That spark, or whatever it was that had flared into life between them, was long gone. He had Clare now, the winsome hippy redhead, sleeping with him in his bed, just a few feet away from her, divided by nothing but bricks and mortar; another thought worth repressing.

Finally sleep claimed her. In what could only have been an hour or so later, the alarm clock startled her awake. Resisting the urge to pick it up and throw it across the room, she forced her legs out of bed.

She was cross with herself. She'd wanted to be on the ball for her meeting with Jack. Instead, she felt as though stringing two sensible words together would be akin to climbing Mount Everest. *The things I do for you, Alex Kline,* she thought wearily, standing under the shower, the water deliberately tepid to blast her awake.

After several cups of tea and a rather heavy-handed makeup session, making particular use of her Touche Éclat, she eased herself into the Mazda and made her way to Launceston.

Jack had said to meet her at The Olive Tree and had given her the postcode for her TomTom so she wouldn't get lost — very thoughtful. She was in no mood for wandering up and down the streets of a strange town, in search of a restaurant she didn't know. The journey didn't take long, less than forty minutes along the same roads she'd be taking when she left Trecastle for good, a thought that made her feel sad. As sad as she had felt as a child every time her holiday had ended, dreading the return journey home, missing Hannah desperately, missing her mother too, knowing that soon Angelica would belong to everyone but her again.

Known as the "Gateway to Cornwall" and sandwiched between Bodmin Moor and Dartmoor, Launceston was a lovely town, full of Georgian houses and quaint, narrow streets. She couldn't think why she'd never visited before; it was so close to Trecastle. Too busy whizzing up and down the coast rather than exploring towns inland, she supposed. There were shops aplenty too, she was pleased to note, as good as the shops in Bude. She may well have to browse after lunch.

The restaurant was bang smack in the center of town, in the shadow of the castle that dominated it. She found the nearest car park and bagged herself a space.

After checking her appearance in the rearview mirror, she made her way to the restaurant, smoothing down her sensible, black, knee-length skirt. She'd bought it at the last minute, not thinking it appropriate to turn up in jeans and flip-flops for a meeting with the managing director of FarScapes. She had also purchased a plain blouse. The black high-heeled shoes she owned already, their first outing since Brighton.

As soon as she entered the restaurant, the waiter approached her. "Yes, madam, can I help you?" he asked, his Cornish accent only barely traceable.

"I'm looking for—" she began but was interrupted.

"Layla Lewis, look at you!"

It was Jack Thomas, rising from his seat by the window and heading enthusiastically toward her. After kissing her on both cheeks, he guided her back toward their table, asking for two glasses of champagne from the waiter as he did so. "You look well," he said, holding a chair out so she could sit down. "Very well indeed."

"Thank you," she said, feeling suddenly very shy.

He looked pretty good, too. What was he? Mid-fifties, she supposed, with salt and pepper hair that really suited him and barely any lines, not even when he smiled. She wondered if he would look as good in casual clothes as he did in a suit, but didn't imagine so. He was definitely the suit type.

"Order what you want," he continued. "My treat."

"Thanks, again," she said before quickly taking a sip of the champagne the waiter had duly placed in front of them.

Appalled at her manners, she held up her glass and said, "Sorry, I meant to say cheers before doing that. It's lovely to see you, too."

"Not a problem," he countered. "See anything you like?"

Perusing the menu, she replied, "The sea bream looks nice. I'll have that."

"Good choice," he beamed. "I'll join you."

After they'd ordered, he sat back in his chair and looked at her, a slight frown on his face. Uncomfortable under such scrutiny, she did what she always did in awkward situations and babbled.

"It's so good of you to come all this way to discuss Easy Travel. And it is a long way. A hundred miles? Probably more. You've definitely done the lion's share of driving. Thanks again. Alex is mortified by what's happened, you know. Really, really upset."

"I'll bet he is," said Jack, the amusement on his face replaced with distaste at the first mention of Alex's name. "As you know, I'm curious, what prompted you to write such an email in the first place?"

Gritting her teeth and longing to shout *I didn't write that bloody email,* she said instead, "Oh, we had a falling out, Alex and I. I lost my temper, hence what happened. It was stupid of me. I'm very sorry."

"Of the two of you, I wouldn't say you were the stupid one."

She was taken aback by this, unsure how to reply. Thankfully the waiter appeared, saving the day as he placed an appetizer in front of them, a tiny espresso-sized cup of fish soup that really did whet the taste buds. The main course arrived soon after, also delicious. Jack tucked in too, their conversation thankfully switching to more mundane matters such as the beautiful weather they'd been having lately.

As soon as he had finished eating, however, he started again.

"I see Alex has got you to do his dirty work for him. He wants you to plead with me for the merger to go ahead, doesn't he?"

Feeling really quite defensive, she said, "It's not dirty work. I caused this trouble in the first place. I'm just trying to put it right."

"But I'm actually grateful to you, Layla. I want to make that clear. That email was a godsend. It gave me the excuse I needed to distance myself from Alex, to buy some time. Everything was going ahead far too quickly for my liking. He's a good businessman, I'm not denying it, but his integrity as a person, now that I find suspect."

Ruffled by his words, Layla replied, "He has great integrity, I can assure you. He's held in very high esteem by those in the industry."

"Not me," said Jack, reclining in his chair.

"Why?" she asked, not knowing what else he expected her to say.

"Because of the way he pestered my secretary, that's why. A young girl, barely out of college, she was. Alex couldn't seem to get it into his head she wasn't interested. Every time he visited my office, he made a pass at her. The poor girl was distraught. Nearly ended up resigning."

Whatever reason she'd expected him to give, it wasn't that. "When?" she breathed, the impact of his words causing her hands to tremble. "When was this?"

"All last year."

All last year? "That can't be," she protested. "We were together last year. That thing with Sarah-Jane, it was a one-off. He wasn't unfaithful any other time. He couldn't have been."

"Ah, so it was Alex having an affair that prompted that email. I thought as much," replied Jack, almost triumphantly. "And no, he might not have been unfaithful otherwise, but it wasn't through want of trying."

She looked up sharply at this, cut to the quick. "Why are you telling me this?" she asked, her voice low but even.

"Because I like you, Layla. Because I think you're a talented young lady with a great future ahead of you, and because I think you're blinded by him. Totally. He's asked you to marry him, hasn't he?"

"How do you know?" she asked, taken aback.

"He sent me an email telling me, that's how. Perhaps he wants me to think he's put his lecherous ways behind him—get me to reconsider the deal. I was pretty angry about his treatment of my secretary when she finally told me about him. I confronted him about it at the time."

"And what did he say?" she asked, bracing herself for the answer.

"He laughed, said it was just a bit of fun, that's all. Dismissed it, just like that. Harassing a member of my staff is not, however, in my opinion, a bit of fun. I told him if he continued, I would call the police."

The police? That was going a bit far, wasn't it? Then again, maybe not. The poor girl sounded terrorized. But Alex wasn't a sex pest. There was no way she, Layla Lewis, would fall in love with a sex pest. No way.

"He's changed," she said. "He's different now. He wants to settle down, have kids, the whole works. Yes, he's asked me to marry him, but I haven't said yes. I've told him to wait for me. If he can wait and wait faithfully, I'll consider it."

"Don't do it, Layla. Don't marry him. You're too good for him."

"Why?" she asked, her eyes blurring at his vote of confidence in her. All those years she had thought Alex was too good for her, and now someone was saying the opposite. "Why am I too good for him? And why do you care?"

"I care because I've got a daughter only slightly younger than you are. In fact, you remind me of her. I don't know what your father thinks, but I'd be horrified if she brought home someone as flashy and arrogant as Alex. And if I knew he had cheated on her to boot, I'd take my shotgun to him, I swear I would. Have you ever cheated on Alex?"

"No, of course not," she whispered, upset by the reference to her father. "I never would."

"And that's why you're too good for him. I know men like Alex. In my line of work, they're a dime a dozen. Drunk on their own power, believing the hype. I've seen them take impressionable young girls, chew them up, and spit them back out again, not once but over and over again."

An impressionable young girl? Is that what I am? Another throwaway comment of his that stung.

"I've told you," she shot back. "Alex is different now. He's changed. His old ways sicken even him."

"Layla —" Jack started, but she cut him off. She'd had enough "fatherly" advice for one day.

"Look," she continued, "I'm grateful for your concern, really I am. I know you mean well, but I haven't come here to discuss my private life. I've come here to discuss the merger. As you said, Alex is a good businessman. FarScapes stands to benefit as much as Easy Travel from the merger. Give him a second chance. Speak to him, at least. Please."

"I don't know," he replied, looking, indeed, thoroughly perplexed.

"Jack?" she prompted.

Sighing heavily, he eventually answered. "Let's get one thing clear: If it wasn't sink or swim in the travel industry right now, this merger would not be going ahead. But as that's the way things stand, maybe it will."

"Maybe?"

"Maybe."

"You'll talk to Alex."

"Get him to call me."

"I will." Then grappling for an excuse to leave, she said, "Gosh, look at the time. I have to go. I'm working a shift at the pub this afternoon."

"The pub? But Alex told me you were in Cornwall conducting research into the holiday market."

Oh, did he now? "Well," she said, as bright and breezily as she could manage, "what better way to conduct research than from behind the bar of a pub. The locals, they're a goldmine of information, you know."

"Ah," he said, nodding his head enthusiastically. "That's what I mean when I say you're a talented girl, Layla. You think outside the box. I like it. Are you sure you won't stay for coffee?"

"No, thanks," she replied hastily. "I really do have to go."

And with that she backed away before turning and literally throwing herself out of the restaurant doors and into the street where she stood for a few moments, breathing in deep lungsful of air. Afraid he'd come after her if she lingered any longer, she started walking, slowly at first and then faster when she knew she was out of sight, finally kicking off her shoes and breaking into a run. It was not until she was behind the wheel of her car that she felt safe again.

Pulling out of the car park, the irony of what had just happened was not lost on her. Far from being a letch, as Penny had worried, it seemed Jack's primary intention was to warn her of one.

Alex had pestered Jack's secretary to within an inch of her life? Could it be true? Alex liked the ladies, but she had never witnessed sexually aggressive behavior before on his part, and she had worked with him for eight years. Then again, she hadn't witnessed rejection, either. The women he set his sights on succumbed willingly. Her included.

No, Jack had to be wrong about this sexual harassment thing. But what if he wasn't? Who the hell was she marrying— *if* she married him, she quickly reminded herself—a monster?

She almost choked on the thought, and she strived to calm down. It wouldn't do to become too emotional when driving, especially when trying to negotiate notoriously twisting, turning roads. Jack had to have got it wrong. Perhaps the secretary had been oversensitive or something, didn't understand Alex's sometimes cheeky sense of humor. Why believe them so readily over the man she loved?

Eighteen miles seemed like eighty. All she wanted to do was throw herself upon the sanctuary of The Outlook. She should phone Alex when she got in, tell him she had spoken to Jack as he had asked her to, that his answer regarding the merger had been *maybe*—the story of Alex's life at the moment. Perhaps she'd hint about the secretary, test his reaction. Perhaps she wouldn't. Even if it were true, it was the old Alex who was guilty, not the new Alex, the one who had come to her door so recently, cap in hand, begging her to take him back. The old Alex would never bow to anyone. It proved how much he had changed. That she had changed him. It went to show that no one was beyond hope.

Alex had said to put the past behind them, and that's what she would do with this latest bit of information: leave it in the past, where it belonged. She wouldn't confront him at all. She would give him the second chance he asked for. But no more, definitely no more.

Layla pulled up outside the cottage just as the rain began to fall. She hurried inside, praying she wouldn't bump into Joseph and Clare en route. That would be the final straw, watching them disappear hand in hand into his cottage, ready to spend another cozy evening together, whilst she, as usual, faced the night alone. Hurling herself onto the sofa, she curled into a tight ball, trying not to think how complicated her life—and that of those around her—had become. How nothing was ever straightforward. At least Penny and Richard seemed to be okay again. That was one thing to be grateful for.

Finally deciding to switch on the TV, some Channel Four reality show in full swing, she felt her mind go numb and was thankful.

chapter twenty-one

The rest of the summer months passed quietly enough. Layla kept a low profile, mostly seeing Hannah, hardly seeing Joseph, and continuing to work hard at the pub. Both her twenty-ninth birthday and Joseph's had been celebrated during this time, but not in each other's company, something Layla couldn't help feeling sad about. In between work and play, she continued to write. As well as having a short story published in an anthology entitled *Where Spring and Centuries Begin*... thanks largely to Rachel who seemed to be championing her at the moment, she'd had a poem, "The Awakening," published in an online literary magazine. She was buzzing with her achievements, but when she told Alex about them on the phone, he had been dismissive to say the least, hardly commenting at all before returning to talk of Easy Travel. So different from Joseph's reaction all those months ago.

If her writing wasn't real to Alex, however, Easy Travel wasn't real to her. It belonged to another lifetime, making it doubly hard to believe she'd be working there again in the not-too-distant future. She had just a few months left in Trecastle, not even three really, as she planned to leave mid-December so she could spend her second Christmas with Alex. Lenny hadn't given exact details of his return date yet, but it was bound to be in January, a year from when he'd left, so The Outlook wouldn't be empty for long. She would miss these four walls, though. Having felt so alien on her first night, they were familiar now, homey.

As Jack had promised, he had indeed spoken to Alex, and they were currently "in negotiations." She didn't probe further. She wasn't really that interested, to tell the truth, which was strange, considering her future depended upon it. Alex seemed pleased with how things were progressing, though. She didn't need to know much more than that. In fact, the less she knew about it, the better.

They were enjoying an Indian summer in Brighton, but in Trecastle the early autumn days were distinctly chill. Alex kept trying to tempt her back, especially over her birthday weekend, but she had said no, she was too busy. "I'll compensate you for lost wages," he had replied. Typical of Alex, no thought toward the people she'd be letting down if she didn't work, just the money aspect.

And it was Hannah she'd be letting down if she didn't work. Her paintings were selling really well, stunning seascapes in colors Layla didn't even know existed in the artist's palette, they were so vibrant. Layla was covering her shifts at the pub as much as possible, enabling Hannah to let herself be absorbed completely in her creativity. An absorption so all-encompassing, it was beneficial in a number of ways, she was sure.

Penny, she must phone Penny. They hadn't spoken for a few days.

Dialing her number, she said, "Hey, Pen, it's me. How are you?"

"Hi, Layla, great minds think alike. I was going to ring you later. I'm fine, thanks. A bit stressed but otherwise okay." She did indeed sound stressed, her usually chirpy voice held a distinct edge.

Concerned, Layla asked, "Why are you stressed? Is it work?"

"Yeah, yeah, it's work. You know how it is, a pain in the arse, as usual."

Layla had no reason not to believe her. She knew Penny was sometimes just as bad as Richard, taking on board too much with work, so why was she doubtful? "Are you sure it's work, Penny? Is everything okay with Richard?"

"Yes, things are fine with Richard, really," Penny insisted, the edge getting sharper. "I've just got a lot on my mind lately, that's all. Don't worry, I'm dealing with it. Anyway, I don't want to talk about me. How are you? More to the point, how is that delectable neighbor of yours?"

Oh, for heaven's sake, why did Penny have to bring up Joseph every time they talked? It was like she was obsessed or something.

"I'm fine and he's fine, as far as I know. I don't see him much anymore, Pen. I've told you, he's too busy with his new girlfriend."

"Still going out with her, is he?"

"I presume so. Although I never see them coming and going; they must stay at hers a lot."

Which was, of course, a relief.

"Where does she live?"

"Oh, I don't know. Not in Trecastle, that's for sure. But there are plenty of villages round and about."

"And it doesn't bother you that he's got a girlfriend?"

"Er, no, of course not. Why do you ask?"

"Just wondered." Penny was a touch too mysterious for Layla's liking. "How's Alex? Spoken to him lately?"

"Just yesterday, in fact," she answered before swiftly changing the subject. She didn't want to speak to Penny about Alex either; she was too disapproving. "When are you coming down again? I miss you."

"Hopefully soon. I've got a week owing, so it's not a problem. Just got to see a project through I'm working on at the moment, setting up an after-school club for the children of single working mothers, then I'll be down. Another couple of weeks, I suppose. I'll let you know nearer the time."

"Don't leave it too long, Pen, or I'll be coming home with you at this rate."

"Not a bad idea," said Penny, and Layla could tell she was smiling, looking forward to having her back in Brighton again. "Look, I've got to go. Speak to you soon. Say hi to Joe for me when you do see him."

"Okay," she replied, feeling exasperated again at the mention of his name.

Passing a momentary glance over her laptop, Layla decided to make a cup of tea. Why had Penny asked if she minded Joseph having a girlfriend? What a stupid question. Surely Penny still didn't think she had some sort of secret crush on him. She'd done everything in her power to alleviate her of that particular notion. Good job she'd never told her what had really happened. Penny would be relentless if she had.

Just as she sat back down at the table, the phone rang.

"What?" she said crossly.

"Hello, dear, it's your mother."

"Oh, sorry, Mum. I thought it was Penny. We've just been talking on the phone."

"I see, how lovely. Anyway, darling, just a quick call. How are you?" Before she could answer, her mother continued, "Do you know, I've been feeling ever so nostalgic about Cornwall and the time we used to spend there. How is life in Trecastle? Do you love it or hate it?"

A bit of both at times, she thought. "It's fine, Mum. It's good. I enjoy my work in the pub, and I've been writing again, even had several short stories published whilst I've been down here as well as a poem, so it's certainly bringing out my creative streak."

"Well done, darling, well done. I never knew you were good at writing."

Forgotten all about the competition I won when I was sixteen, then? she wanted to ask. "I don't know whether I'm good or not, but I've always loved it. I used to spend a lot of time in my room writing when I was younger." Unable to keep a note of sarcasm from creeping into her voice, she added, "Remember?"

Either ignoring the jibe or not noticing it, Angelica replied, "Good, good. You'll be glad to know all is well in *Italia*. Giorgio is wonderful, spoiling me as usual. How are things with you and Alex? It is Alex, isn't it?"

"Yes, it is," said Layla. How many times in the last year and a half had she mentioned Alex, but still her mother had to ask? "It's a shame you never made it over to Trecastle, you know. We could have had fun. I've only got a short while left before I return to Brighton."

"Oh, I know, darling, and I would have loved to have flown over. A trip down memory lane does appeal. But my social diary, it's crammed to the point of ridiculousness. Giorgio says I'm a martyr to it all, and I am, it's true. Still, you're there for a few more weeks if I should find a window, aren't you?"

"A few, yeah," sighed Layla, thinking, *You won't find a window. Not for me.*

"And how's Connie? Do you see her much?"

"I haven't seen her, no. She doesn't live here anymore."

Hannah's mother had moved to Exeter six years ago to live with an ex-dairy farmer. They were very happy together, apparently. Hannah visited every month, and Layla covered her shift whilst she did so.

"Oh, that's a shame. I miss dear Connie and our chats. Anyway, I'll let you go. You must be busy. Writing all those stories of yours."

And before she could say, *It's okay Mum, I can take a break. Stay on the line, talk to me. Give me more than five minutes of your time every now and then,* Angelica had rung off.

Replacing the phone, Layla stood for a while staring at Gull Rock from her kitchen window, a feeling of utter deflation in her stomach, a common side effect of any communication with her mother. She wished they were close; she could really do with a "mum" right now, someone who would listen to her, tell her honestly the mistakes she was making, guide her in the right direction. But Angelica had never been that type of mum, never guided her in any direction. Layla'd been largely left to guide herself.

Still, she had to concede, Angelica had made a good life for herself, living in Milan with Giorgio, holding her own amongst the rich and glamorous in Italian society. She might not be ideal mum material, but she was never dull. She was as bright and shiny as that diamond bracelet Alex had tried to give her—not once but twice—full of sparkle and vitality. In a way, Layla was proud of her. She was the sort of person you could write a book about. *Ironically,* she thought with a sigh.

Thinking of writing, she realized she hadn't produced one single word today. She was working on another short story, this one set in Brighton. A story about two boys in high school: one the bully, one the victim, both refusing to recognize the true nature of their feelings for each other. It felt good, writing about her hometown, and she wanted to finish it, but as hard as she tried, she was getting nowhere fast. She just wasn't in the mood.

She eyed a stack of magazines on the far end of the kitchen table, grabbing a couple of them as well as a big bar of milk chocolate from the cupboard. Throwing herself on the living room sofa, she decided to relax instead. She had the night off tonight, the first in a week, and she was going to enjoy every single minute of it. Engrossed in an article about London's fash pack, she was only vaguely aware that the sky was turning blacker and blacker, as the rain fell harder and harder.

Eventually her eyes grew tired of reading, so Layla decided to have a bath before calling it a night, the plan being to wake up bright and early the next morning, finish off the short story she was supposed to finish today, and get some housework done.

En route to the bathroom, she peered out the window. The weather hadn't cheered up at all. In fact, the air felt decidedly heavy as though a storm was getting ready to roll in off the Atlantic. She hoped not. She hated storms, had done since childhood. Wondering if she should check the weather forecast on the Internet, she decided against it, opting for blissful ignorance.

Layla ran herself a bath and poured a glass of wine, intending to plug her iPod in her ears whilst she soaked at leisure. That should be sufficient to drown out the thunder if it did hit. Lowering herself into the water, she realized how clammy she was. She couldn't deny it; she was nervous. Hopefully, the wine would have a relaxing effect, though. She didn't know why she hated thunderstorms so much, she just did. It was inbuilt. Her father had been such a comfort during bad weather, enfolding her in his big strong arms, making her feel safe again. After he'd gone, she would go to her mother for reassurance whenever there was a storm, but Angelica would always laugh, albeit good naturedly, telling her not to be silly and to go back to bed. Now, as well as scaring her, thunderstorms made her feel sad and lonely, and she hated them.

After an hour or so of listening to pounding rock tunes and heartfelt ballads, courtesy of Pink, she climbed out of the bath and into bed, the iPod still plugged firmly in her ears.

So far, so good, she thought. The atmosphere was still heavy, but all was silent apart from the wind, which was picking up apace. She tuned into Kate Bush's classic album, *Hounds of Love*, next, her high pitched voice the perfect foil to the elements—and amazingly fell asleep. Her last thought before oblivion took her was how doing nothing all day was just so damn tiring.

It was only a couple of hours later that the first low rumble began. Layla woke immediately, as though some part of her had been on red alert all along. She sat upright. *Oh, God,* she repeated over and over again, all rational thought quickly dissolving. She felt clammy once more, beads of sweat breaking out on her forehead. She wiped roughly at them with the back of her hand.

Knowing she wouldn't be able to lie there as the storm took hold, she climbed out of bed and into a pair of yoga pants she used purely for lazing around the house. She pulled a warm jumper on over her mussed-up hair and went downstairs, thinking a second glass of wine might help.

Upon entering the kitchen, another loud crash cavorted across the sky, and this time it felt considerably closer, not quite overhead but almost.

"Get a grip" replaced "Oh, God" as she jumped in fright. Lightning briefly lit up the room, transforming it in that spilt second from the cozy, warm room she loved so much into something from a Hammer horror film.

Although she was desperate to turn on the main light, she recalled reading somewhere that electricity attracted lightning, so she turned on the strip lights under the kitchen cupboards instead, making the room look even more eerie. For extra safety, she unplugged her computer and the television and prayed that the storm would pass quickly. As she approached the kettle, another flash of lightning lit up the night sky, and as it did so, she felt her legs buckle beneath her. The wind was violent too, howling its rage around her. She sank down onto a chair and started to shake uncontrollably. There was no way she could endure this alone.

Alex, perhaps she should phone him? It wasn't too late, just before midnight, but what use would he be? He was hundreds of miles away. He couldn't help her. She could phone Hannah, but it wasn't fair. She'd probably just finished her shift at the pub and wanted nothing more than to go home, crawl into bed beside Jim, and sleep. Which left Joseph.

She had noticed his Land Rover parked next to her Mazda just before she'd gone to bed. She had developed an annoying habit of checking whether it was in situ every night. Hopefully that meant he was at home, unless he had gone to Clare's on his trail bike. The thought of venturing outside to knock on his door was anathema to her; she would have to phone him. Surely he wouldn't mind? He knew what it was like to be phobic about something. He'd understand.

As more thunder kicked off, she hesitated no more, jumping quickly to find the phone and dial his number. It was an agonizing few seconds before he answered.

"Joseph? Joseph, is that you?"

"Er, yeah," said a sleepy voice. "Layla? What's the matter?"

"Are you busy?" she asked feverishly.

"I was sleeping, if that counts," he replied bemused.

"Please, *please,* come over," she begged before letting out a piercing scream as the lightning flared again.

"Blimey!" he exclaimed. "Yeah, okay, give me a couple of minutes."

Not long after, she heard him knock. Another burst of thunder erupted, directly overhead this time. She threw open the door, pulled him inside, and hurled herself against him.

"Oh, thank God! Thank God, you're here," she sobbed.

"What is it? What's wrong?" he asked, confusion and alarm vying for control of his voice.

"Just hold me," was all she could say.

Grateful that he obliged without further question, she focused on the soft rhythm of his heart, willing it to drown out the noise of the thunder, her own erratic heartbeat slowing as he gently stroked her hair. It was some time later before she was brave enough to take a step back.

"Has something happened?" he asked, his whole manner touchingly gentle.

"The storm…the storm happened," she replied pitifully, head down.

His furrowed brows relaxed. "The storm? You don't like storms?"

"Like them? I loathe them! You weren't sleeping through this, surely?"

"Actually, I was," he said. "I can sleep through pretty much anything." Looking away from her and toward the window, he continued, "It looks as though the worst is over. Will you be okay on your own now?"

"No!" she shouted in horror. Forcing herself to calm down, she quickly added, "I don't think I will, actually. Please stay. Just for a while…*please.*"

A look of worry swept briefly across his face, and his eyes darted toward the door. She could understand why he felt awkward being here, but right now her need for company was surely greater than his desire to escape. The thunder might be retreating, but she still felt shaky.

"Joseph?" she pleaded, looking deep into the blue of his eyes.

Softening his obvious reluctance with a smile, he conceded. Almost giddy with relief, she flicked the main light on as he pulled up a chair and sat down. He was right: the storm was subsiding, and for a second, she couldn't believe she was feeling disappointed — she had no excuse to jump back into his arms now.

"Do you fancy a drink?" she asked. "A proper drink, I mean?"

"What, now?" he replied, glancing at his watch.

"I need one," she said, shrugging her shoulders at him. "My nerves are shot."

"Go on, then. Just the one, though."

Layla went to the fridge and pulled out the previously opened bottle of chardonnay. She filled two glasses to the brim and sank down on the chair closest to him.

"Have you always been afraid of storms?" he asked.

"Ever since I can remember." She was glad his face was full of genuine concern. "Don't they bother you, even a little bit?"

He laughed, and as he lifted his glass to his mouth, she noticed endearing little crinkles appearing either side of it. "No, not storms. But spiders, well, as you know, they're another matter. And believe it or not, I don't like the sea much, either."

"What?" she asked in surprise. "Living in a place like Trecastle? The sea's the main attraction."

"I know, and I can swim, after a fashion. Jim insisted on teaching me as soon as I moved down. Said it was important I learn. But I don't like water, never have done. I was impossible as a child. Just stood in the shallow end, refusing to move. I'm a landlubber, I suppose."

The mention of Jim brought Hannah to mind. She wanted to say something about how awkward it had been at the barbecue, but what? She'd only give the game away that she knew they'd once been a couple. Quickly she resolved to stick to neutral subjects; that way no misunderstandings could take place.

"It doesn't matter if you're not a champion surfer; they're two a penny round here. You're brilliant at what you do. I've seen the stuff you've made. With a name like yours, you were obviously born to the profession."

"Yeah, following in the footsteps of the great man himself." He laughed.

"Have you always wanted to be a carpenter?" she asked.

"Ever since I can remember," he replied. "My grandfather was a carpenter. My dad and I spent ages in his workshop when I was a kid, both of us soaking up whatever we could. Furniture restoration was his big love, my grandfather, that is. He spent time working in Italy when he was younger. Florence, in fact, in a workshop there. Had the best time of his life."

Whilst he was lost in the past, she had time to study his face, the depth of his eyes, the natural golden hue of his skin, the clear lines of his jaw. All complemented by that blond mop of hair, not bright blond like a child's, but dark blond, very much a man's color.

He ran his hand through his hair as he continued. "When I was older and studying carpentry, he got me a placement in that workshop in Florence. Just for six months, but he was right: it was sublime. It opened up a whole new world to me. Thanks to him, restoration is my big love too. Taking antique furniture and breathing new life into it."

"You make it sound so romantic." She sighed, visions of him in a Tuscan setting dancing in her mind.

"It was actually bloody hard work," he pointed out but good-naturedly so. "But you don't mind when you love what you're doing. The work I do here, it's not as interesting, but it's plentiful. Thankfully I've got Jim to help me at times."

Back to Jim again and via Jim, Hannah.

"Jim is lovely, isn't he? He and Hannah seem very happy together." It was naughty, she knew, going back on her decision not to talk about them, but ignoring their existence would look weird.

"Yeah, they are. He's a good bloke. None better, in my view."

But not in Hannah's, she thought. It was clear from the look on his face, however, that this was not a subject he was prepared to elaborate on. Hannah was right; Joseph was a very private man. She considered asking about Clare, but decided against it. Clare was the last person she wanted to think about right now. They had drained their glasses.

"May as well finish the bottle," she said, returning to the fridge.

"May as well," he agreed, not protesting that "just the one" was turning into two.

Soon their glasses were empty again.

Digging around in the cupboard rather than the fridge, she retrieved a bottle of whisky. She set it down before him with what she hoped was a tantalizing smile.

"Is that really such a good idea?" he asked, but he was smiling too. Clearly, the wine had had a relaxing effect on him as well as her. Grabbing a couple of tumblers next, she didn't pour hefty measures, but they couldn't be described as small either. He didn't complain, though. They sipped more slowly this time, Layla savoring the atmosphere as well as the fiery liquid. It was how it used to be, before that fateful night. He talked more about his time in Italy. She told him about the short story she'd had published in the anthology and the poem which had recently been published online, laughingly reassuring him he was the first to know about the latter this time and, technically, she supposed, it was true. She may have mentioned it to Alex, but she'd wager it had fallen on deaf ears. Joseph laughed too in reply, a sign, she hoped, he had forgiven her for her previous tactlessness.

More whisky was poured and a second hour passed, although it felt like mere minutes to Layla. He must have felt that too because when he glanced at the clock on the kitchen wall, the color drained from his face and he jumped to his feet in horror.

"Christ, look at the time. I didn't realize. I've got to get back."

"Really?" she asked lazily, feeling warm and fuzzy inside. "Do you have to?"

"Yes," he said, clearly panicked.

Although she rose leisurely from the table, she had to hurry her pace to catch him at the front door. As he turned to her, she said, "Thank you, thank you so much for coming. I can't actually thank you enough."

He was about to reply, but she didn't give him a chance. The same feeling that had possessed her on the night they ended up in bed together possessed her now as she reached up to kiss him. She could feel his hesitance at first, his hands holding her elbows as though he intended to push her away. But then slowly he relaxed into her, his arms creeping round her back to hold her close once again as their kiss deepened. In the distance, she thought she could hear violins. Soon, she was losing all sense of the world around her, melting into him, reveling in the heat of the moment, when suddenly he stopped and stood back.

"What is it?" she asked, a little surprised. "What's wrong?"

"This," he said. "This is wrong. I've got a girlfriend, remember?"

She felt her face flame with embarrassment. Clare, of course. She had been determined to forget all about her and had succeeded. She had forgotten about Alex, too, completely.

"Is it serious between you?" she quizzed again.

"That doesn't matter. What matters is that standing here kissing your next-door neighbor when you're involved with someone else isn't right."

"No, no, of course not," she said, marveling at how different his attitude was to Alex's. "I'm sorry."

"No need to be. No harm done."

Instead of holding her with his arms, he held her with his gaze. "Talking of serious, how are things between you and Alex? I know he was down a while ago, but I haven't seen him since."

So Hannah hadn't said anything to him. Or did he just want to hear it from the horse's mouth?

Chewing her lip, she replied, "Pretty serious, I suppose. He's asked me to marry him."

He looked shocked. "Marry him?" he breathed. "And are you?"

"I don't know. I haven't said yes."

"But you haven't said no?"

"No," she said, lowering her head. "I haven't said no."

"Either way, you're going back with him?"

"I don't see I've got much choice," she burst out. "What am I going to do otherwise? I'll be homeless soon, and a bar job isn't going to cut it as far as bills *and* rent are concerned."

"You've always got a choice," he replied, his eyes searing her. "And that's no reason to marry someone, so they can put a roof over your head. Do you love him?"

"Yes…no. I'm not sure," she said, realizing for the first time it was true.

"You can't marry someone you don't love."

"I didn't say I didn't love him. I said I wasn't sure."

"Well, think about it, and if you realize you don't, let me know. Meanwhile, don't forget the choices you do have."

What choices? What did he mean? She was desperate for him to elaborate, to spell it out, but she couldn't push him because of Clare.

Feeling a curious mixture of elation and confusion at his words, she said, "Thanks, Joseph, for coming over. For everything."

"My pleasure." He smiled, a hint of playfulness in his eyes, if she wasn't mistaken. "And you know where I am if you need me. Don't be a stranger anymore."

"I promise." She smiled back. "See you soon."

"You will," he replied, and it seemed more of a statement than anything else.

As she closed the door behind him, tiredness won over both confusion and elation. Her legs felt like they'd been filled with concrete mix, but nonetheless they obediently carried her upstairs where she crawled under the duvet. She was amazed, considering her lips were still tingling from his kiss, that sleep could encroach so quickly.

chapter twenty-two

Layla woke late that morning from a deep and dreamless sleep. Stretching, she rose from bed and parted the curtains, pleased to see bright blue skies, the storm having successfully cleared the air. *Oh, shit, the storm,* she thought, suddenly remembering how she had panicked, called Joseph over, plied him with drink, and kissed him—*again.*

"Oops," she said, sitting back down on the bed. But whether she was sorry or not, she couldn't tell. She felt unfaithful to Alex, the irony of which was not lost on her, but it was just a kiss, nothing more, although it could well have been if Joseph hadn't stopped it. He had stopped it because of Clare—and rightly so. She liked that, respected him for it.

As she got on with the housework she had put off yesterday, her mind kept wandering back to their kiss. The vivid memory of it led to more memories, memories she had been careful not to entertain until now. Of the night they had spent together, the way his skin had felt against hers, how he had looked at her—really looked at her—stirring something inside, something she hadn't known existed.

Her breathing was getting heavier, and she couldn't continue. She would need a cold shower if she did. Would she ever feel this way with Alex? She was surprised when a little voice inside her, piped up, "*No.*" It was the same voice that had urged her to come to Trecastle in the first place. What did it know that she didn't?

Discarding her duster, she thought she'd immerse herself in writing instead. Perhaps that would occupy her mind more fully. Unable to string a decent sentence together, however, she grabbed a book off the shelf in the living room. She plowed through several chapters, soon realizing she still didn't have a clue what the story was about.

Sod it, she thought, *I'm going for a walk.* Clearly, today was going to be as unproductive as yesterday.

She stepped outside and immediately shivered. It was cold, really cold. Retreating back inside, she shrugged on her jacket. Suitably attired, she tried again. A few houses up, Mrs. Taylor was shuffling her way back from the village—a bulging blue carrier bag indicating a trip to May's. Layla waved to her before starting determinedly forward.

The first thing she should do was go see Joseph at his workshop, apologize for last night. Heck, she didn't want to apologize; she just wanted to see him again, why not admit it? Perhaps even kiss him again, perhaps even more. *Stop!* she almost screamed out loud. *You are not single, and neither is he.*

Yet... that little voice piped up again.

Walking past the fields, the houses, the school, the small quota of village children having learned their lessons for the day, she felt an almost involuntary grin spread across her face. She felt good, better than she had done for a long time, as far back as she could remember, in fact.

Her good mood was hampered by the fact that Joseph's Land Rover was nowhere to be seen. If he was at his workshop, the car usually was too.

"Damn!" she was disappointed.

Oh well, you never know. Several bangs on the door, however, *did* let her know he was not in residence. Frustrated, she glanced sideways at the Trecastle Inn. She'd go in there instead and see Hannah. *Oh, God, Hannah.* Her mind had been so full of Joseph, she hadn't thought about Hannah. If anything were to happen between her and Joseph, and it was a big *if,* they would have to play it very sensitively where Hannah was concerned. There was no way Layla wanted to add to her pain.

There were a few people in the pub, but it could hardly be called busy. Holidaymakers were long gone now the weather wasn't so clement. The quiet was a relief, though. Sometimes she, Hannah, Tom, and Kate had been left feeling dizzy with exhaustion at the end of a busy summer's night. It seemed you needed the winter to recover.

She knew Hannah was working today, and as the door swung open, there she was behind the bar, looking bored stiff. But when she spotted Layla, she snapped to attention.

"Hey, Layla, have you heard the news?"

"No, what's happened?"

"It's Joe and Clare. They've split up!"

Layla could feel every inch of color drain from her face as she got to the bar. That was fast work!

"What do you mean split up?" she asked, careful to conceal just how much the news was affecting her.

"Grab a stool and I'll tell you. What are you drinking?"

"Erm, just a lime and soda, thanks."

Filling her own glass with lime and soda too, Hannah leaned forward conspiratorially. "Joe showed up at ours around ten this morning, looking as though he hadn't slept a wink. Jim's working with him on a job at the moment, and they had to go off and get some supplies. When Jim got back, he told me Joe was out of sorts. Apparently, he and Clare had an almighty row last night, and she walked."

Last night? But he was with me last night, thought Layla before realizing. *Oh no, Clare must have been with him when I called!* In which case, why had he come? He should have just said no. As for rowing afterward, she would have heard them, surely? They were only next door. Then again, after wine and whisky, she'd been dead to the world.

"What's more," continued Hannah, thankfully so wrapped up in her story she didn't notice Layla's growing horror, "it turns out that Clare is the niece of the people who own Hill House. You know Hill House? Up on Bodmin Moor? It's more of a mansion, really. Joe does lots of work up there. That must be how he met her, come to think of it. Anyway, the owners are very influential in this area. They've been putting in a good word for Joe, here and there, for years—that's why he's always so busy. Well, he got a phone call this morning from the owner, Rob Yeates, who tells him to come and get any tools he's left at the house and to never darken his doorstep again. He says he'll find himself another carpenter, too, one that won't use and abuse his niece!"

"Oh no, this is all my fault!" cried Layla in despair.

It was Hannah's turn to look puzzled. "Your fault? Why? What have you done?"

"I had no idea he was with Clare. It didn't even cross my mind. The storm last night frightened me out of my wits. I called Joseph and asked him to come round."

"So?" said Hannah, flicking a few strands of hair out of her eyes. "Why should popping round to yours upset her?"

"Well," Layla was hesitant, "he didn't *pop* round as such; he stayed for quite a while. A couple of hours, in fact, maybe a bit more."

"A couple of hours?" repeated Hannah.

"I *was* scared," Layla stressed.

"Yeah, but a couple of hours? That storm blew itself out pretty quickly, didn't it?"

"Not quick enough," said Layla earnestly. In a rush, she added, "It's not as if we did anything. I mean, not really. There's nothing for Clare to worry about. We just sat and talked. Honestly, nothing happened. Nothing at all."

From the look on Hannah's face, Layla knew her over-the-top protestation had damned her. She slumped against the bar defeated. "Where is he now? Do you know?"

"Joe? I don't know. Probably begging Mr. Yeates and Clare to take him back if he's got any sense. That's a lot to lose just because you did nothing at all."

Staring at each other, the tension between them grew more and more palpable. Layla could have swooned with relief when Mick suddenly appeared.

"Mick!" she cried. "Good to see you. Can I buy you a drink?"

"Now there's an offer I can't refuse. I'll have a pint of Tribute, please."

Hannah turned away to get his drink, still looking distinctly irked. Mick, however, remained delightfully oblivious. As he chatted merrily away, Layla soaked up his easy manner. He was just what she needed right now, his big, friendly presence a refuge from the suspicion in Hannah's eyes, from the huge lashings of guilt coursing through her, from the certain knowledge that she had once more messed things up.

"Come on, let's go and find somewhere to sit," said Mick, taking her arm and leading her to a dark corner at the far end of the pub.

"Oh, yes, please," Layla replied, desperate to escape Hannah's glare.

As they sat down, he patted the seat immediately beside him and said, "Snuggle up. Tell me about your day so far."

"God, no! The last thing I want to talk about is me. Tell me what you've been up to. Don't leave anything out. I want to hear all of it, every last detail," she said, needing to just sit and listen, to have her mind filled with something other than this latest fiasco.

Mick was quick to comply. He told her how he had sailed his boat during the early hours of the morning, along with his dad and a couple of crew members, and hauled another great catch just off Rumps Point, further down the coast—mackerel mainly, but also gurnard, ray, and pollack. Mick was one of the main fish suppliers in this area, servicing restaurants great and small, and clearly he loved his job. Listening to him punctuate his chatter with jokes galore, she relaxed. He was so refreshing. Nothing seemed to affect him; he was always the same, always in the best of spirits. One seemingly very contented man.

Laughing out loud at yet another of his nautical capers, she leaned her head on his shoulder, snuggling into him as he'd suggested. As Mick lent in to plant an affectionate kiss on the side of her head, she looked up at him, and he caught the edge of her mouth instead, lingering there for a second or two longer than he should have. Intending to playfully admonish him for taking advantage of her, she caught movement at the bar instead and looked up.

Joseph was standing there with Jim, looking at her with eyes that even from the other side of the room she could see were as cold as steel. Hastily extricating herself from Mick and sitting ramrod straight, she wondered when he had come in. How long had he been standing there, looking at them both, huddled together and laughing as though they hadn't a care in the world between them? As for that kiss, could he tell it had been a mistake, just bad timing on her part for what was purely meant as a gesture of affection? She chanced a smile at Joseph—a rather worried one, she had to admit—but his face remained severe, resembling one of last night's storm clouds. It was Joseph who looked away first, severing the connection between them. Leaning in toward Jim, he said a few words and then turned and walked out of the pub, completely ignoring Layla and Mick as he did so.

"Oh, heck," she said, not realizing she was speaking aloud, "here we go again."

"Do what again?" asked Mick happily.

"Oh, nothing," she sighed. "It's just me. I can't do right for doing wrong. With some people, anyway. Look, I'm sorry. I've got to go. I've got some explaining to do."

"Don't go," said Mick, looking disgruntled now. "Surely it can wait."

"If only," she said, smiling wryly, "but I don't think it can. Sorry."

She stood, grabbed her jacket off the seat beside her, slung it over her shoulder, and hurried toward the exit. Before she left, she turned to wave goodbye to Hannah and Jim, both of whom waved back, but with very different looks on their faces.

chapter twenty-three

Hannah knew her instincts had been right—something *had* gone on between Joe and Layla. And it was still going on, by the looks of it, Layla's emphatic denial anything but convincing. But why wouldn't Layla tell her? Why keep secrets? Hannah felt hurt at Layla's unwillingness to confide. It wasn't as if she hadn't asked her to. She had said, that night on the beach, that if she had anything to say, even if it concerned Joe, it was okay. She would understand, be glad for them, even. At this rate, she'd have to torture the truth out of her!

After their awkward exchange at the bar, Layla had latched onto Mick as though he were a life jacket and she the drowning victim, moving with him to a table in the far corner. Another thing that had hurt: that outright desperation to get away from her. Every so often she had looked over at the pair of them. They seemed cozy enough, Layla laughing raucously at Mick's jokes, but then everyone laughed raucously at Mick's jokes. It was hard not to. If the fish supply in Cornwall ever depleted, he needn't worry—he'd have a fantastic career as a stand-up comedian. His thirtieth birthday was coming up soon, and the whole village was going to his party. Mick was loved by all; nobody would miss the celebration for the world.

Clearing away empty pint and wine glasses left on the bar for her, she had just happened to glance over again. This time they were kissing. Mick and Layla! Okay, it hadn't been a full blown snog, but it was a kiss, undeniably so. Unbelievable! And poor Joe, after the morning he'd had, walking into the pub at that very moment. Shocked was not the word for it. He'd looked as though his whole world had gone up in smoke. She had so wanted to reach out to him, to comfort him, but she couldn't because Jim was with him. Who was she kidding? She couldn't because Joe wouldn't want her to. She couldn't do anything except stare at him as she tried to fathom what Layla had that engendered such strong feelings in him when she had been unable to summon up anything other than friendship, despite her very best efforts.

And now what was Layla planning to do, following hot on the heels of Joe's swift departure? Appease him? How exactly? That was the problem; she didn't have a clue, because Layla wasn't telling. Nothing at all. Best friend? She was beginning to wonder.

chapter twenty-four

The light was on in Joseph's workshop. *He hasn't gone home, then,* thought Layla, partly relieved, partly disappointed. Recalling how he had looked at her in the pub, her nerves threatened to fail her, but she held firm. Her need to apologize was even more urgent now. Not only had he lost his girlfriend because of her but his most important client too.

Once again she knocked on the door, and once again there was no reply. Knowing he was there this time, however, she pushed it open and walked in. He was tidying some tools away but looked up as soon as she entered, as though he'd been expecting her all along. She hoped to see some sort of welcoming flash in his eyes, at least a glimmer, but there was nothing. Just the cold, hard steel she had encountered a few minutes earlier in the bar.

Swallowing hard, she said, "I'm sorry to barge in. I heard what happened with Clare and her uncle. I am so sorry."

"News travels fast around here," he answered, looking as though the very fact that it did disgusted him. "Who told you? Hannah?"

"Yeah, a little while ago, in the pub."

"Oh, right, in the pub, having a good laugh about it with Mick, were you?"

"No, no, of course not!" She was surprised by the vehemence in his voice. "I would never laugh about such things, nor would Mick."

"Don't worry," he said, actually sneering at her. "I'm not paranoid. I know *he* wouldn't. *You*, however, I'm not so sure."

"Oh, come on, Joseph," she countered. "That's not fair. I came here to say sorry, not to argue."

"You've wasted your time, then. I'm not interested."

Unsettled to say the least but also determined to say her piece, she continued, "I didn't realize Clare was with you last night. If I'd known, I wouldn't have called you. I would have braved it out." She didn't think that was true for one minute, but it didn't hurt to say so. "You should have just told me to get lost."

He snorted in disbelief. "You call me at midnight, screaming down the phone, and I'm supposed to tell you to get lost? You sounded as though somebody had their hands around your neck, squeezing the life out of you. I couldn't just ignore it, could I?"

"Okay, okay, fair enough," she conceded. After all, it had been rather a desperate shriek. "But perhaps you shouldn't have stayed so long, once you'd seen I was okay, I mean."

His face was incredulous as he replied, "So it's my fault then, is it? Last night was entirely my fault. It's got nothing to do with you at all?"

"No, I didn't mean that," she flustered. "I'm just as much to blame as you are. More so, of course."

"Damn right, you are. You're the one who insisted I stay long after the storm had passed, and you're the one who kissed me, not vice versa."

"I know. I know I did. I was just so grateful."

"Grateful? You kissed me because you were grateful?"

She was about to babble again, she could feel it. "No, no, I didn't kiss you because I was grateful. Well, I *was* grateful, for you coming out so quickly during that storm, but—"

"So that was my reward, was it?" he cut across her. "And what about the time before that? What did I do to deserve actual sex?"

Flinching at the sarcasm in his voice, she had to take a deep breath before replying. "Look, discard everything I've just said. I'm talking rubbish. I'm shocked, I suppose, about Clare and her uncle. I came here to apologize for kissing you last night. It was wrong. We're both with other people. And I had no idea it would have such consequences."

"Consequences?" he spat. "You don't know the meaning of the word. You do exactly what you want, when you want, without a thought for who you're hurting. One minute you're engaged to that twat from Brighton, the next you're making moves on me, and now you're all over Mick. He's a simple bloke, Mick. He doesn't need someone like you messing with his head."

"I was not all over Mick!" she protested. "He's just a friend. We were having a laugh, that's all."

"You were kissing him, Layla."

"No, I mean, yes, I know it looked that way, but I wasn't. It was an accident. It's really quite funny. If you'll just listen to me, I'll explain. What happened was—"

Again he interrupted her, his voice low this time and bordering on the savage. "You might find it funny, throwing yourself at just about everyone that crosses your path, Layla, but I'm not exactly laughing, am I?"

She tried to reply, but couldn't. Shock had finally silenced her.

Throwing myself at everyone that crosses my path? Is that what he really thinks? How stupid she had been. She had really thought that when she came here, he would accept her apology, reassure her even that it wasn't warranted, that what happened last night was the start of something long overdue. He would tell her that although Clare was nice, a lovely girl, in fact, there was nothing serious between them, it was just a fling. As for Hill House, well, he had other contracts on the boil, far more lucrative. In turn, she would tell him she had made her choice and it wasn't Alex. If all that was a bit farfetched, at least they would come to some sort of understanding. Build their friendship up again, slowly but surely, see where it led them. She couldn't have been more wrong. They would never understand each other. They were poles apart, separated not just literally by a brick wall but metaphorically, too.

Caught up in this swirling maelstrom of thoughts, it was a second or two before she realized he was speaking again.

"Life was good before you came along. It was simple. I want that back. The sooner you leave the better."

So life was good, was it? Before she showed up? Everything was simple? Not quite. Anger finally arose in her, smashing to pieces every other emotion. "Not for everyone it wasn't. Not for Hannah."

It was his turn to look surprised. "Hannah? What's Hannah got to do with this?"

"I know about you and Hannah."

"She told you?" he asked, his voice unnervingly quiet.

"That night, at the beach, when you turned up with Clare, she told me everything."

"And what, you want to sit down and discuss it with me, do you? Find out the gossip from my side?"

"I don't want to discuss anything with you," she threw back at him. "I'm just trying to point out that everything wasn't so bloody brilliant before I came along. Unless, of course, you get off on the fact that your best friend's girlfriend is more in love with you than she is with him."

Staring at each other in fury, Layla became aware of movement out of the corner of her eye. Turning, she caught sight of Jim.

"Er, hi," he said, his face ashen. "I just came in to drop off the rest of the timber we picked up today. Sorry, I didn't mean to interrupt."

Shit! How long had he been standing there?

"Jim," Joseph said, obviously wondering the same thing. "You're not interrupting. It's fine. I don't know how much of that you heard—"

"Nothing, I heard nothing," he interjected, that smile he wore so readily back on his face, but forced this time, she could tell. "Look, I…I have to go. I'll see you later."

And with that he turned round and left, literally running from the building.

"Fucking hell!" cried Joseph, running both hands through his hair.

"He's lying, isn't he? He did hear us?" said Layla, holding her breath as she waited for his answer.

"Of course he bloody did. Can't you tell?"

Her hand flew to her mouth and tears began to fall. "I'm so sorry," she whispered. "I had no idea he was there. I would never have mentioned Hannah if I did. I feel awful."

"And so you should. Hurting me, that's one thing. Hurting Jim, that's another matter entirely."

"Joseph," she pleaded, but it was no use.

"Just go. Get out of my workshop. I can't stand the sight of you. You and Alex, you deserve each other. You're two of a kind. Now go, before I really lose it."

Really lose it? God, she didn't think it was possible to be any angrier than he was at the moment. As Jim had done, she turned and fled, out into the early evening dusk, flinching as needles of ice in the air stung her face. She hurried past the pub without even glancing at it, past the grocers, past her favorite shop, Harvest Moon, past the closed cafés and the empty restaurants, running blindly until she reached home. Taking the stairs two at a time, she rushed into her bedroom, grabbed a bag from the bottom of the wardrobe, and shoved it full of clothes, shoes, and toiletries until it bulged at the seams. And then she collapsed, big heaving sobs engulfing her.

The way Joseph had looked at her! She couldn't stay to endure that look again. And poor Jim, he must feel so betrayed. Hannah would feel betrayed too when she found out. She had asked Layla specifically to keep quiet, and what had she done? She had broken her confidence at virtually the first opportunity. Hannah would hate her just like Joseph hated her, and rightly so. She had to leave, go back to Brighton, to Alex. She really did have no choice now. She had taken everything that was good in life and destroyed it; unwittingly or not, it didn't matter. The trouble was, she couldn't drive right now, not in this state. It would be downright dangerous to do so. She'd crash before she reached the village outskirts, she was sure. No, she'd have to stay tonight, but in the morning, as soon as it was light, she would leave. She'd leave a note for Hannah, apologizing profusely, and a note for Lenny, doing the same. And then she would run back to where she had run from, the adventure was over.

chapter twenty-five

"Mum! What the…?" Layla stumbled for words.

"There, that surprised you, didn't it? One minute you're talking to me on the phone, the next I'm here."

"But, Mum, I'm leaving."

"Leaving? To go where? Into the village? Not a problem, darling. I'll come with you. Get cracking on the sightseeing straightaway."

Damn, thought Layla, *if only I hadn't slept in this morning.* She hadn't meant to. She had meant to wake early, to be on the road by eight at the latest and back in Brighton just after lunchtime. Instead, it was midday when she'd opened her eyes, the emotional exhaustion of last night obviously having taken its toll. Despite having slept for much longer than normal, she had felt groggy since she'd got up, as though suffering from a killer hangover, albeit minus the alcohol intake. It was only in the last hour that she'd been able to contemplate a long journey. When her mother had knocked at the door, she'd been busy texting Alex to say she was coming "home." Thankfully she hadn't pressed the send button.

"Come on, darling. Don't leave me on the doorstep. I've travelled a long way. I'm dying for a proper cup of English tea. Surely, there's time for one before we head out?"

"Sorry, of course, come in."

"Oh, look at you," said Angelica, hugging her daughter tightly before holding her at arm's length. "Actually, you look dreadful. Are you ill?"

Thanks, Mum. Just what I needed to hear. "It's just a cold. I'm practically over it now," Layla lied, praying her mother wouldn't probe further.

"Hmm," she said, clearly unconvinced. "Goodness! What a lovely cottage. It's so sweet."

Her mother looked around her and noticed Layla's bag sitting prominently on the kitchen floor, all packed and raring to go.

"What's that doing there, darling?" said Angelica, pointing to it.

"That? Oh, nothing. They're, erm…they're my summer clothes. I won't need them for the duration of my stay so I thought I'd get them out of the way, put them into storage, so to speak."

Two lies in as many minutes. *Way to go, Layla.*

"You're so organized, aren't you?" said Angelica airily. "Always have been. Must take after your father; it's certainly not me. Put the kettle on."

Wondering if she were actually still asleep and dreaming, Layla surreptitiously pinched herself as she walked over to the sink to fill the kettle. Wincing at the pain, she couldn't deny she was indeed awake.

"Erm, how long do you intend on staying?" she asked as she filled a china cup rather than the usual mug and handed it to Angelica.

"A few days, if that's okay." Angelica took a sip of the hot caramel colored liquid. "Oh, that's wonderful," she sighed. "When it comes to tea, the Italians just can't compete. Coffee, now that's a different matter, but tea…oh, God, that's good."

As her mother went into raptures over what she was drinking, Layla thought, *Shit, what am I going to do about the pub?* If she stayed, she should work, but she couldn't possibly venture into the Trecastle Inn. If she did, she would have to face Joseph, Hannah, Jim, and Mick. And she couldn't do that; she just couldn't.

Her mother had stopped talking about tea and started discussing her journey from Milan to Exeter instead, home of their nearest airport, from which she had ordered a cab to Trecastle, driven by a lovely man called Dan, apparently. Whilst she chattered away, Layla, as discreetly as possible, texted Tom, telling him her mother had turned up out of the blue and could he possibly cover her shifts for the next week, starting tonight.

An affirmative answer came back straight away, with Tom noting he was glad for the opportunity to earn extra cash.

If Layla had to stay a few days longer, at least she could keep away from the village pub, and when it came to sightseeing, she'd steer her mother further afield also. With a bit of luck and a hoodie thrown in as a means of disguise, she might be able to avoid just about everyone she knew.

Finishing her tea, Angelica said, "Right, I'm almost ready. Just let me freshen up a bit, put a bit of makeup on, then we can venture into the village. Might you want to do the same, darling?"

"No, Mum," she replied tersely. "I'm fine. I'll just wait here for you whilst you get ready."

"Thank you, darling. I'm sure I look a fright too."

She didn't, not at all. She looked a million dollars, despite having just flown halfway across Europe. Decked in custom jewelry and designer clothing, Italian of course, her champagne-colored hair was swept into a sophisticated chignon, and her skin looked as soft as cotton candy. She was breathtaking, significantly younger looking than her very nearly fifty years.

"Before I do, though, show me round this little palace of yours. It really is very quaint. My friends back home, they'd kill for this, you know, despite the fact it's so tiny. English charm, you see. This has it in buckets."

Layla duly obliged. "Well, this is the kitchen, obviously."

"Gorgeous. Oh, look, it's got one of those Aga things."

"It's a Rayburn, actually," said Layla, seizing her chance to feel superior if only for a second or two. "And yes, I had noticed."

The living room also met with enthusiasm, although Layla couldn't think why; it was a mess. There were magazines lying haphazardly around as well as a plate with yesterday morning's half-eaten toast on it and a mug full with tea she'd ignored. She was going to tidy it before she went; she just hadn't got round to it yet.

Pointing to one of Lenny's books, Layla said, "That's written by the man who owns this cottage, and look, on the wall, those are his paintings."

"Wonderful. His artwork is nothing short of exquisite."

Upstairs, she showed Angelica "Penny's Room" first and then her own, Angelica fawning over the antique walnut wardrobe and fireplace just as Layla knew she would. As they were about to leave the bedroom to return to the kitchen, her mother let out an excited yelp. Turning, Layla saw her pointing toward the window.

"Look, darling," she said, as though it were a revelation to her daughter as well as herself. "There's Gull Rock, there in the distance."

Layla walked back toward the window. "I know" was all she could think to reply. She felt sad that Angelica had no idea their days spent on Trecastle Beach, with Gull Rock in the distance, were amongst some of her most treasured childhood memories. This feeling soon gave way to horror, however, as Angelica turned to her with fire in her amber eyes.

"Come on, let's go. Right now. I want to see it."

"See what? The Rock?"

"Yes, Gull Rock."

"But you haven't changed. We haven't unpacked. You must be starving. I am, come to think of it. Can't it wait till later? Maybe even tomorrow? We could take a ride out to Port Isaac instead, have a late lunch there." *There should be no one I know in Port Isaac.*

"No, it can't wait," said Angelica emphatically, "and I'm not hungry. I forced something hideous down on the plane. It quite ruined my appetite. Come on; let's go. *Carpe diem* and all that."

As her mother rushed out of the bedroom, Layla called out, "But your shoes. Change them, at least. You'll break your neck in those."

At the bottom of the stairs, her mother considered this point briefly before finally conceding, rummaging through her Louis Vuitton travel bag.

Holding a more suitable pair of flats triumphantly aloft, she said, "Right, don't dawdle. This autumn sun won't last. Shall we drive or walk?"

"Erm, I'll drive. It'll take about fifteen minutes to walk."

"Fifteen minutes? That's nothing. The exercise will do us good," Angelica stated as she headed out of the door and into the subdued sunlight.

Layla followed suit, feeling a flush of excitement herself and marveling that she did so. This was one of the reasons her mother was loved so much by practically everyone she met: she was just so damned enthusiastic about everything. She was able to incite, even in her begrudging daughter, an incredible lust for living. What mattered to her was the moment and making the most of it; all that had gone before or was to come was superfluous to requirements. *A philosophy that suits me down to the ground at the moment,* thought Layla.

They walked at breakneck speed and reached the beach in record time. The tide was on its way out and the sands deserted. As soon as the path gave way to sand, her mother discarded her shoes and began running, setting an impressive pace as Layla struggled to keep up. As they raced, Angelica's hair began escaping from its elegant bun. Reaching up, she removed the pins that secured it, letting it flow freely behind her, reminding Layla of how she'd been as a younger woman, although her hair had been much darker then, more dramatic. They soon reached the edge of the ocean and began kicking the cold, foamy water at each other, letting out high-pitched squeals of laughter as the ocean hit bare skin. They ran the length of the beach, and despite the age gap, Angelica was not as breathless as she was.

"Come on," she bellowed over the cry of the sea birds. "Time for adventure."

It was like being a child again, following in the footsteps of yesteryear. When they reached Merlin's Cave, her mother went in first, as she always did, Layla following closely behind. Although it was dark inside, they managed to venture impressively far, further than she had gone with Penny and Hannah, encouraging each other on and frequently shouting to hear their voices bounce from wall to wall. After a while, the sandy bottom shelved dramatically and they could go no further; they'd be wet to their knees if they did. Standing for a while, soaking up the eerie silence, it was Layla who started giggling first, joined quickly by her mother before turning back toward daylight. As they emerged, the sun was sinking rapidly, the light starting to lose its battle against the late afternoon dusk.

Facing the ocean once more, Angelica said, "So what do you think? Can we do it now? Is the tide out far enough? Can we reach Gull Rock?"

Stunned to hear the words her mother had said to her so often in childhood, it was a minute or two before Layla could reply. "We can try," she said, her voice quivering slightly.

Standing side by side, just staring at the huge slab of granite before them, it was Layla who spoke again. "You remembered, then?"

"Of course I remember. I will never forget the time I spent here with my little girl. Never."

As her mother turned to her, Layla felt a lump the size of a beach ball catch in her throat. She looked into Angelica's eyes, warily at first but then with increasing trust, and felt herself enfolded in her mother's arms for the second time that day.

Although initially stiff, Layla quickly relaxed, and as she did so, the floodgates opened. Grief for her father, and for the mother she had lost too but in a different way, rose up inside her and burst through the cracks in the wall she had built so carefully since childhood. And she let it. She let the wall just tumble down, brick by brick. All the while her mother held her, and with each new tear that fell the pain receded until she was able to break away and laugh, first in embarrassment but then with joy, real and utter joy.

Angelica started laughing too, and together they laughed and laughed for what seemed like an age before heading home, hand in hand, in silence.

Angelica stayed for the best part of a week, and Layla loved every minute of it. On their first night, after dinner, they had talked into the early hours. Well, Angelica had done most of the talking, but Layla had been happy to sit and listen, marveling at her mother's account of life in Italy, the sort of people she was mixing with, European royalty, famous fashion designers, and billionaire business men and their exquisitely beautiful girlfriends, most of them established models or soon to be. Angelica laughed about them all, able to enjoy the glitz and glamour, without taking any of it too seriously.

"Giorgio is different," she told Layla, "from most men I've known."

"In what way?" asked Layla, intrigued.

"He's genuine with a heart of gold. He has no agenda other than living life to the full, something that you know I try to do as well." Smiling at Layla, she continued, "He's good to me. He's kind. But no one will ever replace your father. Never."

Layla had been surprised at this revelation and gently encouraged her mother to elaborate. Seemingly happy to do so, Angelica talked about how she and Greg had met, fallen in love, and decided to marry, all within a year, despite being so young. He'd been twenty-one, she just twenty. She'd fallen pregnant with Layla straightaway, something they hadn't planned but were over the moon about. For almost seven years, life had been perfect. Angelica had stayed at home to look after Layla. Greg had worked hard to provide them with a good standard of living. As an architect starting out, they didn't have much in the way of material things, but they felt themselves rich in other ways. They did try to have a second child, she told Layla, but it never happened. It wasn't something that concerned them anyway; they were enjoying Layla. There'd be plenty of time to add to their family later on, or so they thought.

"You were the apple of your father's eye," Angelica continued. "He quite literally worshipped the ground you crawled and then later walked on. The feeling was quite mutual. Sometimes I felt like a spare part, you know, an outsider, with my nose pushed up against the window, looking in on something I wasn't actually a part of… but longed to be."

Layla was surprised her mother had felt this way. She started to interrupt, not quite sure what to say but to be sympathetic at least, but Angelica stopped her.

"It's fine. I was rambling. I find myself doing that more and more lately," she said, patting Layla's hand affectionately. "You were just so incredibly close, the two of you, and at times I felt a little jealous of the bond between you. That was my fault and quite unforgivable."

Shaking her head as though to clear unwanted thoughts, Angelica continued with her reminiscences. She told Layla all about her first day at school, how many pictures her father had taken of that special day, his pride when she had played a star in the school nativity.

"Most of the children were stars, for heaven's sake." She laughed. "It wasn't exactly the lead role, but it might as well have been, the way he was behaving. I thought he was going to burst."

After chatting some more about Layla's childhood, she started talking about the accident, as Layla knew she must.

"He was only seventeen, you know, the lad who hit him. Just passed his driving test. Out with a group of friends in his father's car, showing off, no doubt. He plowed straight into your dad's car head-on. Nobody in the other car was hurt, not so much as a scratch, but Greg died instantly, or so they said. I still wonder if that was true or if they were just trying to be kind. If he was alive at the scene of the accident, even for a few moments, what was he thinking? Who was he thinking of?"

"You, Mum," said Layla softly. "He would have thought of you."

Angelica visibly struggled at this, but she nonetheless managed to continue. "I missed him so much. It was as though a part of me died that day, too — and not a small part. A big part. Most of me, in fact. It was agony, sheer agony, and the agony just wouldn't go away."

Layla moved closer to Angelica and took her hand.

"I couldn't see past my own pain. I know that. Don't think I don't. I couldn't deal with anyone's loss but my own. Not even yours. I've always been selfish."

"No," Layla protested, but weakly. There was, after all, truth in those words.

"We struggled on, you and I, but very much in our own ways. I see that now. I wasn't there for you, was I?"

"In a way, you were. But I could never reach you, not really. You surrounded yourself with so many people, almost like they were armor. It became my turn, I suppose, to stand on the outside, looking in."

Angelica nodded thoughtfully. "Armor? I like that analogy…yes, that's what they were in a way. They were armor against my feelings. They stopped me from thinking about Greg. I had to be busy every part of every day, doing something, being with someone, anyone. If I'd had time to stop and think, to contemplate how I really felt, I would have fallen apart, and then I would have been of no use to you at all. I'd probably have been locked away in an asylum somewhere, and you'd have been left to the mercy of Danica."

Mum avoided her sister like the plague. As far as Layla could work out, her aunt Danica was a bitter woman, full of anger over a failed marriage, blaming everything and everyone but herself for the misfortunes in her life. She was someone Angelica had spent her whole life striving to be the complete opposite of and someone Layla hardly knew.

Steering the conversation back to her father, Layla asked, "Do you still miss him?"

"Yes, darling. At some point every day, I think of him. You never recover from losing your soul mate. But you do learn to live with it, eventually."

"I'm so sorry."

"No, no, it's me that should be saying sorry," replied Angelica fervently. "I knew we were growing apart after your father's death, and I regretted every minute of it, but at the same time, I seemed powerless to stop it. I gave up trying to stop it, I suppose. Growing up, you looked so much like your father. It hurt to even look at you. When you retreated to your room, I let you. It just seemed easier somehow, for me, that is, not you. I am truly sorry. So many years wasted."

"But we had this, remember?" Layla threw her arms out. "We had our holidays in Trecastle, with Hannah and Connie, and we were close then, all of us. It wasn't all wasted."

"You're so generous, my love," said Angelica. "You embody the best of Greg and me. I'm so needy. I can't cope with life on my own. But you, you've supported yourself since leaving college, never relied on anyone. You brought yourself up, or as good as. Now you live here, writing away, and holding down a busy bar job too. You're amazing. A life like yours would kill me. I mean, who'd take out the bins?"

Layla smiled at her mother's joke. "I'm not sure I'm *that* capable. But it's nice to know someone thinks I am." *Unlike Penny,* she thought, harking back to their argument earlier that year.

"Don't underestimate yourself. You're extremely capable. I don't think I've ever said this to you before, Layla Lewis, but I'm proud of you. You are one very special girl. And I miss you. I have done for a long time."

"I've missed you too," whispered Layla, swallowing hard. "But it's not too late. We can start again."

"I'll drink to that," said Angelica, tears running freely down her face as she raised a glass of the premier cru she'd brought from duty-free.

"Cheers," Layla replied, her eyes dry but filled with wonder.

Much later, lying in bed alone, Layla had marveled yet again at the magic of Trecastle. At how this place had brought her and her mother together so many years ago, if only for brief periods of time, and how it had brought them together again, hopefully for good this time. And if that was the only purpose for being here, she told herself, it was a fit purpose. It was enough. When her mother left, Layla would leave too and lay to rest this chapter of her life. It was finished; its purpose fulfilled.

They didn't talk about the past again during the days that followed. There was no need; that too was finished, over and done with. It was time to live for the moment, as her mother tried so hard to do. And to get to know each other again.

At long last, she thought. *At long last.*

chapter twenty-six

It amused Layla how easy it was for Angelica to throw off the trappings of her glamorous life and come back down to earth again with a vengeance for the duration of her stay. She would pad around the cottage in Layla's clothes, as she deemed her own too fussy for the wilds of Cornwall, with not a scrap of makeup on and hair unrestrained. Despite her mother's longing to revisit Trecastle proper, Layla somehow managed to steer her to a neighboring village to linger over lunch in a seafood restaurant or to visit stately houses such as Pencarrow and Lanhydrock. Even the Eden Project got a look in, both of them relishing the humidity of the indoor rainforest. There was an incredible easiness between them now that was both comforting and surprising, and Layla found herself feeling as close to this woman as Penny and Hannah. Admittedly, they were more like friends than mother and daughter, but that was fine. It was better than the nothing they'd had.

"Why don't you come and see me again in Milan?" Angelica had asked, promising to scale down her social engagements so she could show off the city properly this time. "I can introduce you to several eligible bachelors I know. I'm sure you'd like them."

Angelica didn't know Layla was contemplating marriage to Alex. Layla wondered if she should tell her, but held back, not wanting to taint their time together somehow. And those bachelors did sound tempting: dark, handsome, and, fingers crossed, completely unable to speak a word of English. Considering how often she put her foot in it with Joseph, that would be a huge bonus!

As her remaining time in England dwindled, Angelica refused to be put off any longer—she wanted to see Hannah again. She also quizzed Layla about all the other friends she'd made in the village, wanting to meet them, too, before she left. Layla had dreaded this. Not only did that familiar feeling of not wanting to share her mother resurface, she wasn't sure she had any friends in the village left to introduce her to, Hannah included.

Angelica insisted they visit the Trecastle Inn on the penultimate night of her stay, and thinking what the hell, she had nothing more to lose, Layla agreed. As they walked in, the usual suspects, as she secretly thought of them, were in residence. All except Joseph, she noted with relief.

"Angelica!" cried Hannah. "Tom said something about you paying a surprise visit, but I thought he must have got his wires crossed."

"No, darling, he was quite right. Here I am, large as life and still full of surprises. Let me look at you," she said, holding Hannah by the shoulders. "Oh, you're beautiful. How wonderful to see you again."

Whilst Hannah and her mother formed a mutual appreciation society, Layla tried to catch Jim's eye, but he was deep in conversation with Curtis, whether deliberately or genuinely so, she couldn't tell. As for Mick, he was chatting animatedly to some woman she'd never seen before, although he did look over and smile at her from time to time.

At least someone's acknowledging me, she thought sadly.

"Layla, darling, what are you drinking?"

"Oh." Layla shook herself out of her reverie. "Erm, a glass of pinot, please."

"A glass of pinot grigio, it is. And Hannah, one for yourself, as well. Introduce me to your friends, then, darling. I'll buy them a drink, too."

"No, Mum. Really, there's no need," Layla started, but it was too late—Angelica had already made her way over to Mick, Jim, and Curtis.

"Hello," she said enthusiastically. "I'm Angelica Lewis, Layla's mother. Are you friends of my daughter's?"

After a surprised but mutual nodding of heads, Angelica said, "Oh, good, I've found some at last. I was beginning to think she was some sort of social pariah."

"Mum," hissed Layla, mortified but spared any further exchange as Mick quickly answered.

"Her mother? You're kidding me? You look more like sisters."

Angelica laughed delightedly at this. If there was one thing she adored, and indeed was used to, it was flattery. The initial awkwardness successfully dispelled, Jim also started chatting, as did Curtis and a few others, Angelica's warmth drawing them like moths to a flame. She kept them all highly entertained with her witty stories and anecdotes, making herself very popular indeed.

Whilst her mother was busy, Layla knew she should go over and speak to Hannah, but she found herself rooted to the spot, unable to. Layla had glanced over a couple of times, and each time, Hannah had been looking straight at her. Had Jim told her about her argument with Joseph? He must have done, considering the daggers in her eyes. Layla would have to explain at some stage, she knew that, but maybe from afar. Most definitely from afar.

Meanwhile, like a little girl hanging onto her mother's skirt, she stood obediently by Angelica's side, marveling at her ability to hold court. If her mother was proud of her, she was proud of her mother. Very proud.

Walking home later that night, Angelica enthused about Layla's friends, remarking on the gorgeous young woman Hannah was now and how friendly the boys were. She loved being back in Trecastle and wondered if Giorgio would be averse to buying a little holiday cottage here, a notion that filled Layla with complete and utter horror. When she left here, there was no way she'd be able to return, ever.

As they entered the cottage, Angelica turned to face her. "Do you know why Joseph wasn't in the pub tonight?"

Layla had no idea her mother knew anything about Joseph. Certainly she hadn't mentioned him; she'd made sure of that.

Feeling herself blush furiously, Layla spluttered, "Erm…er…no, I don't. Why should I?"

"Oh, I just wondered," Angelica replied innocently enough.

"When…when did you meet him?"

"Yesterday. When you were at the shops, I went to inspect the garden. This botanist chap—Lenny, isn't it?—he's hardly going to be thrilled with how you've let the weeds take hold, dear."

"The weeds? Oh, Mum, never mind about the bloody weeds. You actually spoke to Joseph?"

"Yes, I did. He was tinkering in that shed of his. I called over to say hello. We had a lovely chat. What a gorgeous boy he is and those eyes!"

"I know," said Layla, before quickly adding, "I mean, yes, he has got nice eyes, I suppose, not that I've really noticed, not at all, in fact." Forcing herself to stop babbling, she asked, "What did you say to him?"

"Oh, we passed the time of day, that sort of thing."

Layla could tell her mother was playing with her now. She had a sly, knowing look on her face, a look that was striking fear into the very depths of her. They hadn't *just* passed the time of day, she was certain. But if not, what had transpired?

"Come on, Mum." She was desperate now. "Tell me."

"I just asked, not directly of course, whether he was single?"

"Single?" asked Layla incredulously. "Why? Why would you do that?"

"Think about it. He's single; Alex is never around. I wanted to know why the pair of you hadn't got it together. You'd make a lovely couple, you know. I thought that as soon as I saw him."

"Tell me you didn't say as much."

"Actually, I did. He's too good to ignore. I don't know what's wrong with you sometimes. Your boyfriends are almost as old as mine. Sophocles would have something to say about that, I'm sure."

Layla grabbed hold of her mother's wrists. "What have you done? This is a disaster." Releasing her just as abruptly, she turned away, muttering all the while, "Thank God I'm going. It's just as well. I could never stay here, not now. Not only does he think I'm a nutter, he'll think I've come from a long line of nutters. And he'd be right. Absolutely bloody right."

Angelica came up behind her and placed her hands on Layla's shoulders. "Now, now, don't upset yourself so. I was very subtle about it, you know. I didn't just come out with it."

Swinging around, Layla implored, "Tell me, then, every word you said."

"Don't be silly, dear. I can't remember every word I said. But it was interesting. When I mentioned about you two being an item, he went very quiet. Looked forlorn, in fact. Naturally, that aroused my suspicions."

"Naturally," replied Layla, anger and embarrassment taking it in turns to swamp her.

"I asked him if perhaps you'd already been an item at some stage. After all, you've been here a good few months now. He said I'd have to ask you about that, but he thought you were a lovely girl and, having met me, he could see where you got your good looks and charm from."

At this Angelica elicited a girlish giggle, obviously taking his words literally, choosing or failing to see any irony in them.

"I cannot believe you," yelled Layla. "You are actually unbelievable."

"It has been said," Angelica purred. "But seriously, why you've never mentioned your neighbor was so edible is beyond me."

"Because of Alex, of course!"

"Oh, Alex Smalex, your absent boyfriend, you mean?"

"He's absent at my choosing, not for any other reason. I'm going back to him soon, very soon. Tomorrow, in fact. I'm leaving right after you are. I was about to leave when you turned up, stopping me. If it wasn't for you, I'd be gone by now."

Forcing her daughter to sit down, Angelica said, "I knew it. I knew something had happened. You looked wretched when I turned up, and then there was your reticence to introduce me to anyone, to even wander into the village center. I had to insist on seeing Hannah, too. As for Joseph, something's gone very wrong between you two, hasn't it?"

"No," she protested, "it hasn't." And then, fed up with all the lies, with keeping her feelings to herself for so damn long, she said, "Yes, yes, it has. It's gone horribly wrong. I can't believe how wrong it's gone, not when it was once so right."

"There, there," said Angelica gently. "Let it out, every last ounce of anger and frustration. Don't suppress it. It's not good for you. I've spent a lifetime doing that, and it looks like I've taught you to do the same. Enough now. Be honest with me, but more importantly, be honest with yourself. Only then can things start to get better."

Her mother's words striking to the very core, Layla looked up, saw the empathy in the woman's face, and, in a rush, told her everything.

chapter twenty-seven

"And now you're returning to Alex?" said Angelica in astonishment. "I can't stay here, Mum. You can see that's impossible."

"Nothing's impossible, darling. Of course you can stay. In fact, my advice is you damn well do stay. Sort out the mess you've made."

"So you do think I've made a mess, then?" Layla hung her head forlornly. Couldn't her mother lie just a little bit?

"I most certainly do, and believe me, if you leave it that way, it will come back to haunt you. No, you need to do the right thing: make amends with Joseph, Hannah and Jim too. Only then can you make peace with yourself. As for Alex, he sounds truly awful. Dump him."

"He's not, Mum," said Layla, lifting her head defiantly. "I know I haven't painted a great picture of him, but what he did, he did in the past. He's promised it will never happen again. He loves me. He moved heaven and earth to find me."

"Heaven and earth? I'm not sure about that, dear. I told him, or rather I told his secretary."

"You told him?" Layla gasped, unable to believe her ears.

"No," replied Angelica without missing a beat, "I said I told his secretary, not him. She rang me to say Easy Travel needed your forwarding address, something about wages owed. A very nice young lady she was, polite. I told her you lived in Trecastle now, worked in the pub there."

"But how did he…she get your number?"

"Oh, I don't know, darling." Angelica shrugged her shoulders. "It's not that difficult nowadays, is it? Not with the Internet."

So that's how Alex had found her — hardly heaven and earth at all, just clever deducing. Deducing he'd probably got his secretary to do, not even making the phone call himself.

Determined to look on the bright side, however, she said, "Well, at least with Alex I'll have a home, a future."

"With Alex you'll have a lifetime of heartache and nothing else."

"How do you know that?" Layla was getting cross now. "Why is everyone so down on him?"

"Perhaps because they can see what you can't?"

"That works in reverse, too. Perhaps I can see something in him that they can't, something credible, something real."

"Okay then, darling, enlighten me. Tell me one 'real' thing about him."

About to rise to the challenge, Layla was shocked when her mind went blank.

"Darling, you must make your own mind up. I can't and won't do that for you. It's not my place. All I can draw on is my own experience. I'm happy with Giorgio, but I don't love him. No, don't look like that. As I said I'm happy with him, content. And content is all I ask for now. He gives me the world, like Alex will give to you, but there's one big difference: I trust Giorgio implicitly."

"Mum," Layla started, fed up of discussing Alex's infidelity.

"Let me finish," insisted Angelica. "You're twenty-eight, the same age I was when I lost your father. Lost the love of my life. It sounds as if you still might have yours. Okay, he's angry with you, but he's alive. Greg was taken from me. I had no choice in it. You do. Don't throw him away because you think he doesn't want you. I saw something in his eyes yesterday that told me otherwise."

"You're wrong. Only Alex wants me. Joseph doesn't."

"No, *you're* wrong. Find some resolution, whatever that may be. And whilst you're at it, keep in mind you're perfectly capable of standing on your own two feet; you've been doing so since you were seven. You don't need anyone to pave the way for you."

"I am starting to realize that," said Layla, feeling as though she were the one being enlightened.

Angelica yawned. "I'm going to turn in now. All this preaching has tired me to the bone. I've got a long journey tomorrow."

"Night, Mum," said Layla, smiling up at her.

Before she turned to leave, however, she added, "Any time, night or day, I'm here for you. It may be on the other end of the phone, I can't help that, but I will *always* make time to listen. No more rushed exchanges. That's my promise to you, if you promise to do what I ask."

"I promise," whispered Layla, exhausted to the bone herself.

While Angelica got ready for bed, Layla checked her phone. Alex had texted several times.

> Where are you? Why don't you ever answer your phone?
> You okay?

> Layla, speak to me. I miss you. I love you.
> I can't wait til you come home.

> Good news, Jack has signed contracts. The merger
> is complete! The Cristal's on ice.
> Can't wait to celebrate with you.

> I've drunk the Cristal, couldn't wait. Layla, pick up the phone.
> You've no idea how much I miss you. I love you.

After reading them several times over, she switched her phone off, unable to think of a suitable reply.

Despite Layla telling her not to, that she'd drive her to the airport, her mother insisted on calling Dan the taximan, saying she didn't want to put Layla to any trouble. Layla suspected, however, it was the thought of cramming into her tiny little Mazda that was really concerning Angelica. She had clearly gotten used to traveling in style.

As they kissed goodbye, just managing to hold the tears at bay, Angelica said fondly, "Remember, life's too short for mistakes. Think about what you *want*, not just what you need. It may be Alex; it may be Joseph. It may be neither of them in the end, I don't know. Just listen to your instincts, and you won't go wrong."

"Thanks, Mum, for all your advice." Layla tried to smile.

"Better late than never, huh?"

"Better late than never."

As Dan pulled up outside in his shiny blue cab, polished to perfection no doubt to impress her mother whom he looked thoroughly in love with, mother and daughter said their final goodbyes.

As she was about to step into the taxi, with Dan making a great show of holding the door open for her, Angelica stopped. "Isn't that your friend? The blond one, Penny?"

"Penny?" said Layla, looking to where her mother was pointing. "Bloody hell, Penny!"

Screeching round the corner in her Qashqai was indeed Penny, coming to an abrupt halt in front of Dan's cab.

She hadn't known Penny was turning up. There had been no text to say so. Then again, her phone had been switched off since last night.

"Another surprise, darling?" Angelica asked with a wink. "It seems the smoke fairies are doing their utmost to make sure you stick around. Good luck. I'll call as soon as I'm home."

"Bye, Mum. Safe journey," she said, quickly planting one last kiss on her cheek before rushing over to where Penny sat, a look of utter misery etched on her face.

chapter twenty-eight

Steeling herself, Penny got out of the car. "Was that your mum?" she said to a bewildered Layla.

"Er, yeah, she's been here for a week. A surprise visit."

"A surprise visit? That's a turn-up for the books, isn't it?" Before Layla could answer, however, Penny rushed on. "Oh, Layla, what a dreadful journey! How I made it in one piece, I don't know. I nearly crashed about a dozen times on the way."

"Why?" said Layla, her eyes wide.

"You're not going to believe why. Come on; let's get indoors. I'm freezing."

It wasn't actually freezing. It was, in fact, an unusually mild day for late October, but she'd been unable to stop shivering since leaving Brighton, her tremors an almost involuntary action. As she headed toward the cottage, she heard Layla call out behind her.

"What about your bags? Shall I get them for you?"

"Bags?" Penny called back. "I haven't got any. There wasn't time to pack."

Layla came racing in behind her. "Penny, I don't understand. You never travel anywhere without your entire wardrobe in tow. What's going on?"

"No clothes, no phone. It's just me, I'm afraid. Nothing but me." Slumping down at the kitchen table, she whispered, more to herself than to anyone else, "God, I could do with a drink."

Hearing her, Layla went straight to the fridge to find some wine. Quickly Penny said, "No, no, not wine. A cup of tea will do. A really strong cup, though. Big burly builder style. Two sugars. No, make that three."

Layla raised her eyebrows at this and duly made tea instead. Penny took a few sips of the scalding hot liquid before promptly bursting into tears.

Without hesitation, Layla enfolded her in her arms. "Penny, what is it? What's going on? I thought everything was great with you now."

"It is. It was. But it's gone to shit, just like that. Dylan turned up on my doorstep yesterday evening. He found out where I lived. I'm not sure how. I never told him. He won't leave me alone, Layla. He's a head case."

"Dylan? I thought Dylan was history."

Penny breathed deeply in an attempt to calm down. When she was sure she could speak again without dissolving into tears, she tried to explain further. "You remember how badly Richard took it when I told him about me and Dylan?"

"Er, yeah. I'm hardly likely to forget."

"And we weren't speaking for a while?"

"For a while? That's the understatement of the year."

"Well, you know how furious I was with Richard for reacting the way he did? For completely refusing to accept that he might have played a part in pushing me into Dylan's arms. For blaming me entirely."

"I do. It was unfair," soothed Layla, gently stroking her hair.

"It was, wasn't it?" said Penny, grabbing hold of her hands, desperate for validation. "Unfair, I mean. I'm not a selfish cow, am I?"

"Of course not. You tried to tell him a thousand times how lonely you felt. He didn't listen, wouldn't compromise. The fault is as much his as yours."

"Thanks, Layla. I needed to hear that," Penny said with a sniffle, grateful not just for her support but for the box of tissues she had provided as soon as they sat down. They were certainly coming in handy.

"Whilst he wasn't speaking to me, Richard that is, I carried on seeing Dylan occasionally. No, don't look so shocked. It was just as friends. I made that crystal clear to him. He was funny, that's all, and I needed some lighthearted relief from all the crap I was getting at home." Hesitating slightly, she continued, "I'm not blaming you, don't get me wrong, but you weren't around. You'd left by then. Dylan became a bit of a lifeline, I suppose, someone I could have a laugh with."

"I can understand that," Layla said gently. "Really I can."

"After that episode with his father, do you remember? He had a suspected heart attack, and Richard called me whilst I was here, to ask me to come home? And I did, the very next day. Well, we got closer after that, Richard and me. As close as we used to be. Everything was going great, except for one thing: Dylan just wouldn't accept I didn't want to see him anymore. He started bombarding me with texts — friendly at first, like the ones he sent me whilst I was here, asking me about my holiday and stuff, but they became more threatening as I failed to reply or told him to back off. He said I'd used him, and in a way he's right, I did."

"He texted whilst you were here? You didn't say. I thought that was Richard texting you all the time. You said it was."

"I lied," said Penny as she burst into tears again.

Layla continued to try to console her, but it was no good. Penny felt trapped in a tunnel of misery, at the end of which no light prevailed. The walls around her suddenly closing in, she jumped up. "I need to get out. I need some air."

Without waiting for a reply, Penny headed out of the cottage and into the soft sunshine, striding into the village and down to the beach, Layla practically running to keep up with her.

The high street was empty, except for a few people, locals at this time of year she presumed, popping into the grocers or May's to stock up on provisions. She cast a cursory glance at Joseph's workshop and the pub as she marched ahead, praying that neither he nor Hannah would choose that exact moment to appear. Except for Layla, she was in no mood to see anyone; she must look wretched.

Down at the beach, she walked up to the water's edge, big foamy waves rushing at her like galloping horses, the gulls loud and swooping.

Layla caught up with her eventually and stood beside her, staring out to sea also.

"I'm scared, Layla," said Penny finally. "Dylan's acting like a man possessed. He won't leave me alone."

"What happened when he turned up on your doorstep? What did Richard do?"

"He hit the roof, that's what he did," said Penny, the salt air stinging her chewed lips. "Thankfully, he managed to refrain from hitting Dylan, although how, I don't know. I never told you this before, but Dylan had been in trouble with the police when he was younger. He was quite open about it, almost blasé. I just assumed it was for something relatively minor, smoking a bit of weed or something. He never enlightened me otherwise. Not until recently anyway. It was assault he was in for. Did time in Lewes Prison for it. I think he let me know as a kind of threat, does that make sense? Thank God, Richard's not really the aggressive type. If he'd started on Dylan, he would have probably ended up flattened."

"Christ," said Layla.

"Eventually Dylan did leave, but only after calling me a prick-tease and a slut. Heaven knows what the neighbors thought; their curtains were twitching madly. Then Richard demanded I tell him every last detail. And I did. I showed him the texts Dylan had bombarded me with, how I had tried to appease him, to get him off my back, and how he had ignored me. I told him every bit of it, leading right up to the confrontation on our doorstep."

"Oh, Penny, I don't know what to say." Layla was clearly shocked.

"Neither did Richard," said Penny, shaking her head sadly. "After I finished speaking, he left. Just like that, without saying a word. I spent the night driving round Brighton trying to find him. I even went to Beachy Head, can you believe it? Just in case. I drove round and round, went back to the house several times to check, but he never showed up. As soon as the birds started singing, I put my foot down and didn't stop. That's how I ended up here."

Layla held onto Penny's arms. "We have to contact Richard," she said. "We have to let him know you're safe."

"As if he cares," said Penny bitterly.

"It's only fair, Penny."

"Fair?" Penny screamed. "I was out of my mind with worry last night when he left. Hours passed, and still I didn't know where he was. He didn't think how fair that was on me, did he? I told him it was just a friendship with Dylan. Well, it was to me, anyway. My replies to his texts proved that at least. But Richard doesn't believe me; he believes only the worst."

"Penny, calm down. This is not tit-for-tat; this is serious. It's only right we tell him where you are. Everything else we'll sort out later, when we've had a chance to think about it. Now come on; I'm taking you home. By the sounds of it, you haven't slept for twenty-four hours. You can't be thinking straight. You need to rest. Let me take care of you."

As the ocean roared incessantly in the distance, Penny thought, *Yes, that would be nice, someone to take care of me.*

And like a meek child, she allowed Layla to take her by the hand, lead her back down the high street and toward The Outlook, a refuge for both of them now.

chapter twenty-nine

"I know what I need," said a considerably brighter-looking Penny over breakfast the next morning.

"What?" said Layla, chewing on a slice of toast.

"A man's perspective on my predicament. I'm off to see Joe."

Layla almost choked. "Do you think that's wise?" she said, hoping to imply it most certainly wasn't.

"It can't hurt." Penny finished the dregs of her tea. "In fact, I'll go now. Catch you later."

As Penny rushed out the door for the second time in two days, Layla was glad she was sitting down. She would have fallen over with shock otherwise. Penny seeing Joseph, or rather flirting with him, was not going to help. It would only complicate matters further.

Feeling annoyed that she was annoyed, she carried the breakfast plates over to the sink before trying Richard's phone again. He wasn't answering, his silence hopefully due to anger rather than reasons more sinister. She sent a text instead, but got no reply to that either.

Layla had thought she would spend today with Penny, but heaven knew how long she'd be gone for. *What shall I do instead?* she wondered. But deep down she knew what she had to do: she had to seek out Hannah and apologize. *Do the right thing,* her mother had said. And it was the right thing, even if the thought filled her with anxiety.

She headed outdoors, walked past houses and green fields toward the village center, and turned right, away from the pub, toward Hannah and Jim's road. She rang the doorbell, and it was a few moments before there was an answer. Instead of Hannah standing before her, however, it was Jim, with nothing but a bath towel wrapped round his waist.

"Oh, hi, Layla," he said as he rubbed his hair with another, smaller towel. "I've just got out of the shower."

Embarrassed by his near-nakedness, she started to back hastily away, muttering all the while, "Sorry, Jim, didn't mean to interrupt you. It was Hannah I was after. No worries, I'll call back another time."

"It's okay." Jim smiled at her, not with his usual isn't-life-just-brilliant smile but more of an isn't-life-just-totally-fucked-up-sometimes smile. "She's popped to the shops. Come in and wait. She won't be long."

Reluctantly, she followed him in. She had really wanted to see Hannah first, to get a sense of how the land lay, but perhaps this was fortuitous when she thought about it. Jim was an innocent caught up in the mess she'd made. He deserved to top her list of people to apologize to.

"Coffee?" he said amicably.

"Er, yeah, that'll be great. White, please, no sugar."

If she hoped he'd get dressed before he made their drinks, she was disappointed. He had no such intention, clearly unaware of the effect his bare torso could have on a girl. Forcing herself to look around the kitchen instead of at him, she noticed dirty plates, mugs, and bowls piled up on every available surface. On the wall was another of Hannah's paintings, a huge canvas liberally splashed with oranges, yellows, and golds. A Cornish sunset, if she was not very much mistaken.

"Sorry about the mess," said Jim, although it was obvious he couldn't give a damn. "I'll clear up soon."

"It's fine. Better things to do in life than housework." She took the mug from him and continued, "Look, about last week, what I said—or more to the point, what you heard me say—I'm so sorry. I didn't mean it."

He leaned against the countertop, his toned arms folded across his body. "You did mean it, Layla, because it's true. Hannah's my first choice, but I'm not hers. I know that."

Pushing a plate aside so she could place her mug of coffee down, she said, "Jim, Hannah loves you. She's told me how much. God, she doesn't even need to tell me, it's obvious. And who wouldn't? You're wonderful, kind, and caring. She just needs more time, that's all."

"More time?" He cocked his head to one side as though seriously contemplating it. "Yeah, I can do that. I can give her all the time in the world." Just as she thought he might elaborate, he said, "So you've fallen out with Joe, have you?"

"Er...yeah, you could say that," she replied, taken off-guard. "Why?"

"A misunderstanding, that's all. It will blow over, I'm sure. But even if it doesn't, I'm leaving soon."

"Had enough of Trecastle, have you?"

No. It's had enough of me more like. "I've got a job waiting for me back in Brighton, and Alex, of course."

"Yeah, of course you have, Hannah did say."

He ran his hand through his still damp hair, and a bolt of pain shot through her. It was an absentminded gesture typical of Joseph, too.

"Look, I don't want to keep you. Perhaps get Hannah to call me or I'll call her later."

"Will do," he said, but as she turned to go, he started speaking again. "You and Joe, I thought you might hit it off, you know? Okay, I hoped you would, and yeah, for more reasons than one, if I'm honest. I don't know what's gone wrong between you—we don't tend to talk much about that sort of stuff, me and Joe—but I know he likes you. A lot."

No, he doesn't. Not anymore.

Layla bit her lower lip to stem the flow of tears that seemed to be ever threatening lately. "And I like him. He's a nice guy, despite our bust-up. But as for anything happening between us, no. No chance."

Walking toward her, his semi-naked body startlingly close, Jim said, "All I'm saying is don't write him off. Not just yet. If you've got something special and you *both* feel it, consider yourself very lucky indeed."

Not sure how to reply to his words, she was saved from doing so when Hannah walked in.

"Layla, what are you doing here?"

"I came to see you," she said. Hanging her head in shame, she added, "I know it's been a while."

Hannah brushed past her with a bag of groceries in her arms and gave Jim a quick peck on the cheek before replying. "So what do you want to see me about?"

Bristling at the sharpness in her voice, Layla ventured, "Perhaps if we go for a walk, I can explain."

Hannah considered this for a moment, idly watching Jim leave the room, before finally conceding. "Come on, then," she said, brushing past her yet again and making for the door.

A precarious but spectacular path close to the edge of the headland linked the village of Trecastle with the next village, five miles along. Layla had walked it many times with Hannah, with Joseph, on her own, but today they would tackle only a fraction of it, just enough to get away from the village and all in it. At first they walked in difficult silence until Hannah commented on the weather, giving them an opening for small talk, at least. When they reached the headland proper, Hannah pointed to an empty bench, one of several placed along the path for walkers to give themselves a well-earned rest during their travels.

"Water?" Hannah held out a small Evian bottle.

Grateful that Hannah had thought to bring such a thing, Layla took it from her and downed a few gulps, the constantly ascending and descending path having worked up quite a thirst.

The view from the headland was stunning. Rugged cliffs lined the coast, falling dramatically into the sea, which was deep green and only very gently stirring in the sunlight as though still half asleep. On the edge of the bay, they could see a tiny figure of a man throwing a stick to his even tinier dog. Other than them, the beach was deserted. There was nobody on the headland either. It was theirs and theirs alone.

Just as well, thought Layla, unsure how their conversation was going to go.

Just as she had apologized to Jim, she apologized to Hannah, continuing to make amends. "I haven't been very honest with you," she began nervously.

"I know," replied Hannah.

"About Joseph," she continued.

"About Joseph," Hannah repeated.

Turning sideways to face her, Layla rushed to explain. "I didn't tell anyone that something had happened between Joseph and me, not another living soul, I promise. I thought I was still in love with Alex, that I'd made a huge mistake. I reasoned if I kept quiet about it, it would go away. And then later, I didn't tell you because of what you had told me. I didn't want to hurt you. You seemed so hurt already."

"What hurt is that you didn't confide in me, even when I asked you to. Even when I said if it was to do with Joe, it didn't matter, that I would listen, I'd be there for you. But you shut me out totally."

"I know, Hannah. I was wrong. I wanted to tell you, I really did. I'm so sorry."

Hannah kicked at the grass for a moment. "Okay, apology accepted. But on one condition: you tell me everything that's happened between you and him." In a much smaller voice, she added, "I need to know."

Forcing herself to look Hannah in the eyes, Layla did as she was asked, including the night she and Joseph had fallen into bed together, deliberately glossing over how incredible it had been. She told her how their kiss the night of the storm had made her finally face up to the fact that she did have feelings for Joseph. Serious feelings, feelings that rivaled Alex, maybe even surpassed them, feelings she felt he may have reciprocated if she hadn't placed a stick of dynamite between them again. She explained why the kiss with Mick was not a real kiss, despite what it looked like, and how Joseph had taken it entirely the wrong way. And then she revealed her icing on the cake: that she had betrayed Hannah's confidence and told Joseph she knew about them, that Hannah still loved him over and above Jim, and that whilst she was saying this, Jim had been there, listening.

"I had no idea he was there, Hannah, I swear. I'm so sorry."

"Oh, Christ," exclaimed Hannah, her eyes wide as saucers. "That's why Jim's been a bit distant lately. It makes sense now."

"I'm so sorry," said Layla again, staring at Hannah's stricken face. "About everything. I should never have come to Trecastle. I should have stayed well away. I've caused nothing but trouble since I've been here."

"No," cried Hannah, grabbing her hands. "It's been wonderful having you here. We dreamed of this, remember? When we were kids. Being together. Nothing and no one can come between us. And, okay, it's had its ups and downs, but we can smooth things out. We can make it work."

"No, Hannah, I'm leaving. I was always leaving, to be fair. This was never a permanent option for me. Although I have to admit, it does feel strange going back to Brighton. As though I've outgrown it somehow. It doesn't feel like home anymore. But that's just a temporary blip, I'm sure."

"You don't have to go." Hannah was fervent. "When Lenny returns, you can crash with us. There's bound to be somewhere you can rent after a while. Despite everything, I can't imagine life without you now. I don't want to."

Looking into her friend's eyes and seeing the earnestness there, Layla couldn't believe how generous she was being, how forgiving. "But, Hannah, what about Joseph? What about Jim?" *What about Alex?*

"Leave Jim to me. I know we have to deal with how I feel. Something has to happen, one way or another. As for Joe, if you choose him over Alex, you have my blessing. I'd be happy for you."

"Hannah," said Layla, shaking her head, "have you not listened to everything I've told you? I can't choose Joseph over Alex. He doesn't want me. He's made that abundantly clear."

"He does want you."

"He doesn't."

"Yes, Layla, he does."

"How come you're so sure?" Layla said at last, curiosity getting the better of her.

"It's the way he looks at you."

"What way? I don't understand."

"Well, you know the way Jim looks at me?"

"Yeah," said Layla, still confused.

"That's the way Joe looks at you, and that, Layla, is the look of love."

"Love?" spluttered Layla.

"Love," insisted Hannah.

"Oh, Hannah, I don't know—"

"But I do. I've known from the minute I first introduced you, in the pub, after you knocked him off his bike, remember?"

"Oh, yeah, that was awful." Layla managed a shaky laugh.

"And from that moment onward, he was different. He was happier than he'd been in a long while. Always talking about you, in awe of you. And then he changed. It must have been after your night together. He wasn't so happy then. Now he's like a bear with a sore head. You *have* to talk to him, Layla. You can't leave here without at least doing that."

"But what about you?" Layla whispered, knowing Hannah was right: *find some resolution, whatever that may be,* to quote her mother.

"Me? Well, I need to learn to let go."

"If only it were that easy," said Layla, knowing it was anything but.

"But I have to find a way. Rid myself of these feelings. I don't want them," said Hannah, her voice cracking slightly. "I really don't. They... useless."

"I wish I could help," sighed Layla earnestly.

The women lapsed into silence. A few minutes passed before Hannah jumped up, grabbed hold of Layla's hand, and pulled her up too. "I know," she said excitedly, her hazel eyes flashing, "I know what to do."

"Really?" asked Layla, taken aback by her friend's sudden positivity.

"A Letting Go Ceremony," Hannah replied triumphantly.

"A Letting what?"

"It's simple." Hannah rushed to explain. "I'm going to bring all my feelings for Joe to the surface, and I'm going to throw them away, into the ocean, watch them float into oblivion. Afterward, I'll be as free as a bird, free to love Jim the way he deserves to be loved."

"I still don't understand," said Layla. Hannah was a bit alternative at times, but this sounded bizarre, even by her standards.

"Shame we haven't got any incense. Frankincense is good for cleansing, or candles," muttered Hannah, but more to herself than Layla. "Just to set the atmosphere, that sort of thing. Never mind, we'll make do with what we have."

"We have one bottle of water between us," offered Layla, thoroughly bemused.

"No, no, forget the water. Look, let's hold hands. We need to form a circle."

Before doing so, she led Layla closer to the cliff edge. For one brief and surreal moment, Layla wondered if Hannah was going to hurl them both over the edge. She could picture it: the two of them clinging together in midair, a sort of if-I-can't-have-him-no-one-will! moment. Relief flooded through her when Hannah stopped at a respectable distance and turned to face her, arms outstretched. Closing her eyes, she took a few deep breaths and began chanting. Layla, too, closed her eyes but couldn't resist peeking every now and then. Silently, she gave thanks it wasn't high summer, when these hills would have been packed with ramblers and holiday-makers able to observe their strange antics. The "men in white" would have been called for sure.

"I, Hannah McKenzie, bring forth all my feelings for Joseph Scott and discard them. Let the ocean and the air take them. Set me free."

She repeated this mantra over and over again, her face a perfect mask of concentration. As Layla peeked again, she found herself increasingly moved by these words, and after a while, began rooting for the ocean and the air to comply, to magically relieve her friend of the burden she carried.

As last Hannah fell silent. Letting go of Layla's hands, she wrapped her arms around herself as though holding something precious. After a few moments, she turned to face the ocean and then threw her arms dramatically out, casting her emotions to the elements, Layla presumed. She found herself not daring to even breathe whilst Hannah was doing this, not wanting to disturb in any way such a monumental moment.

Finally, Hannah opened her eyes and turned back to face Layla.

"Well...?" prompted Layla.

"No," replied Hannah with a shake of her head. "It hasn't worked. That New Age shit never does."

A burst of laughter escaping her, Layla was relieved to see Hannah grinning too.

"Come on," said Layla as their laughter subsided. "Let's go."

Linking arms, they walked back to the village, in silence again, but not awkward this time, companionable.

Back at the flat, Hannah asked her if she'd like to come in for lunch.

"No, thanks. I'd better see how Penny's doing."

"Penny?" said Hannah in surprise. "I didn't know she was here."

"Oh, sorry, what with everything else, I completely forgot to mention it. Yeah, she turned up yesterday. Quite distraught, actually. She's had a major row with Richard."

"Blimey, we're all in a mess, aren't we? All three of us."

"You could say that." Layla smiled weakly.

"Never mind. At least we can forget our woes at Mick's party tonight."

"Mick's party? Is that tonight?"

"Yeah. God, Layla where you have been? Oh, in hiding, of course." A cheeky smile lit Hannah's face. "Yeah, it's tonight. You are coming, aren't you? It is his thirtieth."

"Erm, yeah, yeah, of course," replied Layla. *How can I not?*

"Good. We kick off at the pub at eight. The guys' band will be playing a short set, and then it's off to Mick's house to revel into the early hours."

"See you at the pub at eight, then? You're not working, I take it?"

"No, Tom is. See you then."

After hugging Hannah once more, Layla made her way home. Mick's party—her final swan song in many ways. She would go, do her best to enjoy herself with the people who had come to mean so much to her over the last year. It would give her an excuse to collar Joseph, too, to apologize to him for everything, for almost killing him when they first met, for sleeping with him and then tossing him aside, for complicating his "simple" life. She wondered what his reaction would be to her words, whether he would sweep her up in his arms and declare undying love. But she didn't think so. Hannah's talk of him being in love with her...Well, that was just conjecture; it wasn't necessarily true. Recalling how he had last looked at her, she didn't think it was true at all.

After she had made her peace, she would go back to the cottage, re-pack her bags and leave, dragging a no-doubt reluctant Penny back to Brighton to face Richard, offering to stand by her side for support if need be. After she'd done that, she might not stay. She might leave again. She didn't know where she'd go, but she had no ties, not cast-in-stone ties anyway. She could go anywhere.

chapter thirty

"So how did you get on with Joseph? Enjoy yourself?" Layla asked Penny as she made herself a sandwich, hoping her inquiry had a really-not-that-bothered-to-be-honest-just-thought-I'd-ask ring to it.

"Yeah, it was good, thanks. Very interesting," said Penny, throwing herself on the sofa.

"What was interesting?" She couldn't resist pressing further. "The male perspective, I take it."

"Yeah, that and other things," said Penny, a touch too enigmatically for Layla's liking.

"What other things?"

"Just things. I can't remember word for word." Penny made a great show of yawning.

"But you must be able to remember something," said Layla, her exasperation building. "Or are you being deliberately obtuse?"

"No," said Penny, indignant now. "Like I said, it was interesting. We talked a lot. He told me things." She quickly added, "Relevant to the male perspective, of course."

Feeling really quite irked, Layla said, "Come on, then. Name one of those marvelous insights you were given today. An insight that I, as a mere member of the female race, am obviously incapable of giving you."

"Oh, Layla, don't get so narky," Penny appeased. "In a nutshell, he said I needed to go back to Brighton, face up to Richard, and salvage what's left of our marriage." And then leaning forward in a conspiratorial manner, she continued, "It's sweet, really. He also said love is too precious to throw away. If you have it, do what you can to hold onto it."

"That *is* sweet, isn't it?" Layla sighed as she sank down onto the sofa too. "Although nothing I haven't told you myself," she said more sternly.

"Yeah, yeah, I know. It's just novel to hear a man say it, that's all."

Changing the subject entirely, Layla said, "It's Mick's thirtieth birthday party tonight. I'll understand if you don't want to go, but I should really show my face, that sort of thing. I doubt whether I'll stay long."

"Oh, and I'm supposed to sit around moping whilst you're having fun, am I? I don't think so. Of course, I'm coming! I know about the party, anyway. Joe mentioned it."

Bully for him, thought Layla tetchily. "Okay, okay. I just didn't think you'd be in the mood for a party, that's all."

"Always in the mood for a party, me," said Penny defiantly before relaxing again.

"But tomorrow or, at the very latest the day after, we're going back to Brighton. To sort the boys out, as well as us."

"If you say so," replied Penny, an unfathomable smile on her face. The girls spent what was left of the day lolling about, flicking through magazines, channel hopping, and deciding what to wear that evening, which took all of about two minutes as all they had between them were Layla's clothes to choose from.

"Jeans then, I suppose," muttered Penny through gritted teeth, "and a T-shirt."

"At least you'll look like one of us this time, not some refugee from a second rate girl group," said Layla with a grin.

As Penny hogged the bathroom yet again, Layla sat and pondered. So she'd be back in Brighton, sooner rather than later. Where would she stay? Crashing with Penny was out of the question, not all the while she and Richard were at loggerheads; it wouldn't be fair. And although she had some money in the bank, it wasn't enough to cover the deposit for a flat. That left Alex. She would have to stay with Alex. And once she'd moved in with him, would she ever move out? Would it just be easier to stay?

Probably, she thought miserably. *Probably.*

chapter thirty-one

The Trecastle Inn was heaving. Layla had never seen it so packed. Nonetheless, she and Penny managed to push their way through copious crowds to the bar, the music from the jukebox completely drowned out by the cacophonous sound of chatter and laughter. All the while, Layla searched for Joseph, but he was nowhere to be seen. It would be impossible to talk to him in this environment anyway. She'd spend her whole time shouting at him, something she hoped to avoid doing this time.

"Layla!" Mick said, coming up behind her and spinning her round. "Glad you could make it."

"Hey, Mick, happy birthday," she yelled back, hugging him tight.

"And, Penny," he continued. "You look stunning. A bit like that actress, what's her name…?"

"Yeah, yeah, Scarlett Johansson," said Penny, obviously sick and tired of the comparison.

"Anyway, glad you could make it. Jim and his band will be on soon. They're just in the back warming up."

"Where's Hannah?" shouted Layla.

"She's around somewhere. Oh, look, it's Kevin — hey, Kevin! — I've got to go. Catch you later," he said before ambling off.

Layla retrieved her purse from her back pocket and dug out a ten pound note. Noticing Penny looking around in keen anticipation, she asked, "What's the matter?"

"Oh, nothing," replied Penny airily. "Just wondering where Joe is."

Amazed at how downright obvious Penny could be sometimes, Layla turned back to the bar, waving her ten pound note at Tom.

Whilst he fetched their drinks, Layla scanned the room again as furtively as she could. She was getting impatient, however, and feared she looked just as obvious as Penny in trying to locate her quarry. Tom was just handing her back her change when the crowd at the other end of the bar parted. Through the gap, she spotted him. In a white linen shirt and black jeans, talking to, of all people, Clare.

"You okay?" Penny asked. "You've gone all funny."

"I'm fine, fine." Layla turned round to face Penny, hoping to effectively block her view. Far from feeling fine, she felt incredibly faint, overwhelmed by what she had just seen as well as the noise and the heat that so many bodies in close proximity could produce.

What was he doing talking to Clare? Had they made up, got back together again? They certainly looked cozy, Clare staring adoringly into his blue eyes, him laughing at whatever gem happened to be falling out of her mouth.

Where was Hannah? Layla had to find her; maybe Hannah could enlighten her as to what was going on.

Leaving their drinks behind, she said, "Come on, Penny. Follow me."

Layla threw herself back into the crowd. She saw Hannah standing to the left of the entrance, talking to Hilda from May's.

"Hey, Hannah, over here," said Layla, waving frantically.

Hannah looked as if she'd been rescued from the jaws of death. She made her excuses and hurried over. "Oh, thank God. I love Hilda to death, but all she talks about is her husband's lumbago. I feel like I've had a medical lesson, which is all very well, but in the middle of a party?"

"Never mind that," said Layla, trying to be as discreet as possible. "At the bar. Joseph. He's talking to Clare."

"Who's Clare?" shouted Penny before her attention was captured by Jim, Curtis, and Ryan, shuffling onto a makeshift stage.

A raucous cheer accompanied their arrival, and everybody clapped. Then there was silence, almost as deafening as the noise had been, everyone waiting eagerly for the band to start.

"He's really cute, your Jim," Penny had time to whisper to Hannah before the first strum of guitar, followed swiftly by the beating of drums, and then finally, Jim's low and gravelly voice.

Everyone was enraptured, everyone except Layla. All she could think about was Clare and Joseph. As the band continued to play, she couldn't resist looking behind her, her eyes desperately seeking him out. And there he stood, a few rows back, side by side with Clare, looking straight back at her. There was no steel in his eyes this time as he held her gaze, just sadness. If Hannah was right, she had caused that sadness. If it were true, it counted as the single worst thing she had ever done, to hurt someone like that. Desperately she wanted to leave the crowd behind, to drag him somewhere quiet—to talk to him, touch him, kiss him. To atone somehow for what she had done.

Another cheer went up, and he looked away, clapping like everybody else around him. She clapped too, but inside she felt as though she were dying, one cell at a time. What she wanted she clearly couldn't have.

After a couple more songs including a rendition of The Waterboys' "Fisherman's Blues," a personal favorite of Mick's, Jim stopped singing and spoke into the microphone instead. "This one you haven't heard before. It's a new song I've been working on for some time now, trying to get it just right. It's called 'Angel's Heart,' and it's for Hannah McKenzie, the most perfect girl in the world."

Hannah's hand flew up to her chest at his words. She looked shocked to the core. Penny, too, looked emotional. As for Layla, she felt that cell degeneration going into overdrive as he sang out about the girl with the angel's heart, the girl he would love until the day he died. It was sung with so much strength, so much feeling, she thought it would probably haunt her forever.

Oh, to be loved like that, she thought, her own eyes blurring. She put an arm round Hannah, and Hannah leaned into her, tears running freely down her face. Penny, too, came closer, gripping them both.

The song marked the end of their set, the crowd cheering wildly again before yelling their disapproval as the band exited the stage. There was a sudden mass realization of empty glasses, however, and the crowd calmed considerably and moved to the bar for refills. Laughter and chatter filled the air once more as did the tinny sound of the heroic little jukebox, rocking valiantly away despite the fact it was being steadfastly ignored.

"You had no idea he had written a song for you, did you, Hannah?" Layla asked, smiling gently at her.

"None at all," Hannah sighed dreamily. A moment later, horror marked her features instead. "Oh, no, what have I done?"

"Sorry?" Layla was taken aback by her friend's sudden alarm.

"Quick, outside," shouted Hannah.

Layla elbowed her way to the entrance, Penny once more following behind. Before she left the pub, she chanced another glance at Joseph. Not only was he still talking to Clare, but a couple of her friends too, who, like her, looked to be about twenty, giggling like the schoolgirls they so recently were.

Although she was fuming, Layla was glad to be outside, glad to be removed from Joseph and his oh-so-young admirers, for the cold night air that blasted her and for the more subdued level of noise.

"Is Joseph back with Clare or something?" she asked before remembering it was Hannah who wanted to speak. "Oh, sorry, Hannah, you were about to say…?"

Clearly agitated, Hannah said, "I'm not sure, but I think I've given Jim the wrong impression."

"What impression? What do you mean?"

"Earlier this evening, just as he was about to leave for rehearsals, I told him things have got to change around here, that we can't go on the way we have been."

"And?" said Layla, thinking that actually sounded quite reasonable.

"When I said that, he looked, I don't know, forlorn somehow, and before I had a chance to elaborate, he rushed out of the door, mumbling he'd be late for rehearsals if he didn't go straight away. I haven't spoken to him since. The thing is, I meant *I've* got to change, not him. I've got to stop living in the past. I think he thought I might be leaving."

"Leaving? After he's written you that song?" said Penny, not helping the situation at all.

"Penny, shush," hissed Layla.

"I didn't know he'd written me that song," Hannah burst out. "He never let on. No one's ever written me a song before, not even so much as a poem. It was…incredible."

"It was," agreed Layla. "It was beautiful."

Sniffing, Hannah continued, "And that's what I wanted to tell him, before he rushed off. That I'm letting Joe go. That I have a choice, and I've chosen to love the one I'm with, absolutely and completely. And you know what?" she said, gripping Layla by the shoulders so hard it hurt. "After that song, I think it's true. It's actually bloody true. I do love Jim absolutely and completely. I realize that now. I would never leave him."

"Oh, Hannah!" Layla hugged her close. "I'm so glad to hear it."

"Me, too." Hannah was sobbing again. "Me, too."

Extracting herself from Hannah, Layla said, "Well, don't just stand there. Go back in. Tell the poor guy. Put him out of his misery."

"I will," said Hannah, turning to go. Just as she was about to disappear, however, she stopped and turned to face Layla once again. "That song *was* beautiful, wasn't it?" she said, a huge grin on her face.

"It was like you. Perfect," said Layla. "Now go! Go and find him. Tell him what you've just told me."

As soon as Hannah was out of earshot, Penny turned to Layla. "What's all that about Hannah being in love with Joe? Boy, he gets around, doesn't he?"

Layla was stopped from asking her what she meant when Penny started speaking again. "Look, who's that in the distance, walking toward us?"

Straining her eyes to see, Layla could just about make out two figures: one tall and slim, the other not quite so tall and not quite so slim.

"The tall one looks like Richard, funnily enough," said Layla without thinking, and then realization dawned. "Oh, God, it is Richard."

"And who's that with him?" said Penny, her voice barely audible.

"Alex," whispered Layla, feeling for the second time tonight like she was about to faint clean away.

chapter thirty-two

Penny only had to look at Layla to see she was as stunned by Alex's sudden appearance as Penny was by Richard's.

Unlike Layla, she managed to recover enough to find her voice. "Richard, what are you doing here?"

"I've come to see you, of course," he replied. "What do you think I'm doing here?"

"But how did you know where to find me?" she asked again.

"Layla texted me to say you were safe. At least somebody had the decency to," he said pointedly. "I was at your mother's in Slough at the time. I thought you'd gone there."

"And Alex? What are you doing with Alex?"

"What is this, twenty questions or something? He arrived at Layla's cottage the same time as me, looking for her. Neither of you were in, so we came here instead. Alex thought you'd be at the pub, and he was right. You and everyone else by the looks of it."

Before she could quiz him further, Richard said, "Look, Penny, can we go somewhere that's a bit more private, please? We need to talk."

Turning to Layla, she said, "Is that okay, Layla? Or do you want me to stay?"

"No." Layla shook her head. "Go. We'll be fine. We need to talk to."

"Okay," said Penny, briefly rubbing her friend's arm. "I'll see you soon."

To Richard she said, "Come on. This way, down to the beach."

What should have been no more than a six or seven minute walk took her around three as she marched off ahead of him. When she was sure they had complete privacy, she turned round to face him. "So, have you come down here to file divorce papers or something? Want to hand them to me personally, is that it? Rub salt into the wound."

"No," replied Richard, appalled. "I've come to say you don't have to worry anymore. That jerk, Dylan, he won't be bothering you again. I've sorted him."

"What?" she cried as her hand flew to her mouth. This was the very last thing she expected to hear. That Richard had "sorted Dylan."

"Yeah, that's where I went, to find him. No man calls my wife a prick-tease and gets away with it."

Even more stunned, she said, "How did you find him?"

"I looked him up, back at the office. I Googled him. Turns out he's got a police record."

"How did you know his surname?"

"You said it, remember? 'Dylan Goodridge,' you said. 'What do you want?'"

Did she? Then she remembered she'd shouted his name in anger when he'd showed up at their house.

"It took a bit of digging, but I tracked him down in the end. Turned up on his doorstep. All the way over in Kemp Town, he lives. Mount Pleasant, a misnomer if ever there was one. That street's about as unpleasant as it gets. Wasn't so brave when the tables were turned, I can tell you. He looked like a frightened rabbit."

"Frightened? But he's done time for assault."

"You knew?"

Penny hung her name sheepishly. "I did know he'd done time, yes, but I didn't know what for. He only told me *that* recently."

"Did you know it was against a girl? No, I don't think so. You need to choose your flirting partners a bit more carefully in future, I think."

She was about to bite at that comment when she realized he was smiling. What was there to smile about?

"I told him I'm a hotshot lawyer. I said that if he set foot within one mile of you ever again, I'd throw the book at him. Get him sent down for harassment. Four years this time instead of two, it being a repeat offence and all that. I don't know what happened to him in prison, but I get the distinct impression he doesn't want to go there again."

"What did he say?" she gasped, wishing she had a chair she could sink down onto, her legs felt so flimsy.

"He stuttered, he spluttered, and eventually he said he'd leave well alone. He was practically crying by this time."

"Oh, Richard," she breathed at last. *My hero.*

"Especially when I threatened to thump him." He laughed again.

"I had no idea," she said, her voice catching in her throat. "I thought it was the end. That you didn't believe me."

"Of course I believed you. You're my wife; he's a scumbag. Do the maths."

Laughing too, she said, "You know something, Richard Hughes? I love you."

"And I love you, Penny Hughes, to distraction. Always have done, always will do, even if you are an outrageous flirt."

"I'll change. I won't flirt anymore, I promise."

"It's not you that needs to change. It's me. I know I drove you into Dylan's arms in the first place, because I was never around, because I was always at work. I just couldn't admit it at first. I was more angry with myself than with you."

"It's okay——" started Penny, but Richard hadn't finished speaking.

"No, I want to explain why I work the way I do. It's because I want things to be different for us. I don't want the life my mother had, scratching around for pennies, what little she did have being drunk by my father. That's what killed her in the end: money worries and his drinking, I'm sure of it. And, no, don't worry; I'm not angry with Dad anymore. He's a frail and lonely old man now with health problems. I feel sorry for him more than anything else. I wanted to give you everything, and working hard was the only way I knew how to do that."

"You're all I want." She stepped closer to him. "We could live in a shack for all I care, foraging about in the woods for food. As long as I've got you, I'm happy."

"I'm not sure about the foraging bit. I hate mushrooms," he said, bridging the gap between them. "But I promise to compromise, work hard, live well, but most importantly, spend plenty of time with you."

"Good." Penny wrapped her arms around him. "Because the last thing I want to do is bring up this baby on my own."

"Bring up what?" Richard looked startled now.

"The baby," said Penny, savoring the moment. "I'm pregnant."

"You're…oh, my God!" Richard picked her up and swung her round. "Oh, sorry, I shouldn't have done that. I haven't done any harm, have I?"

"Of course not, silly," she said, swiping at him. "I haven't suddenly turned into a Ming vase, you know, just because I'm with child."

"You're more precious than any Ming vase," he replied. "How long? The pregnancy, I mean."

"I've only just found out, so two weeks, maybe three at most. I'll need to get it confirmed. Layla doesn't know yet. I wanted you to be the first, the baby's daddy."

"Daddy," he repeated as though the word held some magical, mystical quality. "And you'll be Mummy."

"We'll be a family." She smiled. "A proper family, our kids growing up with happy memories, not painful ones."

"I love you," he whispered again, pulling her close to him.

"I know you do," she said, and she kissed him hard on the lips.

The moon enfolding them in its warm glow, it seemed like an eternity before she was able to pull herself away.

When she did, she said, "Layla. We'll tell Layla next." Puckering up for another kiss, realization suddenly hit her. "Oh, God, Layla!" she cried out in alarm. "I have to tell her."

"All in good time," murmured Richard, clearly intent on more lip action.

"No," said Penny, hurriedly extricating herself from him. "I don't mean about the baby, about Joe. About what he said to me earlier today on the headland. He wants to tell her himself, said it's only right that he should, but he's leaving it too late. She needs to know now. Before she commits herself to Alex, before she makes the biggest mistake of her life." Not bothering to explain any further, she grabbed hold of Richard's hand and, running as fast as she dared given her new circumstances, they made their way back to the pub.

chapter thirty-three

Alex, the last person she had expected to see, was standing before her. Okay, in truth, he was the last person she had *wanted* to see. Not now, not when she only had a day or so left. He didn't belong here.

"Babe, why haven't you replied to my texts? Answered my calls?"

His use of the word *babe*, a term of endearment he tended to favor, made her shudder. Normally, she didn't mind it, but instead of affectionate, it sounded creepy to her ears somehow, unpleasant.

"I've been busy, that's all," she said, trying not to snap. "Come on, let's go."

"Go where?" he asked, trailing behind her.

"To the pub."

In the pub she wouldn't have to talk to him, not in earnest anyway. It would give her time to think, decide what she was going to do next.

She led him round the fringes of the interior where the crowds were at their thinnest until they reached the bar, the opposite side of the bar to where Joseph stood talking to a much bigger group of people this time, although Clare and her giggly friends were still a part of it.

Joseph hadn't spotted them yet, but he would. It was just a matter of time. What he would make of them when he did, she didn't know. Then again she didn't know what to make of him and Clare, so they had that in common, at least. Briefly she looked around for Hannah and Jim, wondering if Hannah had put him straight about all this leaving business, but it was no good; she could barely see past the people in front of her.

Before she could order another drink, Alex grabbed her by the elbow, forcing her to turn round and look at him. "What do you mean you've been busy? That's no excuse."

"It is," she shot back. "My mother showed up unexpectedly and then Penny. I've barely had a moment to breathe."

"I've been worried," he said, and there was indeed genuine concern in his eyes. "I thought something might have happened to you. That's why I'm here. To make sure you're okay."

"Yes, of course, I understand that," she said, feeling suitably contrite. "I'm sorry. I've been thoughtless."

"Well, no worries." He seemed only slightly appeased. "You're alive and well, that's what matters. I've missed you, Layla. Have you missed me?"

She was saved from answering as a sudden cry went up from Mick to leave the pub and head back to his. Quickly, everyone surged forward, eager to continue into the night. Terrified she'd be left in an empty bar with just Alex for company, she said, "Come on, let's go."

Although clearly reluctant, he duly followed, both of them tagging onto the back of the crowd. Joseph, it seemed, had already left.

"How far is Mick's house?" said Alex shuffling forward. "I'm not up for a big walk, you know."

"Not far. Just up the road, that's all."

Mick's was, in fact, a rather substantial fifteen minute walk from the pub. He lived in a rustic two-up, two-down stone-walled cottage further along the headland. Although the cottage was small, he had a huge garden, and she knew there'd be fire pits dotted around so people could enjoy the outdoors despite the early winter cold.

As they walked, Layla wondered if Alex could sense the awkwardness between them just as much as she could or whether it existed mainly in her head. At one point, he reached out to grab her hand. She considered taking it back, but she didn't feel up to battling with him about it. Instead, she bit down hard on the distaste that rose up in her.

As they reached Mick's cottage, Alex was still grumbling. "How long do we have to stay?" he asked tetchily.

"Not long. I need to clear up a couple of matters before we head off." *Matters like Joseph and whether all's okay with Hannah and Jim.*

"I'm tired, Layla." He let out a heavy sigh. "I've driven for hours. A full-on party wasn't quite what I expected when I got here."

What were you expecting? That I'd jump into bed with you? It took only a moment for her to answer herself. *Probably.*

The inside of Mick's cottage was almost as busy as the pub had been, people grabbing beers from the kitchen and drifting outside, toward the fire pits. Where was Hannah? She hadn't seen her since their talk earlier. Was she at home with Jim, putting into action how much she appreciated his song? Strange, though, she'd been adamant earlier in the day that Layla should come to Mick's party, so apart from a brief appearance at the pub, why wasn't she here, too? He was one of their closest friends. She also wondered how things were working out with Penny and Richard. Well, she hoped, knowing she'd find out soon enough.

And then there was Joseph. How the hell was she going to sort out the mess she'd made with him whilst Alex was surgically attached to her? It could wait, she supposed, until tomorrow when she could sneak away somehow. But she didn't want to wait, not anymore. She wanted to know, right now, if there was any truth in what Hannah had said.

Unable to spot Joseph anywhere in the immediate vicinity, she felt panic beginning to build. Perhaps he'd disappeared with Clare, too. Hannah with Jim, Penny with Richard, Joseph with Clare, which left her with...Alex. She groaned as she scanned the room once more, but there was no sight of Joseph at all. No hint of dark blond hair. She wondered if she should push through to the living room, rush outside maybe, holler his name, anything to find him, but decided at the last moment not to. That look in the pub he had given her, that pain-filled, sad, and intense look. Maybe that had been a goodbye look, a look that said *I'm sorry we didn't work out, but we didn't, end of.*

She hated to admit it, but it kind of made sense.

"Layla, please, at least come outside. I can't hear myself think in here. It's deafening."

It was Alex again, the one who wanted her, not Joseph, despite what she'd been told. Alex who could give her the world, and all she had to do was take it from him. No worries about where she might live, what job she would manage to land herself, whether she'd ever get married and have children. A world that was planned for her, every step of the way.

Finally she said, "Okay, okay, let's go. No point in staying."

"Thank God for that," said Alex, clearly relieved. "What kind of music are they playing in there anyway? It's rubbish."

Stop it! Stop it! she wanted to shout, fed up to the back teeth with his moaning. *You sound like an old man.* He looked older, too, something she had noticed last time he was in Trecastle and noticed even more so now. Could it be that Penny was right? Was he older than forty-three, after all?

"Alex," she said tiredly, once they were out on the street again, "what is it you want? I mean, really want from me?"

"You know what I want. I've already told you." A smile lit up his face, making him look younger again.

"No, spell it out. I want to hear exactly," she insisted. *Just like I made you spell out that you loved me once upon a time.*

"I want marriage, children, the whole works. And to prove it…" He paused for a moment to rummage round in his pocket.

Oh, no, not that damn bracelet, she thought. *Not again.*

It wasn't that damn bracelet. It was a ring, a diamond ring—a rock of a ring, in fact—sitting snugly in a ring box, cushioned by golden pillows, glinting at her, as merrily or as malevolently as the bracelet once had.

"There, what do you think of that?" he said triumphantly, clearly mistaking the look on her face for one of wonder. "Impressive, huh?"

"Oh, Alex," she breathed, about to continue when Penny appeared, hand in hand with Richard.

"Stop right there, Layla Lewis," yelled Penny. "Don't you utter another damn word."

"Penny?" said Layla whilst Alex stared in astonishment.

Finding his voice finally, Alex cleared his throat and said, "Do you mind? We're trying to have a private moment."

"A private moment?" spat Penny. "A private moment? You can stuff your private moment."

Taken aback, he was about to remonstrate again when Layla said, "No, Alex, let her speak. I want to hear what she has to say."

She turned toward Penny. "Go on, then. Why shouldn't I utter one more damn word?"

"Because you're making a huge mistake, that's why. I know you think you love him, Layla. You think you need him, but you don't. He's a serial cheater. He'll never change."

Outraged, Alex squared up to Penny. "I most certainly am not," he said. "It was only the once, and I had my reasons for it. Layla and I have forgotten all about it. We're trying to move on."

"Alex," said Layla, angry at his assumption, "I haven't forgotten all about Sarah-Jane actually. Far from it. She comes to mind more and more lately. How you had your way with her, changed your mind, wanted me back, so sacked her as if she were a piece of rubbish you could just discard. I also know about Jack's secretary. He told me everything."

"Jack's secretary?" He looked at Layla, the color draining from his face. "Nothing went on with his secretary. He's lying."

"She almost resigned because of you, because of your constant pestering. I gather she was fresh from college too. A young girl, probably not even twenty, which makes it even more intolerable."

"And then there's me," Penny piped up. She moved closer to Layla so she could speak exclusively to her. "He made a pass at me, when you were going out with him, one night in a pub, when you had gone to the bar. I didn't tell you at first because you seemed so happy to be with him. I didn't want to be the one to ruin things. I didn't tell you afterward because you were hurt enough already. Perhaps if I had told you straightaway, I'd have saved you a lot of heartache. I'm sorry, Layla."

"A hat trick, then," said Layla, as she turned from Penny to Alex again.

"But that was in the past, Layla," he declared, his face bright red with indignation. "I've changed, I told you. Since you agreed to marry me, I've been as pure as the driven snow. Haven't even so much as looked at another woman."

"I haven't agreed to marry you," Layla said firmly. "I said *maybe*."

"You said *maybe yes*."

Tilting her head to one side, Layla looked as though she were pondering what she had said. All the while Alex stood hopefully.

"I did say that," she agreed eventually.

"Layla," Penny warned, "don't go any further, not until you hear what else I have to say."

"It's okay, Penny." Layla smiled at her. "Don't worry."

She walked up to Alex, still holding the boxed ring in his out-stretched hand, ever confident. She stared into his deep brown eyes, eyes that looked a little lost at the moment, eyes that had fooled her so much in the past, and said, "I'm sorry, Alex. I can't marry you. It's not a maybe yes, after all. It's a definitely no."

"Halle-bloody-lujah," Penny whispered from behind her.

Layla's body, tense before, relaxed with relief. It was over. At last she had said goodbye to dreams that were only ever, at best, smoky. She had known it was over as soon as she had set eyes on him tonight and all she had felt was dismay. It had actually been over a long time before that, from the moment she had looked into Joseph's eyes on that cold and rainy day, as he lay in the road looking up at her, drinking her in despite the fact she'd very nearly killed him. Her mother was right: being honest with herself felt good. She could get used to it.

"Come on, Layla." Penny put her arm round her, intending to lead her away. "There's something else you need to know. I've been sworn to secrecy, but these are outstanding circumstances."

Puzzled, Layla was about to follow her lead when a wild-eyed Hannah appeared out of nowhere. Hot on her heels was Joseph, who stopped abruptly at the scene before him, his face distinctly clouding at the sight of Alex and the diamond ring.

"Jim!" yelled Hannah. "Have you seen Jim?"

And suddenly nothing mattered but finding Jim.

chapter thirty-four

"Hannah, Hannah, calm down," Layla said as she gripped her friend hard by the shoulders. "Look at me. When did you last see Jim?"

"On stage, just like you did," Hannah managed between sobs. "We went outside afterward, remember? I told you what I'd said to him…"

"Yeah, I remember. Go on."

"After we spoke, I went back in to find him, but he'd gone. Curtis and Ryan hadn't even noticed. I looked everywhere—in the pub, outside, back at the flat, at Mick's, but there's no trace of him. I bumped into Joe, and we've been looking ever since. I don't know what to do…"

"Perhaps he's just gone for a walk. It's a lovely night," ventured Penny, trying to sound comforting but failing dismally.

"No. He hasn't *just* gone for a walk," Hannah insisted. "Something's happened, I know it. I can sense it." She turned toward Layla. "Looks like he got the wrong impression after all."

"Okay," said Layla, struggling to remain pragmatic, "is his car still at home or has he taken it?"

"It's still there," Joseph said, his strong, steady voice, sending a shiver through Layla.

This is not the time, she admonished herself.

"He hasn't gone far, then. What about the beach? Have you searched the beach?"

"Yeah, of course we've searched the beach," said Hannah. Suddenly her eyes widened with hope. "But not Shipwreck Cove!" Turning swiftly to Joseph, Hannah said, "Do you think he's gone there, to Shipwreck Cove?"

"He could well have done," replied Joseph, his face hopeful too.

"Let's go!"

Both she and Joseph made a break for it, and Layla prepared to follow them.

"Wait!" Richard bellowed, but only Layla stopped.

"It would make more sense to split up," he continued. "We'll cover more ground that way. Who's got their mobile phone?"

"Not me," said Layla.

"Hmm…mine's dead too. Okay, we'll just have to meet back at Layla's in an hour or so for an update. Penny, come with me. We'll search the main beach again. Alex, why don't you go back to the pub and stand guard there?"

"Back to the pub?" Alex laughed callously. "I don't think so. I'm going home, back to Brighton. There's nothing to stick around for now."

"Alex!" yelled Layla in disbelief. "Jim's gone missing, and we need to find him quickly. This coast can be dangerous. We need your help."

Alex shrugged his shoulders. "No cigar, I'm afraid. If you don't want me, I'm out of here. When you change your mind, though—and you will when the reality of life without me hits, when you don't have two pennies to rub together, when that pathetic wage from that pathetic bar job of yours can't even cover the winter gas bill—don't come running. I'll have moved on. Believe me, there are plenty more brood mares out there."

"What?!" Layla was shocked.

"Brood mare?" repeated Penny, looking equally stunned.

"Yeah, brood mare. That's all you ever were," Alex continued savagely. "I want a son, someone to inherit everything I've slogged my entire life to build up. I don't love you, never have done. Don't flatter yourself. You've just got half-decent genes, that's all."

Feeling as though he'd ripped her heart out a second time, not because she loved him but because she had *ever* loved such a monster, she tried to reply, but failed.

Thankfully Penny came to her rescue. "He's lying, Layla. Reacting because he's hurt. Ignore him."

Richard stepped forward as well. "I think it's best you do leave, actually," he said to Alex through gritted teeth. "Right now, in fact. This very minute, whilst both your legs are in good working order."

"Are you threatening me?" said Alex, a vision of anger, humiliation.

"It certainly sounds like it," Penny growled, "but believe me, he's only allowed one leg. I'm going to break the other one."

"Bunch of losers," Alex said, but the fire had gone out of his eyes. In a whiney voice, he continued, "Layla, *please*, let me look after you."

"I can look after myself, thanks!" she shot back.

As Alex backed away, looking quite nervous, Penny came up to Layla and put her arm around her. "Are you okay?"

"I'm fine," said Layla, feeling really very fine indeed, and with that, she was off in hot pursuit of Joseph and Hannah.

chapter thirty-five

Hannah knew Joseph had trouble keeping up with her as she flew over the muddy headland to reach Shipwreck Cove, but she was not going to slow down. She was frantic. This was the last place left to look. If Jim wasn't there, where was he? It didn't bear thinking about.

Peering down at the cove from the edge of the headland, Hannah noted with relief that the tide was out. It wouldn't stay out for long, though, and when it came in, it would do so with a vengeance, often catching even the natives by surprise with its speed and ferocity. From a distance she could hear Layla shouting, running after them, closing the gap. Not waiting for her either, Hannah began the descent, thankful the moon was bright enough to light her way.

Down on the beach, she could hear the ocean rather than see it, crunching over impacted sands until it became more visible. Spotting something in the distance, she propelled herself forward.

"It's his jacket," she yelled as Layla and Joseph drew closer, both puffing heavily, "and a beer can. He's here. He's somewhere here."

But where? As she stared at the ocean, fear engulfed her. "You don't think..." she said before rushing up to the water's edge, screaming Jim's name.

Behind her, a panicked Joseph and Layla yelled his name too.

When Layla reached her, Hannah stumbled into her arms. "He's dead! He's killed himself. I've killed him. I pushed him to breaking point."

"No, no, he would never do that," Layla replied.

Joseph continued searching, running up and down the beach, shouting frantically against the wind.

"Oh, Layla, what am I going to do? I can't live without him. I can't. He means everything to me, *everything*."

"Who means everything?" a familiar voice behind them said.

Startled, both girls swung around.

"Jim!" said Layla, amazed.

"Jim!" Hannah sobbed as she disentangled herself from Layla's arms and threw herself into his instead.

"Jim!" panted Joseph. "Thank God, you're all right, mate."

"Of course, I'm all right." He hugged Hannah close.

"But you went missing!" protested Hannah, taking a step back.

"Missing? I just fancied a bit of peace and quiet, that's all. I've got a splitting headache, have had all evening. That noise in the pub, it was doing my head in."

"You didn't let me know. I looked everywhere for you."

"I told Curtis to tell you where I was going. Didn't he say?"

"No, he flaming didn't," said Hannah furiously. "And I asked him, too. He's such a ditz, that boy, sometimes." The emotions of the past couple of hours had caught up and overwhelmed her. "Christ, Jim, I thought you'd killed yourself. When I saw your jacket and that beer can but not you, I imagined the worst."

"Killed myself? Why would I do that?" Jim was hardly able to hide his amusement at the furor his disappearance had caused.

"Because of what I said earlier, about how things have got to change around here. I thought you might think I was leaving you."

"You're not, are you?" said Jim, a sudden look of worry on his face.

"No, I'm bloody not. I love you and only you. I would never leave you."

Finally she had managed to say the words she had been dying to say all evening. As she did so, she couldn't resist throwing a quick glance at Joseph. On his face was nothing but relief—relief, she presumed, that at last, after all this time, she was able to let him go.

"That's all right, then," said Jim, capturing her full attention again. "Good job I didn't go for a swim."

Hannah laughed and threw herself back into his arms, holding him tight once more.

"That song," she whispered, "it blew me away."

"Plenty more where that came from," he whispered back, "and all inspired by you."

chapter thirty-six

Basking in the scene before her, Layla snuck a peek at Joseph. He looked happy for them too. She turned back to Hannah and Jim who were still clinging together in the moonlight; it was a few moments before she could tear her gaze away again. When she did, Joseph was looking at her.

"Joseph…" she whispered, hoping her smile conveyed exactly how she felt inside.

If she thought he might reciprocate, however, she was disappointed. He simply turned and walked away, disappearing into the distance, his white shirt the only thing marking him as different from the night. Stunned, she could only stare after him.

Hannah and Jim were too wrapped up in each other to notice her leave. Stuffing her hands into her jean pockets, her shoulders hunched against the cold, she started walking too, but at a deliberately slow pace. The last thing she wanted was to catch up with Joseph. Clearly there was nothing left to say.

As she reached the headland, she could hear music coming from Mick's cottage, the sound as jarring to her now as it had been to Alex. All she wanted was to retreat behind four walls, close the door on the world. Then she remembered Penny and Richard would be at home. Another happily reunited couple, if their joined hands had been anything to go by earlier. And although she was as glad for them as she was for Hannah and Jim, it hurt.

She was right. As she walked into the kitchen, there they were: Richard looking relaxed and content; Penny decidedly anxious.

"Layla! Thank God! We searched everywhere for Jim but couldn't find him. What's the news?"

Layla quickly put Penny out of her misery.

"Oh, that's a relief," sighed Penny.

As Layla slumped dejectedly into a chair next to Richard, Penny continued, "So how come you're not with Joe? I thought you would be."

"He's gone," she muttered. "I don't know where."

"Without saying anything?" Penny asked.

A hollow laugh escaping her, Layla replied, "What's he got to say? To me, anyway. It's Clare he wants to talk to, by the looks of things."

"Clare?" said Penny in obvious frustration. "What's Clare got to do with it?"

"Didn't you see him talking to her in the pub? They were all over each other."

Penny looked confused. "Really? Are you sure they weren't just talking?"

When Layla didn't reply, Penny got up and knelt before her. Before she could say another word, however, Richard piped up.

"Pen," he said anxiously. "Should you be kneeling like that?"

"Oh, shut up, Richard. You're going to drive me mad if you continue like this throughout."

"Throughout what?" Layla was puzzled at the sudden change of topic.

"Oh, well, erm—no point beating about the bush. I'm pregnant," said Penny with a smile. "I wanted to tell you yesterday, but I couldn't. Not until I'd told Richard. It wouldn't have been fair. But I am, just a few weeks, not even a full month, but pregnant, nonetheless."

"Oh, Penny." Layla was genuinely thrilled. "I didn't even know you were trying."

"Nor did I," Penny laughed.

"That's wonderful news," Layla continued, throwing her arms around her friend. "I'm thrilled for you." She turned her head sideways to look at Richard, adding, "For you both."

"Thanks," said Penny. She rose to sit on Richard's lap, and his hands immediately snaked round her still-trim waist. "And we can celebrate later, but you've got something to do first. Something you need to do straight away. Go and see Joseph."

Layla's face clouded. "I've told you, we have nothing more to say to each other."

Penny was adamant. "Trust me, Layla. You have."

Irritated by her insistence, by Hannah's insistence, her mother's too, she shook her head vehemently. The memory of him retreating from her, abandoning her, was vivid in her mind.

"Layla..." Penny nudged.

"No." Layla's voice was emphatic.

A look of surprise crossed Penny's face, and Layla tried to take solace in it. Sadly, however, there was no solace to be found.

"That's a bit final, isn't it?" said Penny at last.

"It is final, between me and him, anyway," replied Layla as she plopped down onto a chair.

"Ah, so you admit it, there *was* a you and him?"

Damn it! Penny was too clever for her own good sometimes.

Reluctantly, Layla replied, "Sort of. A long time ago." More determinedly, she continued, "But whatever it was, whatever we had, it was over before it even began."

"Layla, it's not."

"Yes, it is." It was Layla's turn to insist now. "Besides which, I told you, I don't know where he is."

"Next door, I should imagine. Go and check."

"Penny." Layla could feel a tide of anger rising within her. "You don't seem to get it, do you? I'm not going anywhere near him. Why the hell would I?"

"Because...because..." Penny stammered.

"Because what?"

"Because you have to!" Penny shouted back.

The ferocity in her voice astounded Layla. What was wrong with her? Were pregnancy hormones affecting her brain already? Struggling to find the reason behind her insistence, she remembered Joseph and Penny had met on the headland earlier that day. She had already quizzed her about what they had talked about. But had Penny told her everything? Was there something she was holding back? It certainly sounded like it.

"Penny, do you know something I don't?"

"I might do," Penny replied, annoyingly coy.

"About Joseph?"

Penny nodded.

"And me?"

"And you."

Lunging forward, Layla grabbed hold of her hands across the table between them.

"What is it, Penny? What did he say? You have to tell me!"

"No." Penny was surprisingly immovable. "Ask him yourself."

"Penny…" cried Layla in exasperation.

"No, Layla. Mum's the word, I'm afraid."

Unable to believe Penny could joke at a time like this, Layla tried to call her bluff. "And what if I don't? What if I just leave without saying another word?"

Penny was deadly serious again. "Then you'll be running away. How much longer are you going to keep doing that?"

Her words rendered Layla silent, stinging all the more because she knew they were right. How much longer *was* she going to run? And where to? The ends of the earth perhaps? And if something should happen to rock the boat there, what would be her next option? A seat on the first flight to Mars? Soon the entire universe wouldn't be big enough to hold her. And this something Penny knew that Layla didn't, maybe it was something good. Something worth staying for. Maybe she'd stay anyway. Trecastle felt more like home than Brighton ever did.

Pushing her chair back, she said, "Okay, I'll go and see him."

Penny stood too and beamed at her. "You won't regret it."

Praying she was right, Layla turned to go.

Before she left, however, Penny spoke again. "Remember, Layla, stand your ground."

Layla promised she would, even though the ground beneath her felt very shaky indeed.

chapter thirty-seven

Layla knocked on the door to Joseph's cottage, but there was no reply. Damn it! Just when she had summoned up the courage to face him, he had disappeared. She was about to return home, perhaps come back later, when she thought she'd try one more thing. As she turned the brass door handle, it clicked open, left unlocked as was the custom around here. A custom she had never grown used to. Perhaps she would in time, if she were staying, that is.

Should she enter? It felt strange to do so—breaking and entering. Reasoning that there was at least no breaking involved, she continued forward—the need for closure, of one kind or another, giving wings to her feet.

She was relieved to note the living room was not in complete darkness, two lamps burning steadily away. Beyond the living room lay the kitchen. The door to it was closed, but light was seeping out from under the doorframe. Further evidence Joseph was at home.

She prepared to knock again, this time on the interior door, to announce her presence. Movement from within, however, stilled her hand. Rooted to the spot, she braced herself.

"Layla!" yelled Joseph as he opened the door. "Bloody hell! You frightened the life out of me."

"Sorry," she said. She quickly peered beyond him, unable to resist checking whether Clare or one of her giggly friends had followed him home. Seeing the coast was clear, she relaxed slightly.

Staring at her in confusion, he said, "What do you want?"

"Well…to see you," she replied. *Isn't that obvious?*

He doubled back into the kitchen. "I need another drink," he muttered.

Taking a deep breath, she followed him in, watching as he went straight to the whisky bottle. He refilled his glass and downed it one, his back to her the entire time. If he had something to tell her, clearly he was in no hurry to do so.

"Joseph," she said at last, "I know you spoke to Penny, about us, and I'm sorry…"

He turned swiftly round to face her. "Don't be. I'm leaving."

The ground, so shaky before, nearly caved in altogether. Surely this wasn't what she was meant to hear!

"Penny…she…she never said."

"Penny doesn't know," he replied before snatching up a letter from the dresser. "This came this afternoon, after I got back from seeing her. Read it. It explains everything."

She took the letter from him and tried to do as he said, but, although her eyes dutifully scanned every word, her brain just wouldn't compute. The word *leaving* seemed to be shutting down her senses one by one.

Giving up, she thrust the letter back at him. "You explain. Tell me in your own words."

Running his hand through his hair, a gesture she had always found so endearing, he said, "Remember I told you when I was younger I did some work experience in Florence?"

She did remember. It was the night of the storm.

"Well, I've never lost touch with Paolo, the man who runs the workshop. We've been talking on the phone recently, and at his suggestion, I sent him some photos of the work I've been doing — not for Hill House. Private jobs. Projects, really. He loved it. This letter is a job offer."

"I see," she said, really not seeing at all. "When do you go?"

"In January," he replied quietly. "I'm leaving in January."

Layla turned her back to him to hide how devastating his news was to her. She walked over to the kitchen window and looked out. There was no view of the ocean, of Gull Rock. Although they were both out there, there was nothing but darkness, seemingly endless darkness.

"Layla," he said. "Are you okay?"

Almost toppling forward into that darkness, she pulled herself back from the brink. Okay? No, she could not be described as okay. Penny had sent her on a fool's errand.

Layla faced him again, the light in the kitchen blinding in contrast to the night. She willed herself not to say the words, not to take the shine off his "good news," but they fell out of her mouth anyway. "How can you leave? You love it here. You always say you do."

"I know." He took a step closer. "And I do love it here, but Mr. Yeates, he's a stubborn man. Clare may have forgiven me—she's hardly left me alone tonight, in fact—but he's a harder egg to crack, and I don't want to waste any more time trying."

"So it's my fault you're leaving," she said sadly.

"No, it's not," he said, shaking his head. "Even if work was heaving, I couldn't turn this down. This is my dream, Layla. It has been for years."

"And it's a lovely dream." She tried to smile. "One worth having."

"Layla," he said, making her name sound strangely like an apology.

"It's fine," she replied, backing away from him, toward the living room door. The urge to run, to escape, was making itself known again. Not next door where she'd be met with expectant faces, but down to the beach, to Gull Rock, her rock—the one constant in all of this. "It's ironic, that's all. You're leaving just when I've decided to stay."

She yanked the door open only to be surprised as it was slammed shut again, Joseph rushing up behind her and pushing against it.

"You're staying?" he said, the heat from his body searing her.

"I'm staying." She leaning her head against the wood, grateful for something solid to take her weight.

Swinging her round, his hands gripping her shoulders, he said, "Why are you staying?"

"Why do you think?" she said, shrugging him off, tired now, and yes, she had to admit it, extremely pissed off.

"I don't know, Layla. That's just it. I never do with you."

"Because of you," she almost shouted. "Because I love you."

"You love me?" he whispered, his eyes wide with surprise. "But you're marrying Alex!"

"Marrying Alex? Is that what you think, why you walked away from me?"

"I've reason enough to think it," he replied, a hint of anger in his voice, she was sure. "He was holding out a ring to you on the headland. You were about to take it."

"I was about to tell him to get lost," she quickly corrected him. "If you'd stuck around, you would have seen me come to my senses."

"You're not marrying him?"

"No, I'm not," she confirmed.

"So why are you sorry?"

"What?" she said, thrown again.

"When you first came in, you said you knew that Penny and I had spoken about us and that you were sorry."

"Did I?" Layla thought for a moment. "Oh, right…I was going to apologize for taking so long to realize how I felt about you. Ask for another chance. If not now, then perhaps in the future. When I'd proved to you how serious I was. I was going to tell you I couldn't run anymore. Not from you. What did you think I was going to say?"

"That you were sorry for *not* feeling the same way."

"Shame you interrupted me, then."

His face broke into a glorious smile. "If you love me, I'll stay."

"You'll stay?" she said, her turn now to be amazed.

"Of course, I'll stay. You're more important than any job."

"But it's your dream." She shook her head at him.

"You're my dream," he replied, his gaze intent on her.

She was his dream? No one had ever said that to her before. It made her feel…special, valued. This was everything she had wanted to feel for so long—and could have felt sooner had she not insisted in looking in the wrong place.

"Layla?" he prompted, shaking her out of her thoughts.

"You will not stay," she said, an edge to her voice now. "Not because of me."

"Layla," he entreated, but she stopped him.

"No, you *will* go to Italy, to this restoration workshop or whatever you call it, and you *will* pursue that dream of yours. As for me, well, I'll write."

"You'll write?" he said, clearly horrified at the prospect.

"Yeah, but not *to* you. I'll write my stories, my book, in Florence."

"In Florence?" He was beginning to understand.

"In Florence," she replied, smiling.

"You'd come with me?"

"Damn right I would."

"But, Layla, this job, it's a labor of love. It's not brilliantly paid. I don't even know where I'd live. Some hovel probably. It'll be a hand-to-mouth existence. I can't ask you to share in that."

"Why not?" she asked, challenging him.

"Because you're used to better. I can't give you what Alex can give you."

"What *can* you give me?" she said, still challenging.

"Love," he replied, meeting that challenge dead on. "I can give you love."

"Which is riches enough for me," she said, her eyes misting again, but this time for all the right reasons.

"So, I get my dream girl as well as my dream job?"

"It seems we come as a package," she replied. Then, not wanting to speak any longer, only wanting to feel his lips on hers, those full and sensuous lips that sent shivers racing up and down her spine, like Formula 1 motor cars, she reached up to kiss him. Drawing her close, he duly obliged.

After a while, desire taking over, she pulled away and whispered, "Let's go upstairs."

Joseph raised an eyebrow. "I thought you'd never ask...again, that is."

Layla swiped at him playfully, and they left the kitchen and climbed the narrow staircase, him first, she holding onto the back of his shirt. In the bedroom, his hands, his mouth were all over her, but she was more than a match for his passion. Just as she was losing herself, he stopped.

"Are you mine this time?" he asked, still nervous, still unsure. "Really mine?"

"Yes," she murmured, and there was no "maybe" about it.

chapter thirty-eight

After having spent an idyllic Christmas together and this time the most perfect start to the year, Layla and Joseph started packing for the move. They had managed to find a studio flat within walking distance of the heart of Florence, in a bustling side street. Although the flat looked rustic from the pictures on the Internet, it was also beautiful with white-washed walls, lofty ceilings, a half-decent kitchenette, and an antique looking bed with a gilt-framed padded headboard. She imagined long hot nights spent on that bed, the two of them lying in a humid tangle.

Shivering with delight, she turned her mind to the task at hand: readying the cottage for Lenny's imminent return. She was going to miss this place. She had grown to love it, but it was time to move on and not alone this time, either—hopefully never alone again. She would leave it sparkling to within an inch of its life and write a big thank-you letter to Lenny, placing fresh-cut flowers everywhere, welcoming him home, as he had once done for her.

She took a few moments from polishing and dusting to look at Gull Rock from the kitchen window. She would miss that sight too—a comforting sight, a familiar sight, the memory of which she could take with her wherever she went. But she wouldn't just have memories. Hannah had painted her a small picture of it as a Christmas present. "So you never forget us," she had said—as if.

And that was going to be hard, leaving Hannah, Jim, Mick, and the gang behind, a wrench Joseph faced, too.

She had dreaded breaking the news to Penny that she was leaving *again*. Straight away Penny had cried, "But what about the baby, your godchild?" Layla had promised to return for a week or two as soon as her godchild was born, and at regular intervals afterward, and that had calmed her. After that, Penny had been as excited as Layla was about the move abroad.

Her mother, too, had been over the moon. "We'll be even closer," she had said. Layla hoped so, on both counts.

Meanwhile, Joseph was renting out his cottage during their absence, the money more than covering his mortgage payments. A young man from Bromwich was moving in, having just gotten a job as a chef in Trecastle's one and only hotel on the headland. He had never been to Cornwall before. Apparently, his interview had been done entirely via Skype. Layla hoped he would find it as special as she did.

"Hey, babe, you done yet?"

It was Joseph, the word *babe* sexy from his mouth, not offensive like it has been with Alex.

"Nearly," she replied, shaking her bottom tantalizingly at him in French parlor maid fashion as she made a show of dusting the worktops.

"Do that again and this place will stay dirty forever," he said, a big grin lighting up his face.

She threw a duster at him and enlisted his help, and after another hour or so they were done.

They stood together, admiring their efforts. The whole place did indeed shine as she intended. "I'm happy, but I'm sad too. Do you know what I mean?"

"I know *exactly* what you mean," he replied. "But it's not the end. We'll come back one day."

And in that instant she knew they would. They could be gone for years, not only to Italy, but to Spain, too. Further afield even, maybe as far as Australia, despite those eight-legged arachnids he far from adored being prolific there. He would rescue furniture from the point of extinction; she would work on her novels. The premise for her first one, based on three women and the tangled love lives they weaved strangely enough, had already been received enthusiastically by Rachel Aitkins.

But wherever they roamed, whatever they ended up doing, Trecastle would always be home. Not Brighton, not Italy, not anywhere else in the world, but here, a simple little village on the North Cornish coast, washed sometimes gently, sometimes violently, by the mighty Atlantic Ocean. And sprinkled, courtesy of the smoke fairies, liberally with magic.

acknowledgments

Trecastle, I have to thank you. I also have to reveal your true identity: it's Tintagel, a tiny village on Cornwall's north coast, steeped in history and full of magic. You won't find the beach described in this book here though, but don't worry, it's only two miles up the road, in Trebarwith Strand. Push the two together and you've got perfection. Visit them for yourself one day—the magic will stay with you forever.

about the author

One of those rare creatures—a true Brightonian—Shani was born and bred in the sunny seaside town of Brighton on the UK's south-coast. One of the first literary conundrums she had to deal with was her own name: Shani can be pronounced in a variety of ways, but in this instance, it's Shay-nee not Shar-ney or Shan-ni, although she does indeed know a Shanni—just to confuse matters further! Hobbies include reading, writing, eating, and drinking—all four of which keep her busy enough. After graduating from Sussex University with a degree in English and American Literature, Shani landed a job at a well-known holiday company. Although employed as a Brochure Production Executive, she promptly reinvented herself as a copywriter, a new position they were happy (if a tad bewildered) to concede to. At twenty-four, Shani became a freelance copywriter and has been one ever since, in between writing novels, that is. Contemporary romance *The Runaway Year* is her first book and set between Brighton and North Cornwall, the latter a home-from-home for Shani, her husband, and three lovely kids. She also has a penchant for Glastonbury, another magical place, and don't even get her started on Scotland—we'd be here all day!

← ⟶ Young Adult ← ⟶

Shades of Atlantis and *The Ember Series: Ember* and *Iridescent* by Carol Oates
Breaking Point by Jess Bowen
Life, Liberty, and Pursuit by Susan Kaye Quinn
Embrace by Cherie Colyer
Destiny's Fire by Trisha Wolfe
Streamline by Jennifer Lane
Reaping Me Softly by Kate Evangelista

← ⟶ Romantic Suspense ← ⟶

Whirlwind by Robin DeJarnett
The CONduct Series: With Good Behavior and *Bad Behavior* by Jennifer Lane
Indivisible by Jessica McQuinn
Between the Lies by Alison Oburia

← ⟶ Erotic Romance ← ⟶

Becoming sage by Kasi Alexander
Saving sunni by Kasi & Reggie Alexander
The Winemaker's Dinner: Appetizers & *Entrée* by Dr. Ivan Rusilko & Everly Drummond
The Winemaker's Dinner: Dessert by Dr. Ivan Rusilko

← ⟶ Anthologies and Singles ← ⟶

A Valentine Anthology including short stories by Alice Clayton, Jennifer DeLucy,
Nicki Elson, Jessica McQuinn, Victoria Michaels, and Alison Oburia

It's Only Kinky the First Time by Kasi Alexander
Learning the Ropes by Kasi & Reggie Alexander
The Winemaker's Dinner: RSVP by Dr. Ivan Rusilko
The Winemaker's Dinner: No Reservations by Everly Drummond
Big Guns by Jessica McQuinn
Concessions by Robin DeJarnett
Starstruck by Lisa Sanchez
New Flame by BJ Thornton
Shackled by Debra Anastasia
Swim Recruit by Jennifer Lane
Sway by Nicki Elson
Full Speed Ahead by Susan Kaye Quinn
The Second Sunrise by Hannah Downing
The Summer Prince by Carol Oates
Whatever it Takes by Sarah M. Glover
Clarity by Patricia Leever
A Christmas Wish by Autumn Markus

coming soon from
OMNIFIC PUBLISHING

Romancing the Bookworm by Kate Evangelista

Fighting Fate by Linda Kage

Blood Entangled by Amber Belldene

Good Ground by Tracy Winegar

Keeping the Peace (A Small Town Novel) by Linda Cunningham

Until Next Time by Justine Dell

Hold Tight by Cherie Colyer

Forced to Change by Stephanie Caldwell

Hydraulic Level 5 by Sarah Latchaw

CPSIA information can be obtained
at www.ICGtesting.com
Printed in the USA
BVOW08s0926140617
486890BV00001B/31/P